LAST CALL
FOR THE
LIVING

Peter Farris

FORGE®

A TOM DOHERTY ASSOCIATES BOOK
NEW YORK

This is a work of fiction. All of the characters, organizations, and events portrayed in this novel are either products of the author's imagination or are used fictitiously.

LAST CALL FOR THE LIVING

Copyright © 2012 by Peter Farris

All epigraphs are lyrics from the album *The Failed Convict* by Cable. Reprinted by permission.

A Forge Book
Published by Tom Doherty Associates, LLC
175 Fifth Avenue
New York, NY 10010

www.tor-forge.com

Forge® is a registered trademark of Tom Doherty Associates, LLC.

ISBN 978-0-7653-6796-9

Forge books may be purchased for educational, business, or promotional use. For information on bulk purchases, please contact Macmillan Corporate and Premium Sales Department at 1-800-221-7945 extension 5442 or write specialmarkets@macmillan.com.

First Edition: May 2012
First Mass Market Edition: April 2013

Printed in the United States of America

0 9 8 7 6 5 4 3 2 1

Praise for *Last Call for the Living*

"*Last Call for the Living* left blisters on my eyelids and teeth marks on my soul. Combining razor-sharp prose, a tight plot, and characters I could relate to, the narrative tension bites down and doesn't let go."

—Frank Bill, author of
Crimes in Southern Indiana

"This novel comes at you like an abusive parent, succors you like a mother, smacks you down like a bully, then helps you back up to see the light like a blood brother—but one cranked on meth, steeped in whiskey, and gunned-up for a final showdown. *Last Call for the Living* is a debut novel with true regret in its heart, and a poignant sadness at the implacability of fate. It is probably the most ballistic family-values story you'll ever read."

—David J. Schow, author of *Gun Work*

"With one novel, Peter Farris has cemented his place as one of the best new voices in the crime noir genre. Tough, tense, and always heartfelt, *Last Call for the Living* left me breathless. An absolutely stunning debut."

—John Rector,
author of *The Cold Kiss* and *Already Gone*

"Sam Peckinpah meets Flannery O'Connor in Peter Farris's astonishingly good debut. The veracity of violence, the beauty of brutality, and the majesty of the marginalized all align like malignant stars in this disturbing, literate, and authentic novel. *Last Call for the Living* is the manifesto of a talent who deserves your attention."

—Grant Jerkins,
author of *A Very Simple Crime*

For Dad,
who taught me the rules . . . and how to break them

And Mom,
for always believing

Acknowledgments

Some of the finest friends and family a guy could hope for: Nick Muller, Randy & Tanja Larsen, Jeff & Kim Hughes Caxide, William & Autumn Hamilton, Bernie Romanowski, Chris Fischkelta, Christopher Nelson, Phil Abbott, Christian McKenna & Kathlene Hoisington, John Refano, Matt Canada, Monte Dutton, Kerry Fitzmaurice, Wayne & Diane Donaldson, Maude & Agnew Wright, Billy Wayne & Marfa Donaldson, Tim & Sandy Windham, Aunt ("Titi") Norma, Aunt ("Titi") Lydia, Uncle George, Cousin Andrew and Cousin Laura.

I'd like to express my gratitude to all at Tor/Forge, especially Tom Doherty, Eric Raab and Katharine Critchlow.

A ferocious thanks to David J. Schow. Mentor, sage, supreme amigo and fellow lover of all things that go *Click* and *Pow*.

An extraspecial thanks goes to the men and women of the Cobb County Police Department. In particular Sergeant Ray Lang, an early reader and champion of *Last Call*, indispensable resource and dear friend.

I am also indebted to my agent, Susan Gleason, and editor, Robert Gleason, for the years of guidance, friendship and unwavering support. This book would not be possible without their efforts.

And Heather. Always.

LAST CALL
FOR THE
LIVING

I'm just a failed convict. I got nothin' to lose.

ONE

By 6:45 *a.m.* the sun had risen over Jubilation County. Like a drunken eye, it seemed to stare across the highway, ten lanes running north and south that cut like a river between restless walls of sweetgum and pine, oak and maple. It was Saturday. Few cars on the interstate except for a lone state trooper or delivery van. Tractor-trailers rumbled. Eighteen-wheeled earthquakes heading south toward the Piedmont. Passing by low hills and valleys, the exits marked by diners and gas stations and roads that disappeared behind kudzu-covered pastures and thickets of pine trees.

An hour from the big city the highway leveled and straightened. There was a university, the campus surrounded by a sprawl of development that included an airfield, car dealerships, retailers and restaurants and apartment complexes packed on either side of the main strip.

The parkway bustled day and night. The kind of location developers referred to as a "high-growth corridor." And overlooking it all was a mountain where Joseph E. Johnston temporarily blocked

Sherman's march to the sea in one of the bloodiest battles of the Civil War.

Hicklin lit a cigarette and drove due south. Down a winding, tree-lined road where houses rose from the earth like displaced coffins. Past the farmer's market, now in a state of disrepair. There was a rusty water pump off the side of the building, an abandoned well out back. Untended pear trees dotted the property. When Hicklin parked the car he saw in one of the trees a hornets' nest thick as a pumpkin. Its occupants stirring after months of hibernation.

He cut the engine and waited. The grass behind the lot grew waist high and if he remembered correctly there was a creek that ran all the way to the national park. He recalled playing in a standing pool and you had to keep an eye out for moccasins, but the pygmy rattlers were far worse. They didn't sound like regular rattlers—more like insects—and pygmies were never satisfied with just one bite.

Hicklin tamped out his cigarette in the ashtray and promptly lit another. The heat was creeping up on everything. One of those sticky summer mornings that called for a change of clothes. He was used to it, having been born and raised in Jubilation County, his body attuned to breaking that first sweat in May and not stopping until mid-October. But why suffer? Hicklin started the engine and turned on the air-conditioning. He was fortunate the car had a working unit. His own truck didn't.

He checked his watch. The sun had been up for an hour.

For the normals he knew it was all about forty-hour workweeks and two-week vacations, three-month and annual reviews. Time flew by for regular folks. But not Hicklin. He felt every tick of the second hand. A man used to time as if a glacier were pushing it for him. Hicklin tried to control his nerves by sucking down drags, forcing the smoke from his nose. But sometimes, looking at the windshield, he still saw bars.

Living in a cell with no windows did that to a man.

A couple weeks ago, after his release, he'd gone to an agency that supposedly helped ex-convicts find employment. There was the GED program, a little warehouse work for him up in Jasper. Manual labor hauling pulpwood or a job at a poultry plant loading pallets with boxed meat. Twelve-hour shifts. Seven bucks an hour. The lady at the agency made it sound like a decent wage, like he had options. She talked about how bad the economy was, how finding a job as a convicted felon was next to impossible. How they're fighting the system from every direction. She talked about recidivism and formal education and a lot of other things that weren't lost on Hicklin. But after twelve years in places like Jesup, Hays State Prison and the GSP outside Reidsville, he had a clearer understanding of what the future held for him.

He flicked the cigarette out the window. Put a pair of black shooting gloves on. Checked his watch again. There was a shamrock tattoo under the band.

The letter *A* branded on one clover leaf. The letter *B* on another. Inked with a tattoo gun made of guitar string, a pen and the motor from a handheld fan. Some Low Rider from Pensacola had done it. Done them all. They were cell mates for two years. Hicklin hooked the Pensacola dude up with hooch and even orchestrated a hit for him. Never got busted for that one. But last Hicklin heard homeboy had ratted on one of his own and was living in a snitch pad out west.

The back piece was solid, though. The tattoos on Hicklin's neck and chest had hurt the worst. They were all years old now. Etched into another body, it seemed. Like canvases stowed in an attic.

Hicklin looked at his watch again. Then he drove on.

T*he first of* three alarm clocks went off near Charlie Colquitt's head. The alarms were set to chime one minute from each other. At 7:30 a.m. a chorus of digital squawking began.

His momma called him Coma.

Charlie reached for the first clock. By 7:34 a.m. the room was silent again. He forced his eyes open as if the claws of a dream were trying to close them. Be so easy to fall back asleep, he thought. The bedroom nice and cool. Then the phone rang. On the third ring he was up and moving around his modest apartment. Mostly students in the building, living off-campus from a university that largely enrolled commuters. He answered the phone, grouchy as usual.

"Yes, Momma. I'm awake."

Charlie listened for a while.

"Okay, Momma. I'll stop at the store before I come over."

He hung up. The coffee machine beeped twice and began brewing on automatic. He stood for a moment, watching the percolator, picking the sleep from his eyes, absently scratching himself. Sometimes his mind just wouldn't cooperate. He'd have to stare at something just to focus.

Charlie showered and dressed for work. Slacks, a shirt and tie—the Spartan attire of an office drone. He bought most of his clothes at Walmart and never gave much thought to the brands or if the combinations matched. His dress shoes were dusty and scuffed. No matter. The customers at the bank never saw his feet anyway.

Charlie poured a bowl of cereal and ate in silence.

The shopping bag on the coffee table contained a new boost glider with a pop pod and a small-scale Tomahawk rocket kit with a parachute recovery. He went every Thursday to the hobby store. Didn't always buy something. A lot of times he just walked down the aisles, admiring the X-Acto knives and glue and kits in their colorful cardboard boxes. Like an aspiring writer visiting the local bookstore, wishing his name were one of those on the shelves. After some custom modifications, Charlie planned to take his most recent purchase to the park by the mountain. Maybe after work. Maybe after Momma.

School. Work. And Momma. His life distilled.

He owned a television but rarely watched it, having

little use for the shows and movies that his class-mates endlessly referenced. Charlie was never one to share a joke with, and certainly not the person to turn to with a conversation-starting *Did you see that bit on so and so last night . . .* Humor for him was a reaction to humor in others, not an understanding of it. Charlie's laugh—on the rare occasion he let one out—was tempered by vacuity, an embarrassingly idiotic noise, geeky and loud, like a mule getting tickled to death.

Yet Charlie was a fine conversationalist, if a person was willing to discuss point-mass approximation altitude, spin rate and oscillation frequency.

Charlie stayed vaguely current with the Internet and by listening to the small talk of his customers at the bank. The occasional headline of a newspaper in its dispenser. At the doctor's office, the scrolling ticker of a corner-mounted television while Charlie waited for a checkup. In most cases Charlie gave the out-side world, with its fluctuating rhythms and spikes of relevance, a glance before his mind would return to its comfortable obsessions. Model rockets and space travel and an interior monologue that only he might understand.

He filled his travel mug with coffee. Added a table-spoon of creamer, two teaspoons of sweetener. Mea-sured out with precision.

Thoughts drifted to the remainder of his weekend. He hardly had what you could call a social life, be-yond monthly meetings with a local model rocket club, most of whose members were shut-ins like him.

He was close with a professor at school, but the man was pushing seventy, their interactions usually lively discussions on the way to the parking lot. If only he could skip dinner with his mother, work on that new Tomahawk, study for his Biostatistics final, hit the park for a quick launch. Well, then maybe he'd find time to wash the week's worth of dishes in the sink and tend to the pile of dirty laundry in the corner.

Charlie grabbed the car keys. Before he left he looked at his cell phone on the kitchen counter. A light blinked, alerting him to the dozen missed calls and voice mails from his mother over the past few days.

No one but Momma ever called him anyway.

Charlie left the phone.

He *drove north* on the interstate; the radio was on but barely audible. Unlike most of his apartment, Charlie kept the interior of his compact car spotless. An air freshener, shaped like a Saturn V rocket, dangled from the rearview mirror. His mother had bought it for him. A childhood visit to Kennedy Space Center.

If he tried hard enough, Charlie could still recall the scent.

By 8:10 a.m. he had entered Jubilation County. On either side of the highway the hills were thick with trees. Suburban sprawl gave way to what looked like an endless pine forest in either direction, veined with back roads, the occasional truck stop, a processing plant, rest areas off the highway.

He exited and turned right onto Route 20. A mile down the road he passed through the unincorporated community of Strumkin, in the eastern part of the county. There was a drugstore and supermarket, unfinished subdivisions. Finally the two-lane road narrowed. Small country homes and abandoned work sheds gave way to horse farms and pastures. He passed the turnoff that led to Momma's old house before she got her job at the hospital and moved closer to the city. But that had been a long time ago.

Charlie remembered little about Jubilation County—the horseflies, summer thunderstorms, the awful smell from the paper plant, playing cards with Auntie Marfa while Momma attended night school— that and how to get to his job at the North Georgia Savings & Loan.

He'd thought about quitting before, maybe finding work closer to the apartment. He was attending school on scholarship, but there were still books to buy, and the car payment and insurance and rent. Not to mention his beloved hobby. Rocket kits, the parts and pieces, the tools. None of it came cheap. That and it was real hard to find a job. Charlie knew he was better off keeping his and suffering the long commute.

He passed by the barbecue place and a motorcycle repair shop. There was a vacant shopping center, most of the businesses going under in the last year. Charlie made a right, then drove around a bend in the road to the bank entrance. It was a modest building, one story, redbrick with a walkway bordered by flowering azaleas. A flagpole rose above the branch, the Georgia state flag and the Stars and Stripes hanging listlessly, waiting for a breeze.

He drove slowly through the one-lane drive-up window on the south side of the building, looking to see if the lights were on in the lobby yet. They were. Good sign. He circled the building once, eyeing the glass double doors at the bank's entrance, the small alcove where the ATM was. There once had been a gas station and fast-food restaurant on the same lot. But like a lot of local businesses both had closed six months ago and never reopened.

Charlie didn't see any other cars and that worried him. He hated being first. Not interested in opening the branch by himself. But as he approached the employee parking spaces, he spotted the teller manager's car parked next to the Dumpster.

His boss, Niesha Livingston, was not in her car. Charlie figured she was inside replacing the tapes in the security cameras before putting the all-clear sign in the window by the employee entrance. This month it was a pink sheet of paper.

At the corner of the west wall was an employee door with a small window set in the center. Charlie parked his car on the other side of the Dumpster and turned back to look at the window.

He waited.

The countryside flattened. All Hicklin could see were wild tall grasses bordering a tree farm and beyond the crests of yellow poplars and hickory. After a while more houses appeared. He slowed down. In the backyard of a motorcycle repair shop he thought he saw a woman sleeping in a hammock. A coonhound in a run slept while flies played around the dog's water bowl.

Hicklin continued through an intersection. To his left there was a vacant shopping center. Not even the liquor store had survived. Tough times indeed. Around the first bend in the road he slowed and turned his head. The armored car had just pulled up to the North Georgia Savings & Loan. A portly, bearded guard was loading a dolly with cardboard boxes while his partner remained behind the wheel.

Hicklin drove past the bank.

He wheeled the car into the drive of an abandoned house. The yard weedy and littered with the rusty orange wreckage of farm equipment. Hicklin lit a cigarette. Turned the air conditioner higher. He had once spent three days in transit, in a cage so hot and foul he could still smell the urine-soaked heat. It was as if his senses would never let go of the foulness.

But sometimes they never knew where to put him.

Hicklin turned to the backseat. The lid on the aquarium had come undone, but no water had spilled. Next to the tank was a Mossberg tactical 12-gauge with a six-round capacity. The shotgun had polymer grips, a ghost ring and heat shield, a big twenty-inch barrel. He had slipped an ammo caddy over the stock, allowing for five more rounds of high-velocity buckshot.

Hicklin reached for a duffel bag behind him and pulled out a Sig Sauer model P220, a full-size .45 semiauto with Trijicon night sights. Four magazines of eight and ten single-stacked rounds. Hollow-point plus-Ps, firepower that could turn an arm into a flipper at close range. Hicklin slammed in a magazine, released the heavy-gauge slide, chambering a round. He flicked the decocking lever with his thumb, dropping the hammer safely from single to double action.

He placed the pistol on the passenger seat next to a matching paddle holster and a mask made from a sugar sack.

Charlie *cut the* engine when he saw Niesha appear in the window, taping the pink sheet of office paper to the inset. Then she opened the door and stepped completely out, following one of the last protocols of the bank's opening procedure.

Charlie took his time, not really looking forward to another workday. *Only three hours,* he reminded himself. *It'll go by in a hurry.* The door locked shut behind him. He turned right, walked through the lobby and behind the teller line.

Niesha led the way, a three-ring binder in one hand. She made eye contact with Charlie but, as usual, didn't say anything until she was done with whatever task occupied her mind at that moment.

She took a stack of deposit slips from a supply cabinet, a spindle of paper and a handful of color-coded money bands. She brought everything back to her station and went to work in the vault log.

The retail banker's life. Money and its paperwork escort that had to be signed, initialed, accounted for, tallied, totaled, secured, strapped, balanced and banded.

Charlie stopped at his terminal, staring at the blank screen of the computer as if the machine had made an untoward remark. He turned an apathetic face to Niesha, who looked up from the thick binder and flashed a toothy white smile.

"Well, good morning, Coma!" she said, then realizing her error, "Excuse me, Charlie Colquitt."

He smiled.

"Good morning, *Sunshine*—pardon—Niesha Livingston."

It was one of many inside jokes they shared at the branch. A way to maintain sanity after a day's work with the public. Anything to keep from jumping off an overpass during rush hour.

He put the travel mug between the MICR reader and validator at his station. Walked back down the teller line to the big, floor-to-ceiling Diebold safe. Niesha followed.

"You go first, dear."

The inch-thick carbon steel door of the vault had two wheel-combination locks. Charlie entered the combination to his assigned lock. Niesha did the same. No one teller could know the combination to both wheel locks.

The vault unlocked with a *clank* and Niesha swung the heavy door open. She regarded Charlie for a moment. His slouching figure accented by a jowl under the chin. Blond hair in need of a trim. An attitude of weariness wherever he happened to be. She had more or less grown accustomed to it.

Inside the vault there were eight teller lockers, a large cash locker and sealed cardboard boxes filled with rolled coins. Assorted binders and inventory logs were crammed into what available space was left. Another locker housed the consignment items. Cashier's checks, money orders, traveler's checks, gift cards in fancy gold envelopes.

Charlie spun the combination to his teller locker and removed the box and coin sorter. He carried them back to his terminal, the box balanced on his right hand like a meal a waiter was returning to the kitchen. Charlie cycled through his key chain until he found the one that opened the teller box. He popped off the lid, removed his cash bin and slid it into the top drawer. He placed the coin sorter on the counter next to the receipt tray and booted up his computer. Looking down, he saw a penny on the floor.

"Check the night deposit, would you, Charlie?" Niesha said.

He nodded, on automatic pilot, unaware of Niesha's lingering stare. Thankfully the commercial deposit drop wasn't too full. Only one bag from the pharmacy in Strumkin.

Niesha remembered when the bank had hired Charlie and she thought, *What is wrong with this damn boy?* He was tall, with lousy pale skin. Slumped shoulders that reinforced an impression of shyness. His face oval shaped, an enigma of blandness. She thought he might have been slightly retarded. But the human resources manager must have felt Charlie would be okay to handle other people's money.

In a way Niesha pitied him. *Never talked about friends, especially a girlfriend. Just Momma for lunch every Saturday.* He was in engineering school, taking classes year-round so he could graduate early. Wanted to work for Lockheed because he loved rockets. Niesha knew he was bright, honors student smart. Also, he was good with the customers, though sometimes his demeanor could exasperate a person who had never been waited on by Charlie. At times he suffered from a peculiar aloofness, as if caught in a kind of meltdown. But just when someone might lose patience with him, Charlie snapped out of these funks to complete a transaction or laugh that hee-haw laugh of his or say something unexpectedly thoughtful and appropriate. It reminded Niesha that some people are just different but not hopeless.

Destined to be lonely and largely unnoticed.

Niesha usually picked up some donuts and coffee on Saturdays and today was no exception. She offered a coconut glaze to Charlie, leading with her left hand to show off the engagement ring courtesy of longtime boyfriend Da'Sean. Charlie shook his head, opted for chocolate with sprinkles from the to-go box. *I'll find that donut in the trash with one bite gone,* she figured. *As usual.*

While Charlie thought to himself, *Thank god Da'Sean finally asked her.*

Niesha took her coffee and donut and walked back down the line. She logged on to the bank system, unlocked the drawers and mini-vault of the standing-height pedestal at her teller station. Scanned the money supply. They probably had about fifty grand between them.

The bank didn't open for fifteen more minutes. The financial specialist and branch manager were both on vacation. A travel teller was on the schedule but had called out sick. Niesha and Charlie would be the only employees working that Saturday, abbreviated hours that ran from nine till noon.

"You need to order cash?" she said, mouth full, chasing a bite of donut with a sip of coffee.

Charlie opened his cash drawer and did a quick count.

"I should be fine," he answered. "Maybe a couple rolls of quarters. Saturdays are slow."

"Don't bet on it being slow *today*, Charlie," she said, finding some satisfaction in the torment of her favorite teller. "Delivery didn't come yesterday. You should have heard me on the phone. I let that lady down at the distribution center have it. Forgetting us on payday like that! Be glad you took off to take that exam of yours. I thought we'd barely make it when those boys from H and P Construction came in with their fat checks. More of 'em will be by today. That's why I ordered extra large bills . . . *just in case.*"

Charlie sighed, the prospect of a lobby full of check cashers was enough to ruin his morning. Paydays were the worst. Most people didn't have an account with North Georgia S&L. In fact, hardly any at all spoke English. He looked over at Niesha blankly, tried to make a face like he'd heard and agreed with her. But sometimes he knew his expression didn't let people know he was paying attention. As though he was only partially present for any human interaction. Niesha ignored him or was used to his distracted nature. *Just talking to myself. As usual.*

She just wanted to fill the air with something.

The radio was broken.

"There they are now. Late as usual," Niesha said, nodding to the armored car pulling up to the front doors.

The guard was in and out of the bank in five minutes. Charlie helped Niesha with a quick inventory. They both initialed the log and secured the shipment. Niesha still had to verify every strap of cash, and that was going to take some time. But they had to open in five minutes. Which meant cutting corners, bending the rules and, Charlie's favorite of all the middle-management talking points, *doing more with less.*

"You mind taking customers while I verify the shipment?" she said.

Charlie shrugged, knowing it had to be done. And it wasn't worth complaining about. He kept reminding himself it was only three hours. Three hours and he could get back to that workbench, back to his models.

He settled into his pneumatic stool. The lighting

in the lobby made everything look synthetic, like props on a soundstage. The ATM in the alcove emitted a series of beeps. Beyond the panels of bullet-resistant glass not a car or person showed in the parking lot. For Charlie another workday was about to begin.

I'm runnin' out of river, I've seen what the water's
    done to everyone and everything.
I watched Jesus pass me by.
Out here where the river can carve me, too.
He said, "Never surrender, never surrender.
Polish your guns. Polish your guns."

TWO

Hicklin *turned the* car into an empty lot where there had once been a fast-food restaurant. The night before he'd boosted the Toyota Camry from an AMC 12-plex. He imagined the owner, laughing at some dumb comedy inside. His or her car vanishing into the night.

It didn't matter.

To Hicklin, everyone was a mark. Even his own partners.

He watched the bank. Had a good angle on the intersection and entrance. He waited until the armored car disappeared down Route 20. A rural county not yet awake. Not a goddamn car or pedestrian in sight.

Hicklin pulled the sugar sack over his head. The eyelets gave good visibility, a crudely cut hole over his mouth revealing a crooked slash of bottom lip. A long-sleeve black tee bulged from the body armor beneath. He wore black gloves, combat cargos, steel-toe boots.

He drove across the cracked pavement to the employee entrance of the bank, which had no customers.

Hicklin left the engine running. Popped the trunk. Grabbed the Mossberg.

There was also a foldout hand truck in the trunk. He lifted it out, not in a hurry.

Not yet.

Charlie *was hand-counting* two thousand dollars' worth of hundreds, the bills facedown because the grip was better. Had to strap the money when he was done, lock it in his second drawer. The tellers had cash limits and he was right at his. He looked up at the sound of a glass entrance door being kicked open.

Niesha had finished initialing transfer and verification forms for about $150K worth of cash and coin. Half the cash still wrapped in the plastic from the distribution center. The vault door was wide open. She had left her coffee behind Charlie's teller terminal and was reaching for the cup when she heard *it*, too.

And all she could think of in that moment of comprehension was: *They don't pay me enough.*

Hicklin *chucked the* hand truck into the lobby of the bank. Place was as empty as he'd expected. He leveled the shotgun on a white boy behind the teller line. Charlie rose slowly from his stool, as if he might be about to ask a question. Hicklin swung the muzzle to a round black body in a flowery dress, hair done up nice. A hand crept underneath the counter.

"Let me see your fucking hands, nigger!"

Niesha's hand kept moving.

Hicklin squinted his left eye and shot her.

Charlie felt his body spasm at the noise of the shotgun. His vision dimmed for a moment. Legs barely holding him up, Charlie held his hands out to Hicklin, palms up, as if gesturing for a man to stop at a crosswalk. He heard Niesha's body drop to the floor. Some of her head had splattered on the drive-up window behind them. Charlie raised his hands higher, eyes searching for a way out, but the masked man lunged forward, the smoking shotgun closer now.

With his left hand Hicklin hoisted the dolly over the teller line. Charlie caught it on his forearms and staggered backwards from the blow. Hicklin backed up, then bounded like a panther onto the counter, deftly keeping the shotgun trained on Charlie. He turned and gave the lobby a once-over, his focus jumping from the front entrance out toward the parking lot. All clear. The vault door was cracked open. Dead woman sprawled on the floor. *Don't think she reached that button. But she was makin' a move.* Yet anytime now someone was likely to show up. They always did. Hicklin figured he'd been in the building about a minute. He was looking to shave time.

Another two minutes. Not a second longer.

———

Charlie felt himself go in his pants. The training video during employee initiation hadn't prepared him for this.

Just give the robber what they want and this will all be over. . . .

Don't be a hero.

Police should be on their way.

But Niesha was dead and all he could think of was that he had left his mini-vault and the transaction drawer unlocked and there was no silent alarm alerting some remote dispatcher and *I wonder if I can use this as an excuse to get out of lunch with Momma?* while he stared at the 12-gauge muzzle, smelled it, saw Hicklin talking to him, and Charlie not hearing a word.

Hicklin *pressed the* muzzle against Charlie's forehead.

"I said, open that fuckin' safe!"

The muzzle burned the skin near his hairline. Dropping to his hands and knees, Charlie reached with a shaky hand and pulled the mini-vault door open.

"And the fuckin' drawer!"

Charlie reached up and pulled the drawer open. He glanced at the panic button under the counter of his terminal. It was close enough, just within reach. A quick movement and he could push it, hold the button down long enough to trigger the alarm. But then what? Was it worth it? What was Niesha thinking? He looked up at the white mask, the dark eyelets, waiting for more instructions. There was an urgency in the man's eyes. Violence. Capability.

Reaching into the drawer, Hicklin intuitively grabbed straps of hundreds, fifties and twenties. Ignored the loose cash. He figured the paint pack was embedded in the stack of tens but he couldn't know for certain. He shoved Charlie aside, leaned over and took what was in the mini-vault.

Hicklin stuffed the wrapped money in a black duffel slung from one shoulder. Then, strapping the Mossberg over his other shoulder, unfolded the hand truck and began loading cardboard boxes of plastic-wrapped cash. This took less than a minute, but to Hicklin it felt like half a day. He wielded the shotgun and gestured for the boy to take the handle of the dolly and follow him out of the bank.

"Move! Move! Move!"

Charlie pulled the hand truck, struggling over a door runner and threadbare carpeting. He caught a glimpse of Niesha on her side. Blood everywhere. Fighting the urge to vomit, Charlie backed out of the rear employee entrance, where a sedan was parked, idling. He numbly began to load the vault monies into the trunk at gunpoint. Hicklin opened a back-seat door and dumped the duffel bag's worth of teller cash into the aquarium.

Hicklin thought about killing him right there in the parking lot. Leave no witnesses. But the adrenaline had Hicklin jumpy, hearing things like another car or sirens. He stared at Charlie, at his pale blue eyes, the dumpy waistline, the cowardly expression on the teller's face, before impulsively forcing him into the passenger seat. Useful later, maybe. Hicklin had trusted his gut for too long to second-guess the move, as stupid as it seemed.

But his skin prickled with warning. The message loud and clear.

This is all wrong.

When he got into the car Hicklin punched the teller in the head. Charlie's eyes rolled and he slumped against the window. Hicklin put the car in gear and sped off. Away from the bank and down a wooded road. Heading north into the foothills.

Toward a refuge where the living were few and far between.

Put out the fire. There's men in the trees.

THREE

Tommy Lang had just poured himself a cup of coffee from a thermos when he heard the call on his unit radio.

"All units, be advised, signal forty-four, signal fifty, possible signal five issued for North Georgia Savings and Loan, Peach Creek Circle, just off Twenty."

He put his coffee in the cup holder and responded.

"Sixty-six-eleven code eight. Sure that's right, Terry?"

Lang already was backing the Crown Vic to the end of his driveway. He gunned it down a long, flat road that ran parallel to a field of sassafras and alfalfa often visited by white-tailed deer and other browsers. The bucks would be growing back antlers shed in February. Some Saturday mornings Lang sat on the front porch, Remington Woodsmaster across his lap, coffee topped with a splash of Gentleman Jack, thinking of the reddish-brown coat of a healthy twelve-point buck. But not today.

The radio crackled.

"Oh, hey, Sheriff?"

"Ten-four. What's the deal?"

"Yeah, Sheriff. It's bad. Someone killed a teller."

"Copy that, Terry. Who's there?"

"Hansbrough. Deputy Bower is en route."

Lang eased off the gas entering a bend, past a cemetery where the road began to rise and fall. Lang glimpsed the highway, but it was soon out of sight as the Crown Vic drove deeper into the county.

"Tell them not to touch a goddamn thing till I get there."

"Ten-four, Sheriff."

Lang glanced at the driver's side of his squad car, at the posse box full of paperwork, the clipboard, then at the empty mount on the floor. He'd forgotten his shotgun. Left it at home.

"Jesus Christ," he muttered.

L*ang parked beside* Hansbrough's and Bower's units in front of the bank, their flashing light bars signaling big trouble to any passersby. Bower, a lanky nicotine stain of a man, was kneeling by an elderly woman on the walkway. She wore overalls and a big straw hat. A red bandana around her neck darkened with perspiration. She trembled as she rocked, breathing hard, stuttering.

"I j-just come to get my quarters . . . c-cash my pension c-check. Like ever o'er Saturday."

She repeated herself, as if the words were a mantra. Her face was pale and wrinkled. Strands of gray hair drifted from beneath the hat and stuck to her sweaty forehead. The skin under her arms hung from the bones and seemed to tremble with each beat of her heart. Bower regarded Lang wearily.

"Like this since we got here," he said. "Name's Anabelle Walnut. Lives in that big old white house with the horses. Yonder where the creek splits."

"Yeah, I know her," Lang said, looking around. He squatted next to Anabelle.

"Anabelle? It's Tommy. You see what happened?"

She looked up at Lang. Eyes empty. Nobody home.

"Told me before *this* started," Bower said, gesturing to the rocking woman. "Manager's name was Neisha Livingston. Always worked Saturdays. Other teller was usually a guy named Charlie."

"Where's the manager?"

Deputy Bower grimaced, nodded toward the bank. He leaned over and patted the old woman on the back. She'd settled into a gentle sway, hands clutching her knees, eyes focused on a mysterious space that must have held some sanctuary for her

Lang left them and walked into the bank. Lobby door was busted open. Shards of glass on the carpet sparkled in the sunlight.

Deputy Hansbrough stood near the teller line, a crew-cut head cocked to one side like a puppy hearing its name for the first time. He was the son of a judge who'd had a heart attack in court, dying with his fingers taut around the gavel. The kid was taller than Lang, broad shouldered, a tight end on a state championship team his senior year. Lang liked Hansbrough, but when he saw the rookie's hand on the counter he lost his temper.

"Put your hands in your pockets, goddammit!"

Hansbrough jolted to attention. Then he looked at the counter and the glossy finger- and palm print he'd left there.

"Don't touch nothing in here!" Lang said, his eyes finding the blood spray on the drive-up window. He approached the line, stepping around an expended shotgun shell, as a red-faced Hansbrough backed away. Lang looked over the counter at Niesha Livingston's body. She had pretty rings on a couple of fingers.

To his right Lang noticed an open teller drawer. Big bills were gone. The vault door open, too. Looked ransacked. Not his business to check that out.

"Y'all notify the GBI?" he said to Hansbrough. The kid still didn't know what to do with his hands.

"Yes, sir. I told Dispatch soon as I got here. Said it might take 'bout an hour. The bank got people coming up from Atlanta. The lady outside, Miss, eh, Miss . . ."

"Walnut."

"Yes, sir. She said there was usually two or three tellers in the bank on Saturdays. We can account for only two."

"You run the plates from vehicles parked out back?"

"Yes, Sheriff. The LeBaron belongs to Niesha Livingston. Ford is registered to a Lucille Colquitt. There's a 'Charles Colquitt' on a lunch schedule behind that center desk there."

"This the only body?" Lang said.

"That one there's all we got. I looked around some."

"I hope you did your looking around with your hands in your pockets."

Hansbrough whispered something under his breath, apparently upset with himself, looking a little unsure. Lang thought to tell the kid later that it was a mistake he'd made himself once. But not now. He didn't need his deputies contaminating the crime scene.

Lang motioned to him and they walked back outside.

"Look sharp. Pavement, Dumpster, that entrance around the corner. Mark anything seems out of the ordinary. And for Chrissakes, don't touch nothing."

Bower had helped Anabelle Walnut to her feet. She was unsteady, almost tipsy.

Lang walked past them, back to his prowler. He took off his campaign hat, ran a hand through a shock of gray hair, then hustled a pack of Marlboros from the breast pocket of his uniform. He had hoped to wait till lunchtime before he had his first smoke, but he'd had enough of this day already. H lit a cigarette and started across the parking lot, slowly, studying the ground as if there were answers in the asphalt.

"Where you going, Tommy?" Bower said, using Lang's first name as he was prone to when excited.

Lang didn't reply. He turned and faced the bank, inventorying the scene. Front entrance, the walkway, a dozen or so parking spots. Drive-up lane to the right. Employee door, some additional parking behind the building. A year ago the bank and the shopping center across the street would have been bustling this time on a Saturday morning. Now there wasn't a car on the road. The businesses were all closed. And Lang knew that someone could drive for five minutes and disappear into the goddamn wilderness.

Bower watched Lang curiously. The old woman clung to Bower, her eyes still tracking a phantom in the open space of her mind. Near the intersection a pickup slowed. The driver stared. Two black Labs in the flatbed barked. Moments later another pickup, the bed weighed down with day labor, tried to pull into the bank's parking lot. Lang shook his head at the driver, who did a quick U-turn and sped off.

"You gonna tell GBI to get their asses on up here?" Bower said. "We ain't equipped to deal with this, is we, Sheriff?"

Lang walked to his cruiser. Settled in the driver's seat again. He keyed the mic and relayed a request to his dispatcher, careful to follow protocol. Because Bower was right. They weren't prepared to deal with a heist *and* a homicide like this one. Not since Lang had been forced to eliminate two investigator positions due to budget cuts. Their job today was to secure the scene and then stay the fuck out of the way.

Lang watched as Hansbrough popped the trunk of his patrol car, produced a thick roll of police tape. They could faintly hear the sirens of an ambulance. The Sheriff took a sip of coffee, but it'd already gone cold.

Charlie felt hands underneath his arms. He was dragged a long way. He smelled cigarette smoke and sweat-soaked clothing. Inside somewhere, a house maybe? It was a humid place. The rancid odor of squalor. He was dumped into a chair. Hands and feet were roughly bound. Rope paid out by calloused hands. He heard the voice of a woman.

"Oh my! We have a guest," she said.

Then Charlie passed out.

The sun was high and blinding, a yellow scab in the sky ripe for picking. Lang's shirt had sweat stains under the armpits. He stamped another cigarette under the heel of his shoe and pocketed the butt.

The paramedics arrived first and carted Anabelle Walnut off to the regional hospital for treatment. Helluva thing for the old woman to see, Lang considered. He and Bower tried to visualize the robbery, based on what little they had to go on. Fast, violent, probably well planned. Gunman hadn't hesitated to kill the manager. But why take a hostage? Unless the other teller had already been dumped somewhere else. Or escaped? A lot of back roads in Jubilation County, most of them just disappearing or turning to clay or gravel before the woods swallowed them. Old Indian trails, enclaves and hollows where hill people had lived for generations. Folks who seldom revealed themselves to the civilized world.

Hansbrough had walked across the street to the

motorcycle repair shop. A woman came, roused
from sedated sleep. She reeked of stale booze and
was full of attitude. Said she hadn't seen or heard a
thing. Hansbrough believed her.

So he and Lang stood outside the bank and waited.

Finally the state and federal cops arrived. Lang
watched the procession turn off Route 20 and into
the parking lot. The County Medical Examiner, an
Operations Consultant from the bank. Three vans
from the Georgia Bureau of Investigation, followed
by two black sport-utilities with federal plates.

*You'd think the goddamn state fair was comin' to
town. . . .*

But now it felt like a crime scene. Evidence Response Team in blue windbreakers rolled in with
an assortment of equipment. CSIs went to work
behind the teller line, photographing everything, a
cold interest to their expressions. Lang's two deputies stood out of the way, hiding whatever awe they
felt.

Lang spoke briefly with the state's investigators,
told them what he knew, which was next to dog
shit. Then Randy Ingram, the Jube County Medical
Examiner, sauntered over, a toothpick in his mouth,
his round face an irritable shade of pink. Lang had
known the man for twenty years.

"Big boner of a fuckup we got here, Tom," he said.
"Been a while since we had one of these. '91?"

"'94. Hell, I get so used to dogfighting and meth
labs I forget people still rob banks anymore," Lang
replied. They shared a polite laugh, but the Sheriff
couldn't shake that feeling he'd had since arriving at

the bank. As though the wind had been permanently knocked from his lungs.

A photographer walked slowly around the property. There was a lot of action near the employee entrance. The Operations Consultant emerged from the bank, talking nonstop on his cell phone, pacing and distressed. The look of a man mentally sending out résumés.

One of the state agents was a handsome woman who looked to be enjoying the first year of her forties. Hair so dark Lang thought it possible to catch his reflection in it. Light makeup, no jewelry. She wore khaki cargo pants and a blue cotton polo with the GBI logo.

Lang didn't tire of looking at her until she got around to him. On closer inspection he noted her full lips, a long-stemmed neck, cheekbones and a complexion that could have been the gift of Chickasaw bloodlines. He liked the way she wore her full-size Glock, butt-first for a cross-draw.

Presently the woman made her way over to Lang, extended her hand. No wedding band, he observed.

"Sheriff Lang, is it?"

"Yes, ma'am."

"I'm Special Agent Sallie Crews. I'm heading up the investigation."

"Pleasure, Agent Crews."

"Call me Sallie."

"All right then."

"You know this bank, Sheriff?"

"I don't do my business here, if that's what you

mean. County really thins out up this way. Only trouble we get out here is drunks beating on one another, occasional meth lab fireballing. Liquor store holdup. Nothing like this, well . . . ever."

Crews nodded, her expression never losing its intensity. She crossed her arms, hunched her shoulders as though in deep thought.

Off her body language Lang finally said, "You don't think whoever did this is still in the neighborhood, *do* you?"

The look in Sallie Crews' eyes told him she thought so.

A*gents found the* car just past noon. An observant helo pilot spotted something of interest in a stand of bull pines at the base of a ridge, forty minutes from the North Georgia Savings & Loan. Under the rounded crowns of branches a camouflage tarp had been pulled over a Toyota Camry.

It took an hour for the forensic team to reach the vehicle. The road the team took turned from gravel to dirt, then became a weedy track like some coiled snake in the heart of the woodlands. They sealed the car and waited for the tow truck. The gas tank was near empty. With only one way in and out the perpetrator must have dumped the Toyota and escaped. One agent speculated that there probably was a second getaway vehicle.

Heat lightning slowed beyond the valley to the west. The thunderclouds approached, swallowing the sun. It got dark quickly. On the forest floor the forensic team switched on their electric torches and went to work.

Tommy Lang stopped his Crown Vic at the drive-up window of Dixie Liquors. He bought a fifth of Knob Creek, a six-pack of Budweiser and cigarettes. The kid working the drive-up asked him about the robbery. Lang grinned, never surprised at how fast news could spread around the county. He said he couldn't talk about it but advised the kid to report anything unusual. Lang paid in cash and tucked the bottle of whiskey between his legs.

The sky had darkened considerably in advance of a coming storm, lightning backlighting the tapestry of clouds. Lang parked the cruiser in the carport, juggling the brown bag and sixer in one hand, his house keys in the other. He heard the claws of his basset hound scraping against the front door. The hound howled when Lang got to the porch.

She went by the name of Lady.

Lang let the dog out through the back door, regarding the swaying pines in his yard with an unease he hadn't felt since grade school. He watched Lady piss. Then she looked up at the sky and barked.

Yes, you damn fool, it's gon' rain. Git!

Afterward Lang locked the back door. Something he hadn't done in years.

The house was cool thanks to a few open windows. Lang undid the first few buttons of his uniform.

Walked into the bathroom. Saw that Lady had shat on the newspaper he'd laid down for her.

"That's a *good* girl," he cooed. "A *good* girl."

He folded the newspaper and returned to the kitchen. Dumped it in the trash can. Having found her favorite place on the couch, Lady followed him with her eyes. Lang poured three fingers of whiskey in a glass, went into the living room, pushed the dog out of the way. He turned on the television.

Rain pelted the roof, the signal from the dish disrupted by the storm. He caught the tail end of a stock car race from Richmond. There was a weather bulletin for Jubilation County. Tornado Watch in effect until midnight.

Lang started drinking.

The day's events swirled in his memory. He'd watched as Agent Crews reviewed the surveillance tapes from the time-lapse recorders inside the bank. Five cameras in the lobby. No sound.

High, tight angle from the corner-mounted camera. Armored car comes and goes. Minute later a dark figure in a white mask puts a boot to the door. Then comes the hand truck and shotgun. Manager foolishly tries for the alarm and gets her head liquidated. But not the teller? The kid looks terrified. Not like in the movies.

It reminded Lang of the footage captured during earthquakes. Security cameras in a grocery store, a restaurant, an office building. The shaking starts and the people suddenly look frantic, their day going from zero to pole position in the blink of an eye. That was real terror. Nothing to hold on to, trying to find balance in a situation where there's none to be had.

Watching the tapes, Lang noted how quick the robbery went down. The masked man was out the door in under five minutes. Timed it just right. It was as ruthless a sight as Lang had ever seen. A wanton execution. He hated himself for appreciating how remorseless it had been.

Hearing a cousin to the storm rumbling over Lang's home, Crews sat in a cubicle at a regional office of the GBI's Investigative Division, a patchwork of photos from the North Georgia S&L crime scene atop her desk. She closed her eyes and rotated her neck counterclockwise, several hours of built-up tension relieved with a long-drawn-out sigh.

The perp had parked out of sight of the exterior cameras. Forensics got nothing but a tentative shoe size and caliber of the shotgun. Crews already could tell from looking at the tape that the shotgun was a 12-gauge. Double-aught buck judging from the kick and how it had blown that young woman's head apart. No prints on the lone shell casing, probably wiped down or handled with gloves. The robber's sidearm was difficult to identify, but it was definitely a full-size autoloader. *And that son of a bitch was wearing some sort of armored vest*. She figured the man had been prepared for anything, including a shoot-out. His shotgun and sidearm might have been only part of the arsenal in the getaway vehicle.

But a CSI found what proved to be the only solid

lead of the day. Replaying the footage from the surveillance cameras, he'd frozen the action on his computer just as the suspect was about to chuck the dolly into the bank lobby. *There.* The tech sharpened the image. Crews and her team glimpsed the wrist of the perpetrator, a flash of skin, the gray markings of a tattoo just between a gloved hand and the long black sleeve.

Tighter now.

The letters *A* and *B* initialing the leaves of a clover leaf.

Crews had spoken first, the words freighted with meaning.

"Aryan Brotherhood. We have ourselves an ex-con."

She *had left* the crime scene for a few hours, taking two agents with her. They met a detective on loan from another department's Robbery-Homicide Division, himself working a year-old heist that had—according to him—gone colder than his "ex-wife sucking on an ice cube."

They headed southwest from Jubilation County, toward a city north of the Chattahoochee River. They drove past the naval air reserve base and Lockheed Aircraft, where F-22s and C-130s were assembled. Then came the historic business district. Government buildings. The courthouse. Parking islands and traffic. Railroad tracks.

She turned onto a street lined with old frame houses and square manicured lawns. White oaks provided some shade from the sun. Two shirtless kids, showing off physiques sculpted in the high school weight room, tossed a football in what wasn't so much a cul-de-sac as it was a dead end.

Crews stopped in front of Lucy Colquitt's house, immediately noticing the big oak in the front yard. It didn't take but three steps to spot the touches of a quaint country décor. The bird feeder hanging from a tree branch, a steel handcrafted weathervane mounted on a pole. A copper rooster that pointed west. Charlie's mother had planted hydrangeas along a brick walkway that led to the front door. The house needed painting, but it hardly detracted from the charm of the little residence.

Next to the screen door a folksy sign read: *The Colquitts. Do Drop Inn.*

An official from the North Georgia Savings & Loan had arrived and joined Sallie's team. They stood like sentries behind her as she knocked and waited. Knocked again. Crews watched a spindly woman with blond hair slowly approach the door with an expression of muted anxiety. The door was opened. Still wearing her scrub pants and top from the hospital, Lucy Colquitt stared at them and braced herself.

"I visioned this! Clear as the voice of my own mother, God told me you'd come!"

Crews raised a hand palm up and said, "Miss Colquitt, I'm—"

But Lucy Colquitt only moaned, shuffling backwards. Crews reached for her as she slumped to the floor.

The man from the bank looked as if he wished they'd come to the wrong house.

Thunder shook the house like a loose drumhead. Tommy Lang poured another drink. Whiskey over ice and a splash of Coca-Cola. He sat at the kitchen table, occasionally glancing at the television in the living room. Earnhardt's kid had won the stock car race and was getting doused with beer in victory lane. Lady snored, twitching as if she was deep in a dream, tracking some critter up a tree or down a hole.

He decided to clean his duty weapon. More an excuse to go on drinking than a necessity. He got out bore cleaner, some gun oil, and a .40-cleaning rod and brush.

Lang listened as the local news from Atlanta followed the race. Rote and depressing as always, the broadcast led off with a rash of carjackings, preceded by a story about a couple who had jumped from the roof of a flaming apartment. Someone drowned at Lake Lanier. A school bus driver exposed himself to fifth graders. A big drug bust on the city's Southside. The Braves lost their seventh straight.

Lang switched to beer. Empty bottles began to clutter the tabletop as though he were erecting a small city. He left the gun loaded and holstered on the kitchen countertop.

Opened another beer. And another.

Hours later Lang lurched around his house. At the mantle he eyed framed pictures. His fingers came away dusty when he touched them, the glass retaining his prints from other times.

There were photos of his ex-wife and three children. One photo taken years ago at the Tennessee Aquarium in Chattanooga, when the kids were still in high school. He'd had a nice life once. Sold the land his folks had left him to send the girls to college. The boy had gone off to Los Angeles to become an actor. Tommy's wife had remarried and moved to Orlando.

Said to Lang: *We don't want anything, Tom. All we want is to not have anything to do with you.*

It occurred to him that their marriage hadn't ended because of some catastrophic event or unforgivable offense.

It was just a slow deterioration.

And it had begun with the girl, he speculated. But no, earlier, when crystal meth invaded Jubilation County.

Lang had never seen such devastation. Families torn apart. Lives ruined. There was no recovery from a drug like that. Cooks had set up shop in the woods, sometimes in abandoned trailers or vans. Some dealers even drove around in their cars, mixing ingredients on the go like kamikaze chemists. Often the only knowledge the Sheriff's Department had of their location was from the fireball produced when a makeshift lab exploded.

Fed up and thinking of future elections, Lang initiated a task force. Put some local pharmacies under surveillance, popped a gang of addicts smurfing SUDAFED for the dealers up in the hollers. He exhausted himself, but he got results and still managed his home life okay. At times he felt impervious, with a firm grasp on his political life—law and order restored—and a loyal, loving family waiting for him every evening.

Until the girl.

Tourists from Connecticut, older couple hiking the Blue Ridge Mountains, reported it first. They saw a man walking with a little girl, off the trail, before disappearing into the woods. The couple swore that the man had been leading the girl on a leash.

And that the little girl had been walking on all fours.

Lang and two deputies investigated. Deep in the woods they came upon a trailer. They heard cries from inside. The door was unlocked.

There was a cage in the bedroom. Looked handmade. About six feet square. The little girl was naked and filthy, covered in her own shit and piss. There were bowls full of scraps on the floor, baby food, tainted water. The girl howled when Lang approached the cage. He asked the girl for her name, but she could only grunt and squeal.

She had ticks under her arms as big as raisins.

They waited.

The parents drove up in an old pickup.

The girl's father shook his head. Shrugged his shoulders. As if he really couldn't believe it was wrong to keep his daughter caged. The mother only leered, clutching at her husband's arm. It was immediately obvious to Lang that she was feebleminded.

And it took all the restraint he could muster to keep from shooting them both dead.

Lang *continued to* excel at his job. Failed miserably at home. He drank to forget the little girl. Meaningless arguments with his wife were countered by long stretches of silence. Months of this. They stopped sleeping together, but they kept up appearances.

Pure theater.

In private she cried in the bathroom. Lang more or less moved out, the living room couch replaced by a corner table at Kalamity Bibb's beer joint.

His nerves went from bad to worse, and he had recurring nightmares about the girl. He'd step out of his cruiser and there she'd be, naked, on all fours. Then she'd open her mouth to scream and her tongue would drop from her head like an expelled placenta.

Awake, sleeping, the look in the little girl's eyes disturbed every concept he'd had of right and wrong. Of human decency. Lang once thought of himself as a protector of good people. A righteous agent of the civilized world.

But he'd lost his faith in the accountability of human behavior. Lang now viewed his former family, his job, even himself, as a cruel and pointless experiment.

He knew Sue longed for something better. The mother of his children, a loyal woman who had designed election posters and directed his first campaign for Sheriff. His wife was the first girl he'd kissed. Halloween, thirteen years old in the corn maze after the Autumn Harvest Dance. His father officiated at their wedding five years later. Then Diane, Donna and Danny arrived. The good years.

He wanted to tell Sue, rehearsing the words one night after nine beers of a twelve-pack were gone. *Just go,* he imagined saying. *I can't cut it anymore. I'm miserable. I need to be alone. Move on with your life while you still have one. I'm a terrible husband. A terrible friend. I'm haunted. I drink to forget awful things. I need help you can't provide.*

Just go.

Three days later Sue left him. She called from her brother's place in Florida. Lang couldn't remember the speech he'd rehearsed.

In the closet he kept shoe boxes labeled *Christmas* and *Birthday*. Periodically Lang pulled a couple of them out and rifled through some cards. He was still close with his elder daughter. She had a job at a TV station in Tallahassee and was engaged to the owner of a coffee shop. Diane called Lang at least once a month, sometimes sending long e-mails instead, taking it upon herself to update him about the others. *Danny auditioned for a TV show. Got a bit part. Donna went back to school to get her graduate degree. Mom took up golf, says she's writing a romance novel.*

Diane was compelled to keep Tommy in her life and for that he was grateful. If it hadn't been for her he'd never know.

But his daughter was the only one who forgave him, never judged him as harshly as the others. The oldest of the three, she was always a daddy's girl. Raised by two loving parents still unfazed by life's complexities. He knew she and Sue talked often. He imagined long, tearful conversations of which he was the main subject. Knowing his wife had depended on their daughter as the marriage fell apart.

Lang depended on Anheuser-Busch.

Lang *tripped in* the dark, dropping a full beer and losing half to the bedspread. He rolled on his side, tried to get his shoes and socks off, feeling the wetness of the beer-soaked sheets. There were empty bottles on the nightstand. Lady growled from her corner of the bed. He managed to find the remote and turned on the television. Dribbled beer down his chin when he took a sip. His white undershirt was stained, stretched and crinkled around the neck.

Lang's mind churned.

He wondered if doing his job was worth it anymore.

There was that one stretch of his life when Lang really believed he could accomplish everything he tried. Remembering when he and Sue kissed in the corn maze. *Anything you put your mind to,* they agreed. All those clichés and platitudes. The youthful motivations and dreams.

His eyes closed. His breathing grew heavy, wheezy, his lungs thick with years of abuse. Lady snored next to him. Moments later Lang joined her in sleep.

Brushy Mountain ain't no place for a man like Jim.

FOUR

Charlie opened his eyes and saw through a pall of smoke foothills thick with pine. He was in a different vehicle now. An old truck. A snake was sunbathing in the road, stretched out on the asphalt like a leathery stick. The driver of the pickup accelerated.

Charlie felt the snake die beneath the wheels in two sequential bumps.

He worked his jaw, feeling sluggish, dazed, disembodied. He wanted to scream but couldn't muster the energy. From the corner of his eye he saw a tattooed hand on the steering wheel. A cigarette pinched between two fingers. He didn't want to look at the driver, who Charlie sensed wasn't wearing his mask now. The sun was bright on the windshield. Charlie closed his eyes against a starburst of pain. Minutes later the truck turned. Another road, uneven and bumpy. Ascending.

Intimations of what could happen kept him conscious.

Another road, another turn. The driver lit a cigarette and yawned.

Charlie was dreaming about the thrust and drag coefficients of one of his favorite model rockets—the Viper III. He was turning the Viper over in his hands, inspecting it, on some cloudless day when the rocket began to play music. . . .

He woke up in a room, a radio blaring somewhere behind him. He heard voices. Looked around, slowly focusing, realizing quickly he was tied to a chair, his ankles and wrists bound. There was a mattress on the floor, a moldy-looking rug beneath it. Newspapers had been taped over the only window. He didn't know if it was day or night. The room smelled of cigarette smoke and something else. Something acrid, chemical. The wallpaper was curled and peeling, water stains looking like giant Rorschach blots.

Someone had put tape over his mouth.

Charlie tried to move. He swayed, right then left, before he tipped over in the chair, falling face-first to the floor.

He stared sideways into an open closet littered with dirty clothes, shoes, cassettes, crumpled cigarette packs. Someone had taken apart a portable stereo, the parts scattered here and there. A stack of what looked like schoolbooks leaned against the door frame. Charlie watched a spider scurry across his field of vision, disappearing among the detritus in the closet. Then he felt one crawl over his ear, across his cheek and up to his nose.

He shook his head, working the tape loose on one side. His mouth filled with vomit. He spit it out and blew his nose, snot getting all over his lips.

Charlie listened to the voice in the other room for a while. Heard cans clinking together. He took deep breaths, his mind droning from concussion. He was overcome by a feeling of helplessness. Like an infant left to fend for itself. He tried to picture the model rocket from his dream—attaching the fins on that Viper III, sanding the nose cone, launching it at sunset. It was the only thing that provided some comfort. But the thought returned, a notion that'd been eating away at him since he opened his eyes.

What a terrible place this will be to die.

Hey, sweetheart. For Chrissakes. Come help me get 'im up. Motherfucker done throwed up. I swear I'll break a bottle over your head ye don't put that pipe down, get off that couch and help me. Grab his legs and git him up on the bed. That's right. Boy sleeps like the dead. Go on get me 'nother beer. And a wet cloth. I'll stay.

Poor thing never had a gun pointed at him, Hummingbird said. Never been tied up.

These things happen, Hicklin replied. These things happen.

Charlie lifted his head. He was back in the chair, having been moved in his sleep to the main room.

Someone had taken off his dress shirt. Wiped him down. His white undershirt was soiled. Only his wrists were tied at the moment.

"What's your name?"

Charlie looked in the direction of the voice. A woman sat on the couch Indian-style, wearing jean shorts and a tank top. He was pretty sure she was the one who'd asked. The woman raised a pipe to her lips and lit the bowl. She inhaled deeply, holding the smoke in her lungs for a moment before exhaling. A chemical smell not unlike burnt plastic filled the room. She turned her head slightly and favored Charlie with a smile. There was a saucer-shaped sore at the corner of her mouth. She scratched herself, a behavior that appeared involuntary.

"Water?" Charlie said.

She uncrossed her legs.

"Your name's *water*?" she said with a giggle, a juvenile glint in her eye.

Hicklin reached down to a cooler at his side. Grabbed a beer and opened it. Charlie saw bottled water in the cooler, but before he could ask again the lid was closed. The woman had picked up a remote control, but Charlie didn't see a television anywhere. She was eyeing the remote cautiously. Then she put it down and hopped off the couch like a chimpanzee, mysteriously energized.

Inches from Charlie's face, she said, "He talked sweet to you. But he was just drunk. He don't talk when he's not drunk."

Charlie saw a mouth full of bad teeth. He winced.

"I asked your name, but he says we can't say our

names because, well . . . how come we can't say our names?" she said, looking back at Hicklin.

But Hicklin ignored the question. He took a sip from his beer and watched them indifferently.

"You can call me Hummingbird," the woman said to Charlie. "I used to be a schoolteacher. What's your name?"

"Ch-Charlie. My name's Charlie."

"Charlie? Charlie. Charlie!" she said, as if swirling the name around in her mouth.

Hicklin hustled a cigarette from a yellow hard box. He rolled it between his fingers to loosen the tobacco and then lit it. He wore black jeans. No shirt. Seemingly at ease in the hot, shabby cottage. For a moment Charlie thought the man to be flexing. His torso and arms had hard ropes of muscle hidden under sleeves of green ink. An upper body covered in tattoos, some crude and amateurish, others rendered in amazing detail. The symbol of the Luftwaffe on a trio of Stuka dive-bombers. Junkers Ju 88s and twin-engine Messerschmitts soared over a shoulder, crossing his chest in formation. Elsewhere there were Nordic symbols. Spiderwebs. Swastikas. A pair of lightning bolts prominent at the pit of his neck.

Hicklin took another sip of beer.

"Could I have some water, please?"

Hummingbird straddled Charlie. She ran her fingers through his hair, petting him like she might stroke a kitten. She kissed him. A girlish peck at first.

Then she started to lick his neck.

Charlie begged her to stop.

"That's enough," Hicklin said.

As if she was used to such orders, Hummingbird unlocked herself from Charlie's lap and returned to the couch. She reached for the pipe. Hicklin gave her a long look. She disappeared, pipe and lighter in hand.

"You have a nickname?" Hicklin said to Charlie.

"A nickname?"

"I never had much use for real names."

Charlie considered an answer.

"My mother calls me Coma."

"*Coma*?" Hicklin said. "Because of the way you sleep, right?"

Charlie nodded.

Hicklin mashed his cigarette against the heel of his boot and dropped it to the floor. He reached for the pack and lit another, looking at Charlie as if that was the boy's cue to say something. Hicklin coughed into his hand. Whatever came out he wiped against the front of his jeans. Eventually he spoke.

"What's your last name?"

"Colquitt," Charlie said.

"I knew a Colquitt once."

The comment was flat, apathetic, as if small talk pained him to no end. Hummingbird giggled from the bedroom.

"This party won't last," Hicklin said with a sigh of resignation.

They both could hear the songs of Carolina wrens, undercut by a racket of katydids up in the trees.

Charlie had got a clear sense of being up in the mountains, near the state line probably. Which state? the better question. The light dimmed, but it felt like dawn was upon them. There was newspaper taped over the windows in the main room. A filthy woodstove. Somewhere a generator hummed.

"Are you going to k-kill me?" he finally asked his captor.

Hicklin turned the bottom of a beer can toward the ceiling.

"Like I did that nigger lady earlier?" he said, a smile pulling to one side of his face. "I'm done granting favors today . . . but they'll be other days."

Agent Crews held Lucy Colquitt's hand. Charlie's mother cried from one eye, dabbing at it with a wad of tissue. The other eye was artificial—porcelain or acrylic—with very little motility. When the good eye moved, the artificial twin stared straight ahead. The effect bothered Crews.

"Do you have anyone you can call?"

Lucy Colquitt shook her head. Still in her nurse's scrubs, she got up to refill her coffee from a percolator on the counter. Didn't offer any more to her guests. When Lucy sat down again she took a drag from the half-smoked cigarette in the ashtray. Crews had quit smoking, but she wanted one now, Lucy reminding her of how many doctors and nurses and EMTs couldn't kick the habit, simply didn't care, even if they knew better. A cell phone went off and one of the detectives excused himself to answer in another room. His murmur was the loudest sound in an otherwise uncomfortably silent house.

Earlier while Lucy used the bathroom Crews had walked around the home, noting the pictures of Charlie everywhere. The woman kept a clean house, favoring a flea-market country décor not unlike that of the house Crews had been raised in. There was a big braided rug in the living room, tin oval lamps, wall pockets with sunflowers. An old sideboard and a plaid-upholstered queen-size sleeper in the living room. Jelly cupboards in the kitchen. Colquitt had a penchant for roosters, too. Matching salt- and pepper shakers, napkin holders, a suncatcher, ceramic cookie jars. The detectives even drank their coffee from decorative rooster mugs. Little figurines with Scripture on them stood at attention on a shelf in the kitchen. It reminded Crews of her own mother, who'd had a ladybug fetish that turned absurd as the years went by.

"Coma was the nickname I gave him," Lucy told Crews. "He slept like a angel. You know the kind of sleep that comes from a pure conscience? Deep, undisturbed kind of sleep."

Lucy had thin lips, a pale complexion only made paler from shock. Her hair was a copper-blond shade, probably dyed from a bottle. She wore her hair parted down the middle and combed over the ears. Eleven years on the job, she'd mentioned. The graveyard shift at the big regional med center. Lucy had the slightly abstracted manner of a caretaker, Crews noted. A brain accustomed to dark rooms and pained faces, to bodily fluids and the smell of sickness.

A quick background on Lucy revealed that she paid her bills punctually. She had a little money in an IRA at North Georgia Savings & Loan. Pension waiting for her. Not so much as a speeding ticket or another citation in twenty years.

". . . When he was just born, there were times I thought he was dead, he was so still. Could barely make out him breathing. I remember one time I got scared and I held a mirror under his nose. He was two years old and I just stood there hoping he was alive. You know to this day it takes three alarms and a phone call to wake him. Used to be late for school all the time. Just all the time."

Crews listened, nodding. "What's Charlie like?"

"You think he's still alive?" Lucy said, her voice quavering.

"Yes, I do."

Lucy took a long drag from her cigarette. Crews couldn't read her face: the false eye, the heavy makeup. She'd expected her response to temper Lucy's fears, instill some hope. *I'm telling you I think Charlie is alive,* she wanted to scream. But Lucy looked oddly detached, almost disappointed.

"Coma, he's such a good boy," Lucy continued after lighting a Virginia Slim and cradling it in an ashtray. There was an open carton on the kitchen table. "He's my *only* boy. So smart. He's going to be a college graduate. Loves rockets and space and science and such. Nothin' I was ever good at."

Lucy paused, holding back some emotion. She

had one of those expressions. Perpetually on the verge of hysteria.

"I raised him myself," she said with particular pride. "He was always a bit peculiar, kept to himself, never had friends except for some kids from the rocket club at school. Charlie wants to build rockets and jet planes, work for Lockheed or NASA one day. I sent him to Space Camp over in Huntsville. He loved it. Just *loved* it. But I never did have the nerve to tell him that some things are just beyond the reach of people like us."

"He's an overachiever?" Crews said.

"Oh yes. It's just the money, and, well, the scholarship he's on is okay, but that college ain't like the schools rocket scientists graduate from."

Crews mentally added to her impression of her victim from Lucy's explanations. She already felt bad for Charlie. And a little angry. Lucy Colquitt both bored her and made her uneasy. The artificial eye, the quaver in Lucy's drawl, the damn roosters, that half-empty bottle of schnapps next to the microwave. She had all the signs of a functional alcoholic. The functionally unstable.

Crews could spot a badly damaged human being when she saw one. So what was Lucy's real story? No family to speak of. No husband. Probably the product of a broken home. A history of abuse? Alcoholic father? Promiscuity? Drugs? An unwanted pregnancy?

"Did Charlie mention anything about work?" Crews asked. "Any rude or unfriendly customers he must've dealt with? Strangers he noticed hanging around the bank?"

"He never talked about work much when we had our lunch on Saturdays."

"What *do* you and Charlie talk about?"

"Nothing, really," Lucy said with a shrug.

There was a pause. The detectives exchanged looks.

"Did Charlie have any enemies? Students at the college he didn't get along with? Or maybe neighbors at his apartment complex? Anyone who knew where he worked?"

Lucy said, "We never really talked . . . about things such as that."

"Any family he's close to? His father, maybe?"

Lucy Colquitt took a drag from her cigarette, then leveled her working eye on Crews. Her artificial eye looked off, as if distracted by something over Crews' shoulder. Tears caused recently applied mascara to run. Crews frowned, struck by a particularly mean thought. *You could have put her in a field to scare off crows*. Crews already had a hunch that her last question would be evaded.

Lucy exhaled. Smoke drifted from her mouth like woodsmoke off a hearth. It lingered around her head.

"Long dead," she said. "Oh, he's long dead."

I *thought ye might be dead. But I see you're breathing. Used to talk to my celly when he was asleep.*

Know how I still dream about the inside? It's about all I do dream of. State of Georgia . . . we had our misunderstandings, sure. Should still be locked up. The things you got to do to survive which ain't legal no prison I know of. Keep your mouth shut after. That got you solitary most of the time. Unless you snitched. That got you a ticket to the dance.

Funny how they put you away for breakin' the law and all ye do inside is break the law again, over and over. Them niggers and beaners, the baton-happy prison guards. They will push and if ye ain't inclined to push back then there's no helpin' ye. I was never one to be pushed, and when I was I pushed back harder and meaner. Should still be there. But I'm an anomaly. I learned that word. It means slippery. Means I ain't been a snitch or just some dumb piece of meat.

I miss the games we played with the warden. Them gangbuster screws thought they was smart. Thought they deciphered our code and could catch all the drugs and contraband. Yeah. Well, Nature finds a way.

We used to throw cereal in the drain, let it ferment for a couple days with some water and then eat it. Enough to get drunk. I wouldn't wish that taste on anyone. Take fruit from the kitchen, little bag with water. Apples mainly. Bananas. We called it Pruno. Prison wine. It's just rotten is all. But it did the trick. Anything to make time move quicker. Made a small fortune selling stuff that made time disappear. Heroin, speed, OxyContin, cough syrup. Warden might say drugs are a problem, but it's isolated. Yeah. Hardly.

Drugs ran the show inside. And we were the show.

But they are a-comin'. Friends of mine are co-min'.

This room we're in, no different than what I'm used to. Playing by my own rules and look what it gets me. Right back in another room. With no windows I care to look out of. Brothers will come lookin' for me because I jumped on this one. Got greedy. Ye don't just walk away from jumpin' a score. It was supposed to be three men.

Reckon how many of us ye see here, Coma?

Sometimes I wish I never got out. Maybe that's why I took ye alive? I'm still trying to figure that one out.

I know how to play the games, though. I know the angles. You're just one of many. Do ye feel like an angle? I do. I guess eventually we all do. Something playin' us. Workin' us over. We're all marks, I suppose. I'd like to know who's in charge. Because this life is just one big score. All of it.

Been a long time since I had a cooler full of cold ones. I might just puke tonight. Then we might have somethin' in common after all. Ain't that right, Charlie Colquitt?

Hicklin took short pulls from his beer, eyeing Charlie with a mixture of curiosity and resentment. Charlie's head had drooped forward again. *Damned if the boy didn't look dead,* Hicklin observed. *Has a face that might've been trapped under ice and drowned.*

He felt the alcohol buzz from his fingertips to his sternum. And right between his throbbing temples. He'd been lighting one cigarette after another, thinking on what his next move should be, but answers seemed in short supply.

Hicklin rose and walked to the radio in the corner where a long orange extension cord disappeared out a cracked window. Newspaper kept most of the light out. Could have been any time of day. He didn't care what time it was. Just like he was used to.

He turned up the volume and returned to his chair, feeling thoroughly drunk when he sat down. A traffic report from Chattanooga crackled in and out. He heard Hummingbird talking to herself. She was in the bedroom, rummaging around, looking for something. She was always looking for something, real or imaginary. *That woman is no earthly use to anybody,* he told himself. She was slowly killing herself anyway.

A goddamn shame, too.

An impulse struck him. *Walk in thar and stick her. You'd be doing her a favor.*

Hicklin reached inside his boot for a three-and-a-half-inch folding knife. He locked it and ran the tip of his thumb along the black edge of the drop-point blade. He knew anatomy. It was one of his prison hobbies, sizing a man up, looking for the weak spots. Another hobby was to know when to act on these impulses, when to put them aside.

But the impulse grew stronger. Hicklin pressed the edge of the blade against his forearm until it sliced the flesh. Blood appeared, thin as a paper cut. Yet cutting himself quelled the awful notion his mind was entertaining. He folded the blade and put it on the coffee table. Looked around instead for where he'd put his beer.

The night dragged on. Hicklin found himself humming along to a tune from the radio. Charlie slept, his head down, lifting gently as he snored. Otherwise, he was like a statue in a courthouse square. Something you'd just walk past and never notice. Hicklin looked around the living room, stopping to watch moths as they fluttered behind a lamp in the corner. The light had a weak saffron-colored pulse, like it was keeping time, counting down the minutes.

This party won't last.

He stared at Charlie for long stretches. Thought about waking him, maybe with a slap. He could free the boy, drop him facedown across the coffee table, pull down his pants.

Hicklin entertained the idea of raping him, but his attention drifted. He stumbled to the couch, suddenly very drunk. He moved the shotgun, laying it across the floor next to him, thinking if anybody— the law, some disgruntled co-conspirators—came through that door, well, he'd be in deep shit. But they didn't know about this place, Hicklin reminded himself. They didn't know.

Outside the cottage there were chirps and cries, the world rallying around another morning.

We are caged men, ready to watch each other die.
The thief is in your spotlights.
Come and get me you righteous pigs!

FIVE

Nathan Flock turned up the volume on the radio. He was driving his Chevy Silverado, heading west on I-285, skirting traffic as it backed up near the exits. The lighter popped. His passenger cracked the window and lit a cigarette.

"It's a brand-new truck, Preach," Flock objected.

"You smoke, don't you?"

"Yeah, so?"

Leonard Lipscomb pulled a soft pack from the breast pocket of his work shirt. Shook out a cigarette. Nathan glanced at the filtered tip, then took it.

He tried to keep up with a brunette in a convertible. She wore a visor and was talking on a cell phone, a wake of hair flapping in the breeze. Nathan could see her painted nails. She wore a blue tank top and white tennis skirt. She looked rich and well put together, but he'd already convinced himself she was dirty in bed. Probably liked to be choked or cut or both.

He couldn't keep up with her, though. *Bitch must be doing ninety.*

"Why don't you turn this nigger shit off," Lipscomb said, yanking Flock from his fantasies. It wasn't a suggestion, either. In the joint Lipscomb had been known as Preacher. He had a way with words, his musings and philosophizing as legendary in facilities like Hays State Prison as was his ruthlessness.

"What's wrong? You don't like rap?" Flock said.

"I said turn it off."

"Ain't you ever listened to it, though?" he argued. "Not like we haven't done plenty of business with the spooks inside . . ."

Lipscomb pulled a Randall knife from a scabbard and pressed the tip against Flock's jeans just above the femoral artery. Flock flinched and swerved across the next lane, eliciting a chorus of horns before regaining control of the pickup. A tractor-trailer blasted its air horn. Flock turned the radio down, then flicked off the trucker. Lipscomb put the knife back in the scabbard. Not a hint of humor on his face.

"Jesus Christ, Preacher!"

"You don't know nothing about the inside."

A long silence followed. Lipscomb produced a folded sheet of paper. Studied directions written down for him.

"It's the next exit coming up," he said.

Flock threw his cigarette out the window. He glanced at the radio.

"Well? What you want to hear then?"

"How about some Jimmie Rodgers."

"Huh?"

"My thoughts exactly."

Flock abruptly drove his pickup between an 18-wheeler and a limousine before exiting. They came to a stop at the top of the off-ramp. Traffic blocking the intersection. Afternoon rush hour around Atlanta was notorious. Flock could burn half a tank of gas getting anywhere. Lipscomb just stared straight ahead. Nathan didn't remember him disposing of his cigarette. *Crazy asshole probably ate it.*

Nathan made a left and crept toward a bus stop packed with Mexicans and blacks. They were stopped momentarily near the crowd. Lipscomb rolled down the window and spit. Looked around. Everyone with a lick of sense averted their eyes.

Flock drove past a gas station and liquor store and taqueria. Hung a right on a street with the whimsical name Wispy Willow Court. Women walked with their children along the sidewalks, pushing strollers, everyone carrying grocery bags.

Flock turned left into an apartment complex, the parking lot full of vans and used compacts. Work trucks with ladder racks. Imports with tacky paint jobs. Little decorative flags hung from the rearview mirror of almost every vehicle, announcing their owners' origins. Mexico. Nicaragua. El Salvador. Guatemala. *A community of illegals,* Lipscomb mused. *Left alone by the cops until somebody got mean drunk or a wife got battered or a drug deal went sour. Then the cops show up and try to recall their high school Spanish.*

"Who we meeting again?" Flock said.

"Hicklin."

"I heard about him. Y'all did time together, right?"

"Ten years," Lipscomb said.

"What's he like?"

"Ask him yourself if he don't shoot you first."

They got out and walked. Lipscomb led the way up a staircase. The walls of the complex were peeling and cracked.

"So you trust this beaner?" Flock said.

"Yeah, we do."

It was Friday afternoon and a group of day laborers piled out of a minivan. Cases of Budweiser, Pepsi and fast food in tow. They'd been on a roof all day, Lipscomb figured. In some tony neighborhood, skin sun bronzed, hands hardened from years of hammering and hauling and sanding and gutting and mowing. Denim jeans flecked with concrete dust and paint, their shirts tar stained and stinking. Some wore their hair in ponytails. Others wore hats from sports teams for which they had little concern. None of the workers acknowledged Flock or Lipscomb.

But Lipscomb admired the work ethic of folks like them—at least *they* worked, unlike those welfare zombies—even if these wetbacks were what he'd deemed the racial equivalent of a fruit fly.

Rich smells wafted from open windows as dinner was being prepared in a dozen units. A dirt lot doubling as a courtyard served as the recreation center for the neighborhood. Teenagers kicked a soccer ball around while younger kids amused themselves along the sidelines. Some of the children tended to infants in strollers.

A couple of young thugs on the second tier had been watching Lipscomb and Flock since they parked. The thugs hung over the railing and smoked, the sort of cocksure posturing corner kids assumed when they were trying to impress their superiors. One of them sent a text message on his cell phone. The other, brown and stout, turned to face the two white men as they approached. He wore khaki Dickies and a wifebeater, Chuck Taylors. A protégé of some Southern California sect, getting a B.A. in gangbanging, apparently.

"Yo!"

"Yo, yourself," Lipscomb said. He and Flock stopped five feet away.

"You got business here, *Abuelo*? Better hope you do."

Flock flexed some attitude, locking eyes with the mouthy gangbanger. The kid looked not a day over sixteen. Lipscomb stood his ground, clearly not impressed. For sure the boy was strapped. Maybe even fired his little popgun once.

"Lose the attitude, *Hay-soos*," Flock said, then complaining to Lipscomb, "This place is a day-care center."

"I don't want you to talk," Lipscomb said over his shoulder. He turned to address the sentry, saying more with his six-foot-four frame, the hard fat and muscle, than any words could. Body language that suggested he was the type of man to lift a burning car with his bare hands, only to drop it on the trapped victim for laughs.

He noticed the kid glancing at the tattoos that

unwound down each forearm. Lipscomb held up his palms like he was trying to coax a kitten from a tree.

"Now listen here, Jorge or Javier or . . ."

"My name's Paulo, motherfucker."

"So it's Paulo. Tell Cueva we're here. I'm expected."

"And who the fuck are you?" Paulo chirped.

Lipscomb glanced over the railing to the parking lot below, as if judging if the fall would kill a man. Then he smiled.

"Somebody that doesn't give a shit if you live or die in the next ten seconds."

Paulo elbowed his buddy. Another text message was sent out on the cell phone. Then Paulo looked up nervously at Lipscomb. The smile hadn't left the ex-con's face, like a used-car salesman with a secret.

"Make that five seconds, Paulo. My watch is fast."

Someone cut the music inside a nearby apartment. A door opened. The two Hispanic kids walked away. Flock could smell rice and chorizo. He was hungry. Wondered if dinner was part of their deal.

Nathan Flock *followed* Lipscomb inside the apartment and shut the door behind him. The main room included living space and a side kitchenette. Sitting on a couch was a stocky Salvadoran wearing khaki work pants with a white T-shirt. The slippers on his feet were the kind the state issues, known as Nikes by the boys in county lockup. There was a black polymer handgun resting on his knee. A boom box thumped softly on the floor. Flock hesitated near the door, tickled by the fear they were about to be ambushed.

Cueva and a woman sat at a table in the kitchenette. Fifty or so money orders were neatly arranged in front of the woman, a bookish pair of reading glasses on the end of her nose. A menthol cigarette smoldered in an ashtray.

"Thought you'd have guards posted," Lipscomb said. "What about the pigs?"

Cueva smiled. He rose, raised his arms and turned around. There was a pistol snug in the small of his back. An A4 .223-caliber rifle was within his reach, propped in a corner.

"I only use this place a couple hours at a time, Preacher. *Policia* know better than to come around without an appointment."

The man on the couch chuckled. The woman did not look up from the money orders. Somewhere a fire truck siren blared.

Lipscomb noted the black rifle cases stacked six high next to the couch. One was open. Custom interior. Military green ammo boxes. A rucksack with spare magazines pushing against the canvas.

Cueva offered Lipscomb a chair at the table. Flock stood behind them, finding himself ignored now by all in the apartment. He studied Cueva. The Mexican gave up a couple inches to Lipscomb but was no less wide. Cueva's face was pocked around the neck and ears with scars like the chewed-up face of a pit bull. Indeed, the Mexican's eyes had the ferocity of a fighting dog. The potential for reckless abandon. That fearless extra gear inside him that fascinated criminal profilers and penologists.

His body was adorned with prison-gang tattoos. Flock recognized the call signs.

There were hands clasped in prayer, Aztec warriors, naked *mamacitas* with long black manes and pear-shaped breasts. Roses and skulls and the word *Esperanza* from collarbone to collarbone. An ominous blue-green handprint the centerpiece.

Mexican Mafia.

"Hicklin in the shitter?" Lipscomb said.

"Your homeboy came by already," Cueva replied.

Lipscomb reacted with disbelief.

"Say again."

"Yeah, man. Homeboy, eh, Hudson?"

"Hicklin."

"Yeah, Hicklin. Came by late. Two nights ago. Lucky he found me here. This is just temporary 'cuz all the cholos round here lookin' for peashooters to avenge the honor of their old ladies or some shit. That's why I'm relocatin' up-country, where I can move the heavy shit to all you Aryan militia end-of-the-world *pendejos*—"

"What about Hicklin?" Lipscomb said. He was squeezing one hand into a fist like a junkie trying to produce a vein. Flock thought any second Lipscomb would start destroying furniture.

"Came by early Friday. Said he couldn't make it today. The score was set up on the inside, so everything was taken care of. I was paid in advance for the steel and ammo, the Kevlar. Everything else is your business, Holmes."

Cueva sensed something was seriously wrong, Lipscomb's eyes betraying any comfort at this recent development. The Mexican looked to Flock, then addressed his confederate on the couch and his female companion.

"*Ustedes me esperen en el cuarto.*"

The woman took her cigarette but left the money orders. She and Cueva's partner walked down a hall to a bedroom. Flock inched forward but continued standing. Lipscomb lit a cigarette. He couldn't suppress his anger anymore.

"You catch the news today, Cueva?"

"Nah, man. Don't watch TV."

Lipscomb took a couple of deep drags on the cigarette, his mind working to grasp the unbelievable.

"Give us the rest of our gear and we'll be on our way," he finally said.

Cueva shrugged and without a word gestured to the ammo boxes and rifle cases by the couch.

"It's all there, homey. I cleaned the pistols for you, too, 'cause I believe in good customer service."

Cueva pointed to the rucksack, said, "Two HK USP .45s. Nylon holsters and extra mags. Kevlar in that black duffel. I stripped the two Mossys so you could get in and out of here without looking like Special Forces."

Lipscomb and Flock gathered up the duffel bags and left. Neither of them said a word in parting to Cueva. The Mexican sat back down, watching from the table in the kitchenette as the door shut. He picked up the rifle. Fingered the trigger guard of the A4, stroking it as he would a house cat in his lap.

"*Vayan con dios, Ministro.*"

Lipscomb *and Nathan* loaded the truck and Nathan drove them back to the motel. At a gas station Lipscomb bought a newspaper and a carton of cigarettes. Back in the pickup he flipped through the "State/Metro" section and found what he was looking for.

"What is it, Preach? Why did Hicklin pick up his guns before us?"

"Because he jumped the score."

"What?"

Lipscomb folded the paper in half and pointed to the single column of coverage on page 1.

"He jumped our fucking score."

"But we still had a week?"

Nathan cracked the window and lit a cigarette. Both men were silent for a while, Lipscomb smarting from Hicklin's betrayal, Flock taking stock of their situation.

"So what are we going to do?" he finally said to Lipscomb.

"Hicklin knew better. If that sumbitch don't smell the blood, he will."

They *ate at* a Waffle House, the two men brooding in a corner booth. They took turns reading the newspaper article again, scouring for details that weren't there. They sipped their coffee and smoked and said little to each other.

Two police officers came in for refills. Neither man acknowledged the cops, but Lipscomb was acutely aware of their presence, deciding which one he'd shoot first if they attracted unwanted attention. The police left.

They ate guarding the plates of food with their forearms, a jailhouse habit the server had seen in other customers but had no explanation for.

In the motel room they took inventory. The six boxes of buckshot, the five hundred rounds of .45-caliber hollow points, the seven 12-shot magazines. Later Lipscomb paid for the room in cash and walked out to the idling pickup. He tucked the handgun under his thigh and studied a road atlas by the dome light.

Sensing Flock's confusion, he spoke of Hicklin and his stint. Twelve/twelve, Lipscomb called it. To serve an entire sentence without parole.

Other stories followed. How Hicklin once made a garrote from his pillowcase and choked an inmate nearly to death. Took two weeks for the broken blood vessels to heal, Hicklin's victim avoiding mirrors on account of the tomato juice where his eyes had once been.

Hicklin did things that would have guaranteed an extended sentence, but he slipped by, Lipscomb explained. Unnoticed by everyone except the brothers who mattered. Hicklin was known as far west as Lompoc and Pelican Bay, up the coast to Lewisburg, points in between. A reliable man. Smart. Muscle *and* brains. Lipscomb did almost eleven years with Hicklin and a lot of convicts talked the talk, but Hicklin had an aura. Lipscomb described it like a great white swimming, always moving. Searching for prey. An animal with no known enemies.

But the score was set up by brothers inside and it was their money more than Hicklin's or anyone else's. Lipscomb told Flock all the shot callers took a percentage. Scores set up all over the country, and more work for Lipscomb and his crew if the North Georgia S&L job went smooth.

Too fucking late now.

Lipscomb reminded Flock how they were *polishing the rock for the lifers.* Like it was a retirement fund. Hicklin had committed more than just a slight against the Brand.

He had to be found. Things needed to be set right.

Lipscomb had some ideas where Hicklin might have gone, too. Mentioned a point person on the outside, some tweeker from Jubilation County who went by the name of Hummingbird. She took care of Hicklin's finances while he was inside, sent him care packages, even muled some contraband on occasion, all in exchange for drugs and play money. If Hicklin wasn't hiding out with her in the county of his birth, he wasn't anywhere.

This thing just got royally fucked.

Flock listened, his own anger simmering. He merged onto the highway and drove north toward the connector. Brake lights and hyper-color forever circling the big city.

They hit patches of construction, then a long stretch of interstate that rose and fell and eventually ended in Jubilation County.

Lucy met the man and spent half an hour with him. Then he dropped her off at the intersection. She waited while the traffic coupled up and flowed toward some unremarkable goal.

After a while Hicklin pulled his truck over and gestured for her to get in. He seemed preoccupied. Lucy was seventeen. She'd known Hicklin three months. She handed the money over to him. He pocketed the cash. Then lit her cigarette like a gentleman and drove toward home.

Home was Hicklin's trailer. Nothing to brag about, but his momma had left it to him. Lucy never asked about how his momma died. He parked the truck on the gravel drive. Walked around the pickup to her side and opened the door. Lucy liked to give him money. It was as if "they" earned it. When Hicklin made love to her she thought it was love by the way his face contorted and twisted. He made noises that sounded like love.

She didn't know for sure.

Lucy figured he must love her considering she'd been with men all day with their things between her legs, but he didn't care one bit. Even with her defect, that eye the boys in school mocked her for, but he said she was beautiful in a unique way. That was the only way to be beautiful. When Hicklin pushed himself up inside her and the way his arms looked *bracing themselves and the way he grunted Lucy thought for sure this must be love.*

That's all that mattered.

Hicklin got his first tattoo that summer. She washed it for him and when he said he had to go to work she believed him. But he made it clear that her day wasn't done yet and he'd pick her up the same time and just a few more weeks she'd be his and his alone, so she put on makeup and a sexy dress he'd bought for her and walked that familiar route where the trucks slowed and pulled over and she saw brake lights that always looked like a question being asked and when she approached they got their answer. Then the passenger side door would open as if the language they spoke was a nuance of perception and intent and she always expected it, to have to explain her eye to the men, but for the most part they said nothing, not then or after, and she took the days rolling over into each other as some solemn oath to a world not perfect until she could shower and drink coffee and smoke a cigarette while the tractor-trailers pressed on toward their unremarkable destinations.

Charlie raised his head to the sound of grunts. Hicklin had his feet leveraged against the threadbare couch and was pushing his body off the floor. He counted up to fifty before he stopped and righted himself.

Hummingbird waved a plate of hot dogs under Charlie's nose.

"Don't mind him. Been at it all morning. Is that a thousand, yet, baby cakes?" she said.

Hicklin didn't acknowledge either of them. He wore only a pair of white boxer shorts. His torso was slick with sweat, every muscle clearly defined as he walked past them. A trail of nicotine and alcohol seemed to burn off in his wake like a blanket of clouds on a summer morning.

Hummingbird waved the plate of hot dogs under Charlie's nose again, scolding him when she said, "You got to eat, Coma."

Charlie looked down at his rope-bound wrists. He thought about swinging his fists at Hummingbird, but there had just never been any fight in him. He reached up and took an uncooked hot dog and ate it instead.

"Want a cigarette? I like to smoke while I eat. Helps the digestion. Did you know that?" Hummingbird said.

She held a lit cigarette in front of Charlie, but he waved it away. He ate hungrily. When he finished the first hot dog he reached up and grabbed another. Hummingbird stood patiently, holding the plate.

"This ain't no way to live," she said. "But what is?"

When he'd finished eating he asked for water. Then he started to cry. She tousled his hair playfully, as if smitten with a long-lost nephew.

"I've got to use the bathroom," Charlie said, embarrassed, wiping tears from his eyes.

"Number one or number two? Because we shit in the outhouse out back."

"I've got to pee," Charlie whimpered.

"You can't go alone."

"Why not?"

"It's against the rules. . . ."

Hummingbird looked to Hicklin for direction. He nodded. She led Charlie to the bathroom.

"I can't go alone?" Charlie asked.

But she ignored the protest. Ushered Charlie in front of the toilet. She undid his pants and pulled out his penis, watching him with the temperament of someone walking a dog.

Hicklin *had bathed* himself with a washcloth and changed into fresh clothes. He sat down in the recliner to read a book, one of three or four he'd brought with him along with a dictionary. *Tactical Advantage: A Definitive Study of Personal Small-Arms Tactics. A History of the Vikings.* A Donald Westlake paperback. *The Psychopathic God.* Hours reading. Smoking. The shotgun and semiauto always within reach.

Charlie slept for disorienting stretches.

Sometimes he could feel Hummingbird running her hands through his hair. Charlie kept his eyes closed, picturing a supersized Estes Interceptor E model rocket, almost forty inches long with laser-cut balsa fins and a parachute recovery. In his mind the rocket was ready to launch, weather conditions ideal, comforting dreams ready to accept him once again . . .

. . . himself in an open field. A slight wind out of the east . . .

. . . awake again. Hummingbird on the couch smoking her drugs, staring at him as though he were an animal at the zoo. A song on the radio was interrupted by static, the signal strength fading, then surging. Hicklin was gone. Charlie closed his eyes and tried like hell to get back to his dream.

Day *turned to* night. Charlie feigned sleep, always listening, stealing glances when he could. Hummingbird was in the kitchen making sandwiches. He didn't see Hicklin anywhere.

Charlie bolted upright and ran toward the door, hobbling, the chair hanging from his waist by a loosened knot. He tried the knob and the door opened. Charlie could feel Hicklin over his shoulder. Hummingbird taunting him, her voice the only one for miles.

"Git 'im. Git 'im. Git 'im!"

Charlie made it into the open air. Dense, moonlit woods ahead. He stumbled, icy with alarm.

Hicklin's hands were on him in a matter of moments. He was picked up, chair and all, and carried back inside the safe house. Hummingbird clapped her hands, applauding the show. He struggled, but Hicklin was too strong. He punched Charlie in the head and Charlie went limp.

He *woke on* a bare mattress in one of the cottage's small bedrooms. A ratty blanket had been thrown over him. His wrists were tied.

A throbbing headache was accompanied by waves of nausea—pain on par with getting dropped off a roof.

Hummingbird appeared in the doorway wearing only her underwear and a tank top. She slid under the blanket with Charlie. Undid his pants. Kissed him. Charlie turned his face away and moaned, a sound stifled by the duct tape covering his mouth.

He felt her sweat and spittle against his cheeks. She reached inside the waistband of his underwear and grabbed him, started tugging. Satisfied with the result of her efforts, she stopped to unbutton his shirt, Charlie thinking, *Stop,* as if he could will her to consider what she was doing. But there was no reasoning with someone who lived for what was in front of her and nothing more.

Flush with embarrassment, Charlie pushed his tongue against the tape, but it didn't budge. He turned his head from side to side. Hummingbird worked at him with her hand. Then she went down and swallowed him.

She slid up his body until they were face-to-face like lovers. Her breath was fetid. She pulled the tape off his mouth and silenced him with a finger to her lips.

"Stop," he said, ignoring the request. "Please stop."

Hummingbird adjusted her underwear, then reached down and angled him inside her. She made a sound when she settled her weight on him. He instinctively pushed back, thrusting, ashamed and helpless to the wants of his body.

His face froze when he ejaculated. Shocked by everything his trembling body was doing.

"It's okay, baby cakes. I used to be a schoolteacher," Hummingbird said, cooing, her movements slowing now. She hunched over and nuzzled Charlie's cheek.

A soft kiss on an ear. A caress with a fingertip.

She whispered something else.

"He's watching us."

Blood runs black and cold.
Sirens come to life.
Search lights blind my eyes.
The mountains are in sight.

SIX

Tommy Lang *didn't* know what to do with his hands, so he clasped them behind his back. He looked over the knot of reporters, the two linkup vans. Affiliates from Atlanta, their curt, polished correspondents holding those funny-looking microphones. He said a few words to begin the press conference, answered some preliminary questions and stepped aside. Rain clouds hung low. A rep from the Georgia State Patrol took questions. Then Sallie Crews took over at the steps to the government building.

She spoke of what they knew, Lang curious if "they" included him. She didn't elaborate on leads or what the house-to-house searches turned up, or the helo flyovers with their thermal imaging. Crews declined to reveal what suspects, if any, *they* had.

Lang thought the same thing as everybody else there.

This guy's in the wind. Forever. And Charlie Colquitt is probably dead.

What's the point?

But Sallie Crews was a commanding presence.

Her voice had a practiced authority that let everyone know this wasn't her first rodeo. A picture of Charlie Colquitt was released to the media in Atlanta, Birmingham, Chattanooga and Asheville. An agency liaison was pushing the story to go national so that a picture of Charlie might appear on a couple of million TV screens. A photograph of a pale, nondescript young man. With a face that unfortunately warranted little compassion.

In private Crews had shown Lang a list of recent parolees, probationers and absconders who had ties to white supremacist gangs. She had already been in touch with gang units at prisons statewide and as far west as Victorville and Pelican Bay in California. In the Southeast alone the number of potential suspects pushed two hundred.

The news conference ended. A female reporter in high heels giggled as she botched one take after another. Another reporter checked his hair in the reflection from a van's side mirror. They were never as impressive in person, Lang thought.

He hung back a few feet while Crews scrolled through e-mails on her mobile. Always seemed to be something important being messaged to her. Lang studied her and wondered if she took a drink now and then. The fantasy of a boozy night with her occupied him briefly. She turned in his direction.

"Beer joints?" Crews said, as if she'd read his mind.

Lang cocked his head. *Say again?*

Crews frowned. "You mentioned a pool hall and liquor store where the highway dead-ends," she explained. "Ten minutes from the bank?"

"Well, there's KB's Billiards and Bird Dog—that's the package store. Both of 'em right off Route Twenty. That's the end of Jubilation County, as far as most folks go. Nothing but the national forest and mountains beyond it."

"Know those places?"

"They're both for the paycheck-to-paycheck, hard-timin' country folk. Everybody knows everybody in those joints."

"Let's take a ride," she said.

They walked to his patrol car. Crews wore a windbreaker despite the August heat, khaki pants, black boots, her hair pulled back smartly. Lang almost opened the door of his cruiser for her and immediately felt like a fool. He radioed Bower and instructed the deputy to meet them.

Sitting next to Crews made Lang nervous when he had no reason to be. She studied the case file, occasionally resting her eyes on the passing landscape, her mind preoccupied with a multitude of theories, possibilities and considerations.

They passed fencerows. A tin-roof town. Rain dotted the windshield.

Deputy Bower met them in the parking lot across the street from the liquor store.

"Anything?" Lang said.

"Nothing new at Bird Dog," his deputy said, flicking his cigarette toward a puddle of rainwater. "Just the usual riffraff buying thirty-packs of Schlitz and lotto tickets. If there was a white ex-con who's mean as hell in the neighborhood, he ain't been in there."

Lang cast a weary glance at the parking lot of KB's Billiards, the asphalt littered with plastic rings and cigarette butts. The place was a dive, a joint popular with locals looking to drink their lunch, and no stranger to fights of the knock-down drag-out variety. Off the Sheriff's look Deputy Bower walked back to his patrol car, but not before offering Crews a polite tip of the hat.

Lang paused to admire a jet-black Chevy pickup parked out front, a vehicle out of place among the half-dozen beaters and motorcycles. Crews looked back once at the Sheriff, noting the peculiar reservation on his face before they entered the pool hall.

The air was smoky-stale. The cars parked outside seemed to match the appearance of their owners, three of whom racked balls and nursed beers at a nearby table. Any excitement dimmed at the sight of police. There were televisions mounted in two corners above the bar. The volume was muted, replaced by music from a jukebox—some twangy anthem sung by a pop-country princess.

The patrons eyed Lang in his for-the-cameras forest-green polyester uniform, Crews in her GBI windbreaker. No fuss, but Lang sensed their uneasiness.

The bar was front and center in the deceptively large hall. Rows of pool tables on either side. Booths and tables along the walls. Cushioned bar stools. Some of the cocktail tables looked as though they hadn't been cleaned since the previous night, most of them cluttered with glasses of melted ice and browning limes. Crumpled napkins. OxyContin residue. Mirrored advertisements for whiskey and rum, tobacco, neon beer signs sputtered in the darkness.

A couple of regulars hovered over their drinks. A conversation had been suspended in mid-sentence, their eyes on the Sheriff. Lang was certain there were a couple of potential DUIs, no doubt narcotics and an outstanding warrant or two in the room. It wasn't important now.

Lang and Crews approached the bartender. Del Slaton poured a cup of coffee and slyly topped it with Evan Williams.

"Where's Kalamity at today?" Lang said to the bartender.

Del raised coal-colored eyes and smiled. He had about half his teeth.

"Kal's gone to the Costco. I'm Del."

The bartender turned to Crews and smiled but didn't offer his hand.

"Don't believe I seen you in here before, Del," Lang said.

"Don't believe I seen you here this early. Time for a quick one, Sheriff?"

Del smiled again and winked at Crews. Lang felt a cold urge to climb over the bar and pistol-whip him. The drunks seated on stools resumed their conversation, one of them chuckling at the exchange. Del hooked a thumb inside the hammer pocket of his carpenter's pants, ashed his cigarette on the floor with a quick flick of a forefinger. Crews looked around, uninterested in Del.

"This is Agent Crews," Lang said curtly. "You heard about the robbery?"

"I did, Sheriff. Folks been talking 'bout it." His voice had a childish pitch. The disposition of a supreme smart-ass.

Crews smirked and shook her head. Del cradled his cigarette in an ashtray and took to wiping down pint glasses with a dishcloth, stowing them in a plastic crate next to the icebox. He paused to savor another sip of coffee. If Lang had seen Del in there tending bar, he must have been too drunk to remember. Crews leaned in and rested her elbows on the bar.

"I like your pants, Del," she said. "Carhartt's?"

"Only brand worth wearin'," the bartender said.

"You know most of your customers, Del?"

He gave the hall a once-over.

"Regular crowd, I suppose. Last night was purdy busy, but I didn't see no one stuck out."

Lang excused himself and walked to the men's room, passing a man and woman shooting a game of eight ball near the jukebox. Smoke hung over the table. The man smiled and nodded to Lang. The woman ignored him. Lang noticed the wedding ring on her finger but no ring on her companion's hand. Typical for this place. But Lang couldn't be judgmental. He had been one of them.

The trim around the bathroom door was chipped, amusingly repaired with hardened bits of chewing gum. Lang turned his head. He saw the two men in the far corner. Big, mean-looking assholes shooting a game of nine ball.

A memory stirred. The place was so familiar to

him, telling him stories he didn't want to hear. *Christ Almighty the shame . . .*

. . . that one waitress was young enough to be your daughter, wadn't she?

Lang suddenly felt hopeless, emotionally disabled. In the bathroom he washed his hands. He might've punched the mirror, if it weren't already broken.

I*f it weren't* for the buzzing neon sign reading *Pool Tables* and the dingy white *KB* placard tacked up over a tinted window, Nathan Flock would have driven right by the place. The building had all the charm of a broken ankle. He pulled off the highway and parked next to a Pontiac Fiero that looked as though it had recently been stored at the bottom of a lake.

Inside Lipscomb ordered a pitcher of beer. Then he slid a hundred-dollar bill across the bar to Del.

"And what's *that* for?"

"Wondering where the boss is at?" Lipscomb said with a friendly smile.

"Kalamity?" Del said. "She's taken the day off."

"Then we're just looking on how to find her. If we was actually here. Which we wasn't."

A few seconds went by. Lipscomb stared at Del with a cool amusement.

"I follow," Del said.

"You look like a man who understands how to," Lipscomb said, and jerked a thumb at Flock. "My friend over there said I was to be sure to tell you how good-looking you are. Follow?"

Del folded the hundred-dollar bill twice and nodded bashfully.

"Next pitcher's on the house."

"Pour 'em and rack 'em, peckerwood."

Flock finished his first glass of beer to Lipscomb's third as he sized up a cut shot on the six ball. Then Lipscomb murmured something else and Flock looked up at the front door. KB's was dark save for the cones of light illuminating individual tables. Cigarette smoke drifted like a layer of sea foam. The sudden blast of daylight only magnified the arrival of Lang and Sallie Crews.

"Roll down them sleeves, son," Lipscomb said.

Flock took the shot on the six and missed. He made a face. Like he really cared. He walked around the table, casually adjusting the sleeves of his mechanic's shirt. Flock didn't think the county mountie or the chick agent were scoping them yet. Earlier Lipscomb had told him to keep his tattoos hidden. *People remember that kind of shit, he said. The heat in this part of the state is going to be focused to pale blue India ink and yard postures.*

Lipscomb clutched the end of his pool cue, covertly sizing up the room, entertaining scenarios. *Hope Flock's man enough, because I'll kill every damn person in here 'fore I go back inside.* Then he leaned over the table and cut the six ball into the side pocket.

The Sheriff and the woman were talking to Del. Flock circled the table, out of turn, while Lipscomb watched the bar without seeming to. At one point Del glanced at them. After years in prison Lipscomb had developed a talent for intimidation, just a subtle look—maybe a twinkle in his eye, a glint like that coming off the razor edge of a hunting knife. He locked eyes for a brief moment with Del, as if waiting for the ramifications of a wrong answer to register with the bartender.

"Danny Romanowski was a brother from down near Statesboro," Lipscomb said out of the side of his mouth, returning his attention to the game. "Usually ran into him in courtroom bullpens. But for a while we shared a cell on North Block at Hays before I eventually raised. Years ago it was. Danny took a score on a bank once. Noticed a chick every Tuesday and Thursday going in for change orders from a burrito joint. Coming out with a burlap sack that looked heavy with green."

Lipscomb paused. The Sheriff had walked away from the bar. He was four tables from them, eyeing something. The bathroom door? An empty booth?

Flock cradled his cigarette in an ashtray and watched Lipscomb run the cue stick through his fingers a dozen times before attempting his next shot.

Flock practiced a quick draw in his head, thinking of the .357 concealed in a spine holster. Lipscomb was armed, he knew, a piece clipped on his belt. Lipscomb continued his anecdote—hand to his mouth, part habit as a way to deter possible lipreaders. It was a skill many inmates learned in prison, hovering over catwalks and railings, walking the yard. *Guard your tongue,* Lipscomb always said. *The hacks are always watching.*

"Now Danny, he was a goofy brother, a gas huffer. Made him fearless . . . and reckless. So he put on his 'outfit' and got good and high before the bank score. Met this girl inside her car. The shock of seeing Danny in drag caused her to pass out. He never even touched her. Then Danny walked into the bank, his blond wig and lipstick smeared like a whore's. That and a week's worth of stubble. He walked straight up to the teller with that change order. But Danny wasn't so smart, see? He saw those hundred-dollar straps and thought he'd scored big . . . but those straps were for one-dollar bills.

"Was wearing the biggest bra he could find in his momma's closet. He just scooped that money up inside the bra, stuffing cash up in the shoulders of his dress like the pads on a football player. Finally he lit up out of that bank, but by then the assistant manager had came to in her car and flagged down a cop. When they caught up to Danny he was huffing paint, space brained, feeling up his titties, but there was nothing but George Washingtons for cleavage."

Flock smiled nervously. He crouched down in the cone of light and blew a shot on the seven ball.

"Never could hit that corner shot myself," Lang said, stepping into their light, his badge gleaming.

"I*'m learning the* kid, but he's just a touch clumsy."

"How y'all doing today?" Lang said.

"Just fine, Sheriff," Lipscomb said, in character.

"Just pulled an all-nighter repairing our car after Saturday night."

"Dirt?"

"Only thing worth racin' on."

Lang nodded.

"Pony stock? Limited?"

"Nah, super late-model. Raced over in Rome."

Lang nodded again. Lipscomb figured he bought it but was irritated by Lang's knowledgeable line of questioning. The Sheriff knew his shit. But Lipscomb looked the part. He'd been under the hood of Flock's Chevy. Hands were a little grimy. Even had a Hoosier Racing Tire patch on the breast pocket of his twill shirt. Pure fucking luck he'd pulled it from his duffel to wear that morning. Flock took his shot, looking annoyed as he missed again.

"Say y'all from over Rome way?" Lang said.

"Yeah."

"Where y'all been racing?"

Lang was leaning against the adjacent pool table. Lipscomb tried to gauge him. *Is he really just shooting the shit with us?*

"Bulls Gap," Lipscomb said after a moment's hesitation.

Lang nodded an acknowledgment, still friendly, grinning as though it were an election year.

"I didn't see a trailer out front. Just that new Silverado."

"Left our race car at a buddy's garage," Lipscomb answered. "Right front was tore all to hell. You know Frank Dutton?"

"Can't say I do," Lang said.

"Good mechanic. We're looking at four grand to the winner next Saturday night . . . unless Tim Richmond over there don't jump the cushion and throw her into the wall."

Lang laughed, but he was already walking away.

"Enjoy your game," he said with a curt, not-so-courteous nod.

Flock acknowledged the dig from Lipscomb. *Whoops, bud. You know me.* Plus the reference to the NASCAR legend seemed to have humored Lang and sold the lie. As did mentioning the cushion of dirt that racers use as a driving line. Flock took a sip of beer and shrugged. Not sure who was buying what.

Moments later they watched Lang and Crews leave. Del looked over and grinned at Flock like he'd just eaten a big bowl of shit. The jukebox kicked in, as if it'd been waiting for the Sheriff to go. Waylon Jennings sang "Anita, You're Dreaming."

Lipscomb lit a cigarette. He smoked slowly. A weird ecstasy burned onto his face.

"That there was better than any sex I ever had, son."

Lang *drove his* cruiser slowly along the row of parked vehicles, stopping at Nathan Flock's Chevy.

"What did you make of those two?" Crews said.

"I've learned not to be judgmental about prison tattoos."

"Want to run the Chevy's plates?"

"It's Floyd County. Where they said they was from." Lang paused, straining to see inside the truck's cab. "I'd still like to get a look in there," he said.

"Probable cause?"

"None. Just a bad case of SDLR. Let's eat."

Lang pulled out of the parking lot, spraying gravel as the Crown Vic sped down the highway.

"Mostly locals in there the last few nights, according to that queer bartender," Crews said, finishing a cheeseburger. "Nobody throwing money around, asking for girls or drugs or gambling heavy . . . no one bragging about all the jail time they've done."

She sighed. Lang thought it to be the first time he'd seen Crews express frustration. He drove north toward Route 20, a stretch of lonely-looking land with not even a road sign for company. They left the foothills, passing barns and tree farms and the wood-processing plant. An abandoned development with empty lots, a few foreclosed homes, signs from a dozen Realtors. He turned right onto the highway, eventually passing the North Georgia Savings & Loan. Crews turned her head but said nothing. Plastic sealed the broken front doors, police tape crisscrossing the threshold. The bank had hired security guards to patrol the branch until it could reopen, which Lang figured with any corporation that only cared about the bottom line would be sooner rather than later.

Hopefully, they'll wait for the blood to dry first.

He and Crews were quiet for a while, the police band radio the only sound. The inside of the cruiser smelled of fast food. He cracked a window and lit a cigarette. It didn't seem to bother her.

"And how about those two graduates of Felony U. shooting pool?" she said.

"They had a nice story."

"What does 'SDLR' stand for?"

"'Something Don't Look Right,'" Lang said.

"Seems like you know KB's pretty well, Sheriff."

"I used to," he said. "Not anymore."

Little else was said, Crews realizing regrettably that her last comment might have been a conversation killer. She worked her mobile instead, pressing for results from the state's notoriously slow Northeastern Lab.

There was a clapboard church ahead, passionflowers in bloom throughout the small property. Picnickers gathered in a brush arbor. Lang raised his hand in greeting, but no one waved back.

He broke the ice again, wanting to put the sour memory of KB's behind. Topics mostly professional, but hints of a personal life peppered their conversation. He mentioned his ex-wife. Crews mentioned a separation. Odd hours, bad coffee, lack of sleep.

"The occupational hazards of anyone in law enforcement," she said.

She elaborated on the case, speaking of how ruthless and organized prison gangs were. She told him in confidence that more than a dozen other banks in the Southeast had been hit in the past sixteen months. Usually two or three men who had precise knowledge of security features, floor plans and cash delivery schedules. Crews was convinced the heists were being planned in prisons.

Lang tried to focus on what she had to say. He wished the road wouldn't end.

But the same thoughts kept repeating.

Why me? Why here? And why now?

Newspapers *still covered* the windows. Charlie tried to distinguish day from night by watching Hicklin and Hummingbird. She cleaned the kitchen often, even when there was nothing to clean. She'd also taken to organizing little things in the living room. Old magazines, packs of cigarettes, matchbooks. Her rolled-up Baggies filled with crystalline powder. She folded dirty clothes in front of him as if he needed to be taught how.

Charlie figured these activities for morning.

Hummingbird was obsessive. She scrubbed and dried and stacked dishes in a way that suggested guilt or remorse. Then she would shrink to some corner of the cottage, that odor of chemical smoke not far behind.

Hicklin disappeared for hours. Occasionally he opened the front door, appearing with food and ice from risky missions to procure more beer. Charlie was shocked to feel relief when Hicklin returned from these late-night excursions. The air swelling with the sounds of crickets and treehoppers. Chirps. The wind. Thunder. Darkness.

Other times Charlie would close his eyes and

listen to the sounds of the cottage. Hicklin exercising. A fourth set of leg lifts. Then crunches. Push-ups.

The sound of a match flaring against the tip of a cigarette. The whine of the filter.

That burnt plastic smell.

The binges of sleep continued.

He had terrible nightmares. One in particular where all of his veins broke free through his skin. Charlie screaming as a branchwork of blue-green twisted from his forearms and sprayed the cottage with blood. Veins near his ankles and feet, in his neck, burrowing through the flesh like earthworms after a sun shower. It was as if his entire vascular system was making a run for it. He'd never had dreams so violent, so vivid. Not before. Not ever.

When he woke, his muscles ached. Pain shot across the middle of his back, under his breastbone and down across both thighs. He had to urinate. After he asked a couple times Hummingbird untied him. She went with him into the bathroom and as before watched him. Only this time with a covetous smile.

There were hours of interrupted sleep where Charlie grew disoriented. Could have been day or night. For reasons unknown to him Hicklin put a hood over his head. Charlie remembered screaming. Then he felt Hummingbird's hands on his shoulders, her cotton-drawl whispers, offering promises and favors. He shook violently, knowing he wanted to kill her. He wanted to kill them both.

Her laughter haunted him. As did Hicklin's silence.

Charlie dreamed of rockets slicing through the sky. Tools and parts spread across a blanket, a salmon-tinted sunset, a breeze . . . he worked heartily, attaching a tapered swept fin to a Bulldog FS-500. When he looked off into the distance he saw dark figures shimmer before the dream turned over and he was now back at the bank . . . during those lulls when the lobby was empty. He would pass the time entering customer account numbers. On the computer in a flash were several months' worth of check card purchases and withdrawals. He thought of it as financial voyeurism, knowing what people spent their money on. Sex videos and bar tabs and motel rooms and gas and fast food. The patterns and pathologies of people amused Charlie, as though he were spying on an alien race.

A species contrary to his own.

His mind became like a movie screen—his best and only company—complete with reel changes, jump cuts, dissolves. The bank lobby again. Charlie faced a line that never shrank, yet there was his mother, like a stranger, patiently waiting. He greeted her, but there was something different about Lucy Colquitt. *Her eye! She never left the house without her glass eye!* She presented a check for Charlie to cash. He scanned it once, twice, but his equipment would not read the magnetic ink of the check's MICR line. He looked across the teller window at his mother, into a small half-moon socket that was her left eye, accompanied by a look of indifference. And across the lobby, a hooded figure appeared and raised his weapon.

———

The bedroom was silent and dark. Charlie's head and neck ached. Just opening his eyes induced nausea. But something had moved on the floor. At first he thought it was a toy car rolling by his foot, a big black toy car with six legs. When his vision cleared he realized the object was in fact a wood beetle. Oily and sleek-looking in the sparse light, it took a few cautious steps, the beetle's antennae slanting toward Charlie as if it meant to lend him an ear.

The insect made it to the wall and started to climb, then fell. Dull black wing covers fluttered. It righted itself and met the wall again. This time the beetle climbed higher before falling again.

A tenacious insect, the beetle kept this up for a good twenty minutes. Charlie watched, wiggling his own toes and fingers, wincing from a pulled muscle in his lower back. He felt as if he were rooting for the beetle at a ball game, as though the beetle's success would somehow translate to his own. And the bug was steadily improving. Two, three, then five feet up the wall. The ceiling within reach.

Then the beetle seemed to hesitate, those wings fluttering again, but it dropped to the floor, landing with a small thud. Charlie extended his leg. Nudged the insect with a big toe. It couldn't even right itself with his help.

He stared for a long time, watching the legs quiver and bend. He finally kicked it away with a foot, out of sight, the bug crackling across the floor like a peanut shell.

———————

"*Charlie Colquitt . . . but* they call you Coma."

Charlie opened his eyes at the sound of Hicklin's voice. He looked around the cottage, figuring it for day three, maybe day four. Easier to lose track of time than he'd thought possible. Hummingbird sat on the couch in a daze, absently scratching her forearms.

Hicklin reached into the cooler and retrieved a beer. Empty cans were stacked in pairs atop the coffee table. Charlie wriggled, finding the ropes looser than before. He managed to raise a hand and rub his chin, feeling patches of stubble, a tender bruise that ran the length of one side of his jaw. He sucked his teeth. They felt mossy, complementing the rotten taste in his mouth.

It hadn't sounded like a question, but Charlie nodded anyway. He watched Hicklin drop a cigarette in an empty can. It hissed when it hit the bottom.

"It's a great nickname," Hicklin continued. "Nicknames all I know. They sum you up better than any tax return or driver's license or C file. Course I called it like I saw it inside 'less I knowed 'em, meaning you was either a nigger, a wetback or a bitch. Funny I never had me no nickname inside. One celly called me Chef on account I was a pretty good buck master."

Charlie's face dimmed with confusion.

"Made alcohol in prison," Hicklin explained. "Gate time round my cut could get like happy hour. Wasn't no Pabst, but my moonshine did the trick."

Hicklin raised the beer as if to propose a toast, better times replaying behind his eyes.

"You want a beer, Charlie?" he said after a moment.

"No."

"Ever had one?" he asked, holding a can out for Charlie.

Charlie shook his head at first. He was thirsty, though. The can of beer looked ice-cold, water dripping from the sides. He finally reached out and took it.

"Got any water?" Charlie said.

"They's water in that beer you're holding."

Charlie opened the beer and looked over at Hummingbird, remembering her visit from the night before, the way she put her hands on him. Tonight her eyes were glazed, the pupils as big as buttons. Wherever she was, Charlie hoped she stayed there.

He took a sip, the beer tasting sudsy and peculiar. But it was cold and that's all that mattered. He took another sip—and another—before holding the can against his aching jaw. He looked across the room at Hicklin, as if seeing him clearly for the first time. He focused on a greenish-black swastika tattooed on Hicklin's chest.

"You're a Nazi?" Charlie said.

"Thank you."

It was the only thing Hicklin thought to say.

The boy—*Hicklin could* think of him in no other terms—had been a curious hostage. Hicklin had considered ways of disposing of Charlie since arriving at the safe house. But something had kept him from doing the kid in. Hicklin wanted more from Charlie. He needed more.

"So *you hate* black people?" Charlie said after a minute of silence.

"You done had a heart check, huh? No, son. I hate *niggers*," Hicklin said sharply.

Charlie flinched at the word. The *N-Word*. He'd heard his mother use it all his life but had never grown accustomed to it. Hicklin finished his beer and lit a cigarette. An odd, satisfied look on his face.

"You know what a *nigger* is, Coma?" he said.

"An African-American person?" Charlie answered. The beer can in his hand was almost empty. His head had begun to swim.

Hicklin laughed loudly, political correctness not a popular concept inside the Georgia penal system.

Hummingbird giggled, too. She sat Indian-style, chewing on a fingernail. Hicklin gave her a look. She took her finger out of her mouth, repentant as a scolded child.

He said, "A nigger is *anyone* who acts like a fool. A loud, obnoxious fool. I respected many Negroes and Hispanics. A man stands tall and walks hard and I'll respect him."

"But n-nobody has a choice," Charlie said, stammering, trying to inflect a challenging tone. "To be born white. Why hate people because they're different?"

Hicklin rose and stretched, fetched another beer from the cooler. He began to pace, tiger-walking as if the cottage were a cage. The muscles in Hicklin's forearms and shoulders seemed to pop and writhe with every movement. Charlie watched him, noticing Hicklin's tattoos in greater detail, a few so intricate they seemed like a picture show on flesh, a righteous hatred in the details. He found Hicklin's gait strange. The man walked with a swagger, guarded, like a lion stalking the fringes of a pride area.

Hicklin turned on the radio, tuning to a country station. Country Gold out of Chattanooga. Charlie felt something cold over his shoulder, looked up at Hicklin offering him another beer, a peculiar grin on his face. Charlie took the beer without a word.

Hicklin sat down and opened his own, taking three gulps. He reached for the pack of cigarettes, hustled one out and lit it. There were more than twenty butts mashed in the ashtray, God knew how many more floating in the empties.

As if following a cue Hummingbird produced her glass pipe. After smoking her movements became manic, involuntary. Her eyes slapped back and forth. She seemed to be chewing on an imaginary meal.

Charlie tried to ignore her, instead taking a bigger sip of beer, the taste growing on him. The pain in his lower back lessened, as had the soreness along his jaw. His mind felt like water in an ice-cube tray.

"You asked me why I hate people because they're different?" Hicklin said, easing back into the recliner.

"Uh-huh."

"Because I can."

His reply was defiant, more protest than explanation. He drank the rest of the beer, pouring it down his throat. He knew Charlie was right about not having a choice. About how arbitrary one's race was. And Hicklin didn't have an answer for him. Just a blind faith in his superiority.

And Charlie held his beer with both hands, as if afraid that someone would take it from him. Hicklin leveled his eyes on Charlie then, studying the boy's body, idly thinking of ways to improve it with exercise. He rolled an unlit cigarette between his fingers to loosen the tobacco. Then he coughed and spit a saucer of mucus onto the floor.

When Charlie met his gaze he saw a mischievous grin and fought to keep from smiling himself.

Later that evening Charlie found himself thoroughly drunk. Hummingbird had retreated to one of the bedrooms, a compulsive laughter heard through the walls the only reminder she was still in the cottage at all. Country Gold had gone off the air, replaced with a classic rock station from Greenville. Thin Lizzy's "Ballad of a Hard Man."

Hicklin popped the tabs on two more beers and stumbled over to Charlie, kicking several empty cans across the floor as he did so.

"I'll wager we got time for one more 'fore you pass out?"

He held out the can, as if to coax Charlie out of the chair.

"Come on, son. Come and get it."

Charlie felt as if he'd been nailed to the floor. He got to his feet warily, like an old man attempting a steep flight of stairs. Rising with a wobble, he took a perilous first step.

"Get over here. Walk, goddammit!" Hicklin said, waving the can of beer at Charlie like dangling a carrot before a horse.

And Charlie walked, listing to port, his shoulders sagging. He almost fell but caught himself, barely, a drunken chuckle his only sound.

"Stand up and walk straight. Be a man, Charlie!"

Charlie lunged for the beer but grasped nothing but air. His knees buckled and he almost went down again.

"Don't go down on your knees, son! You go down on your knees, reckon what I'll do to you?" Hicklin barked.

Just then Charlie shook his head and righted himself. He stood reasonably straight and walked toward Hicklin again, making a couple passes at the beer. Satisfied, Hicklin let Charlie have his prize. He smiled, holding the beer with both hands against his chest, swaying a little.

"Charlie Colquitt. Damn if I don't think you got the makin's," Hicklin said, saluting Charlie with his own can, followed by a long, slow sip. "I knew a woman named Colquitt once," he added, almost absentmindedly. "Had a glass eye that didn't fit right . . ."

"Glass eye?" Charlie said with a slur, his eyes twinkling with vague recognition.

"Once I fucked her so hard, damn thing popped out a her head!"

Hicklin's drunken laughter filled the cottage. Loud and from the belly. Charlie laughed, too. At first with hysterical and blind enthusiasm, but some underlying truth gave him pause, and the laughter slowly emptied from him like the air from a balloon.

Cold steel and gun metal grey.
Nightmares, another night has turned to day.

SEVEN

They *walked the* catwalks down to the first tier. Wolfen eyes peered out from behind bars. They heard the fleshy sounds of a man masturbating. They did not stop. Some men called out. Shouted warnings to the other inmates that echoed around the cell block. The tactical team knew they were closely watched by the prisoners. Almost anything they said could be lip-read or intuited. They kept quiet.

Four abreast now. The tactical team worked their way down a long corridor, the walls of which resembled the hull of a sunken vessel. They wore flak jackets and gloves and green cargo pants. The lead officer spoke into a walkie clipped above his collarbone. The last gate opened with a *clank* and the men entered the Secure Housing Unit.

The *kite swung* from one inmate's hands to another. They timed the movements of the guards, watching the camera and counting. The cutovers were known like the rising and setting of the sun. Going fishing, they called it.

The line dropped down from one floor of the SHU to the next before it was gathered up, sucked under the door and repositioned. Correctional officers appeared and disappeared behind the acrylic detention windows. With the kite folded, an inmate counted in his head and then flicked the line through the space under the door, arcing it around the column to the adjacent cell. He felt a tug and let the line go. The kite disappeared under the door. The inmate knew he would be rewarded. A skilled messenger always was.

The convict took the message and read it. He was going to flush it down the toilet but sensed something and tight-rolled the slip of paper. He pulled down his boxer shorts and pushed it up inside his rectum as far as it would go.

The tac team was at the window.

"Do me a solid and take off the shades," the lead officer said.

He raised his arms in a mock stretch and complied, tucking his sunglasses in a soft case. Then they told him to cuff up. He turned in a circle, his back to the door, and when the latch popped he found the metal tray of the service slot with his palms. His hands dangled for a moment.

Two pairs of cold metal handcuffs clamped around his wrists. Another pair for his ankles. They told him to walk forward and turn around. When the door opened he stepped out of his cell in his state-issued slippers. They patted him down and made him squat. A shiv or shank would have punctured internal organs. But he was smarter than that. He expected them to inspect his anus, but they didn't.

He stood aside while they tossed his cell.

Two officers remained with him, watching him with respect. Everyone knew who he was. What he was capable of. The convict thought briefly about attacking them both but decided against it. He had names and addresses. He knew that the guard to his left had a mother in a rest home and a sister in Colorado Springs.

Plenty of weapons at his disposal despite the shackles. Teeth, forehead, knees and feet. He just was not in the mood.

The lead officer flipped through photos and letters. Shined an ultraviolet light through greeting cards and notebook paper. He studied the script, the tight lines of ink, the spacing. The words were clear, the meaning ambiguous.

If only these supercops knew the code, the convict thought. *But us poor white trash just a little too smart for 'em.*

The lead officer reached for a stack of books, flipping through one entitled *Discipline and Punish* and another called *Look Homeward, Angel.* Nothing unusual revealed itself. The other guards ran their gloved hands along edges in the cell but found nothing. One officer reached down into the toilet. Another tapped against the wall and bed frame with the end of his Maglite.

The convict did not talk nor did his expression

ever change. The lead officer told him he was taking the letters. The convict nodded. He wished the officer good luck. The guards uncuffed him and locked the door.

The convict stood at the small acrylic square that served as the lone window of his cell, watching the tac team ascend a staircase on the opposite side of the SHU. He ran a forefinger and thumb along his bristly mustache and thought of the kite and its meaning.

Later. He fingered the slip of paper from his anus. Studied it. He felt a sharp pang of betrayal, of bloodlust. He read it again.

H. jumped the score.
?

The prisoner looked around his cell. At the beige walls, his cot and rumpled belongings. A calendar on the wall marked the month and day. Just one of many for him. Time was his currency, the days his most prized possession.

He'd read all the philosophies and musings concerning time, its stagnant flow, all meaninglessness.

Don't leave me now, brother.

Time was nothing but a mark he hoped to manipulate, work the angles on. Because he would be remembered for the will he exerted and not the years it took to do it.

The universe did not decay without company, brother.

They all looked up to him. One of a select few who ran the whole fucking show.

And disrespect was not tolerated.

It was Monday. Nothing surprised him. But the unannounced visit from the prison's tactical team gave him pause. Something was up.

He recalled the thunderstorms and humidity. Clouds boiling over with phosphorescent flashes of light. The smell of grass in late Spring. Running water. The ample shade of a white oak. The land belonged to his foster father, the man responsible for the helplessness that defined his youth. Bent over the chair like that. Such a young man, too. His insides swelling. Those hands on his shoulders, calloused and powerful. The pivotal point in his life when it all went bad and he found his calling.

At sixteen he brained his foster father with a pipe wrench.

Leaving one family for another. Abuse in perpetuity.

I am forever a walk-alone, brother.

But the empire needed leadership. There were issues with the rugheads to address, a mule talking to the guards, two scores and a hit awaiting a vote by the council, a brother getting tuned up for no obvious reason, but there was always a reason.

And then there were the bank heists. The prisoner thought about Hicklin. A man he'd never met, only corresponded with. Knew him by reputation. Word of mouth.

A brother is a brother until that brother dies. . . .

He dug for hate.

He smelled the blood.

He composed a reply using a toenail, dipping it in a small cup of his own urine. A convict's version of invisible ink.

Then he decided to overnight it.

The house was nestled between a stream and a curtain of iron oak. Wire mesh fencing formed a loose perimeter. Kalamity Bibb parked her Dodge in the driveway, checked herself in the rearview and got out.

A neighbor's quarter horse had wandered up to the fence, its tail sweeping back and forth as if it was happy to see Kalamity. She mashed a cigarette in the ashtray. A bead of sweat dripped from her brow and landed on the seat cover.

She popped the hatch. The cargo space was packed with cardboard boxes from a wholesale buyers club off the interstate. Enough groceries to last a decade. There was cherry-red meat, wrapped in plastic and cold to the touch. A rack of ribs, beef tips, pork chops, roasts and steaks. Kalamity unloaded everything into a storage freezer in the carport and walked back to the Durango. Robber flies weaved and whistled through the air. She looked at the front yard. The grass needed cutting. Then she saw the swarming pockets of gnats and figured it could wait.

She slid another cardboard box to the edge of the tailgate—this one packed with canned goods. Soups and broths. Enough bread crumbs to batter an ox. Fresh greens. Snap beans, squash, bell peppers. It was her quarterly shop. She loved to buy in bulk.

Exhausted, she left the paper towels and cleaning supplies for the morning. Before she closed the driver's side door Kalamity reached for a bag from the convenience store with her carton of Marlboros inside. A pack of chewing gum. Some lotto tickets. A lighter with the logo of the Georgia Bulldogs on one side, the team's schedule printed on the other. Season opener was just a couple weeks away. Business at the bar really picked up, but everyone knew you didn't bother Kal on game day, not when her Dawgs were playing.

It was her favorite time of year. Football and booze and lazy Saturday afternoons.

Tommy came by more often.

She never locked her doors. She walked into the kitchen carrying a box of groceries and placed them on the table, the thought of taking a drink and cooling off a welcome one. She'd given herself three days off. Told them not to call unless the place was on fire, but she didn't put her clientele past it. Owning a bar was hard goddamn work. Had to start interviewing for bartenders and waitstaff. Lucky to get six months out of someone before they flaked or got arrested or stole something. Kalamity tried not to think about it. She'd paid her dues, paid off the loan, and by God was going to start making more time for herself.

She'd found the house luxuriously cool, having left the AC units cranked on High before she left that morning. Hard not to think about the relief they provided from the heat, and her enormous electric bill running up like the nation's debt. Local forecast called for thunderstorms to pop up before sundown. The thought of watching one from her front porch—cold drink in hand—was as appealing a scenario as Kalamity could imagine.

She took out the bottle of vodka from the freezer. Poured some over ice. Added pineapple juice and 7Up. She considered drawing a bath, maybe masturbating. Spend the rest of the evening drinking in front of the television.

Throw on a couple steaks. Call somebody special.

She heard the screen door swing open.

When Kalamity turned around he was already standing there. The man had the face of a hedgehog, breathing through his mouth with a mean energy. A tattooed hand grabbed her by the hair. She dropped the glass. It shattered on the floor. The man jerked her head back. The first sip of vodka backfired from her windpipe.

He hustled Kalamity toward the living room and threw her over the couch. Her body crashed onto the coffee table, the glass top breaking under her weight, legs and arms getting hung awkwardly in the metal frames. Coasters and knickknacks and a ceramic ashtray flipped into the air. She reached up and touched her ears, then her kneecaps. Her hands came away with blood. She worked her tongue around her mouth, running it along the edge of a newly chipped tooth.

Then a pair of boots came into view.

Kalamity's eyeballs felt like hot coals, brain churn-
ing on panic overload. She looked up at the man
who had assaulted her. But there was someone else
there in the living room now. Another man, the
younger of the two. He sat down on the couch, a
beer and cigarette in one hand, his other groping for
the TV remote, only to be startled by a cranky *meow*
from her cat, Hershel. The cat spit and hissed, then
disappeared in a flurry, the man angrily stomping
down the hall in pursuit.

Prompted by a voice, she turned her head to the
left.

Leonard Lipscomb was kneeling beside her. The
worst type of smile on his face.

Her vision blurred. Then she passed out.

"Nice little place you got here."

A spike of pain brought Kalamity Bibb to consciousness, only to find her arms tied together at
the wrists and stretched high above her head. A
length of rope ran to the nearby radiator. There
was very little play, as Kalamity found out when
she tried to wrestle free of her bonds. In fact, the
more she struggled, the tighter the knots seemed to
get.

She looked down at her legs, feet dangling, tight
knots attaching her ankles to the edge of the table's
metal framework. What she thought was sweat
soaking her shirt was actually blood. She tasted it

on her lips, that copper and salt, felt it accumulating beneath her.

Not really knowing why, Kalamity started to cry when Lipscomb took her socks and shoes off.

H*e wiped her* forehead with a dish towel. Then at the tears streaming down her cheeks. When Lipscomb spoke his voice was calm and low.

"Where's your sister, Kalamity? Where's Ellamae?"

She winced at the touch, blinking through a mess of hair. She could hear a commotion down the hall. Her bedroom. That man on the couch. Hershel. She looked back at Lipscomb, who was gazing at her. He spoke again, quietly, with the controlled rasp of a heavy smoker.

"Where is Ellamae?"

Her sister's name prompted a surge of emotion. Fresh tears appeared at the corners of her eyes. She knew this day would come, even as any loyalty and concern for her sister eroded to complete apathy.

Goddammit, Ellamae. Goddamn your junky ass.

"Ain't seen her in two years," Kalamity said. "She's an addict. Hooked on meth."

Lipscomb held his gaze.

"She's a family disgrace," Kalamity added. She could feel her face flush with anger. "I stopped giving her money years ago. Wouldn't even let her in my home. I don't associate with people like that. I swear to you I don't know where she is. . . ."

She struggled for air. A sharp pain accompanied

every breath. She looked away from Lipscomb, praying her half-truths and denials would appease him. But there was an overwhelming sense he wasn't buying any of it. Truth was Ellamae had been living in the family cottage for three years. Kal had be-grudgingly brought her food and supplies numerous times in the last eight months, but that constituted the extent of her relationship with Ellamae Bibb.

Lipscomb's expression never changed, however. After a few moments he leaned in close and kissed Kal on the forehead. The gesture was so unsettling she felt a violent tremor run the course of her body.

She watched Lipscomb take her left foot in his hand. She started to sob, fighting her restraints, her body twisting against the sharp bed of glass in which she lay. But the screams didn't come again until Lipscomb reached behind him and produced a meat tenderizer.

Flock *swept a* row of books to the floor with his left arm, straining to get a hand on Hershel's scruff. He was met with a big paw and even bigger claws. The cat spit at him, then scurried to the corner of the topmost shelf. The antique wooden bookcase once belonged to Kalamity's grandmother. It reached almost to the ceiling and weighed two hundred pounds even without the Nora Roberts and Janet Evanovich hardcovers that now littered the floor.

The cat's eyes jittered nervously in its head as Flock knocked aside more books, cursing at Hershel, an ugly sneer on his face. He turned his head anxiously toward the hall.

To the sounds of Kalamity Bibb begging for her life.

H*is hand was* as strong as a pair of vice grips. Lipscomb grabbed the lower part of her left foot, then struck the top with the meat tenderizer three times as if he were hammering a nail through her ankle. The talus and navicular bones popped like firecrackers. The motions were so quick Kal didn't feel anything at first, just a sandpaper sting around the joint. But it only took a few moments for a deep throbbing pain to emerge, followed by a terrible swelling. Kal struggled mightily, an outburst of thrashing that only seemed to entertain Lipscomb. But her efforts were futile and a resignation set in, Kal assuming the look of someone about to doggy-paddle into a tidal wave.

Lipscomb took a couple more quick, hard swings at her dangling feet. She felt a toe pop out of place; then a painful numbness spread across her hind foot.

Physically exhausted, Kalamity was surprised to find herself yelling at Lipscomb. A howling invective that included calling him a faggot son of a bitch and a couple other choice insults. She gathered a shot glass worth of blood and mucus in her mouth and spit right into his face.

Lipscomb didn't even flinch. Nor did he make an effort to wipe it off. The bloody spittle hung like a stalactite from his chin. He dropped the meat tenderizer and knelt down beside her, leaning over to brush away the hair that had fallen across her eyes. He caressed a cheek with his finger.

His voice was steady and assured when he said, "Where's Ellamae? Where is your sister?"

"I told you I don't know!" she pleaded. "Swear I ain't seen her in years!"

But the wheels had already begun to turn. Those time-honored ideals like loyalty among blood kin now quaint when facing her own annihilation.

So why on earth am I protecting her?

Lipscomb only smiled, his eyes glinting with disappointment. He turned and reached for something and held a finger to his lips as if to silence Kalamity. She gasped at the sight of the hammer. He casually flipped it to the claw side, and quick as a viper he snatched Kal by the mouth, squeezing her cheeks to reveal the teeth and gums.

"I'm about as good a dentist as I am a podiatrist," he said with a chuckle. He primed the claws of the hammer before her eyes and gently scraped the surface of a front tooth.

Any notion to continue protecting Ellamae evaporated in an instant. Kalamity had reached her limit. She found herself involuntarily sobbing, a rattle in her chest courtesy of her smoker's lungs. She closed her eyes and said, "She's up in the mountains."

"Go on."

"Been living in the family cottage for three years. I got a map in the drawer of the nightstand . . . next to my bed."

She must have passed out. When Kalamity opened her eyes again Lipscomb was standing by the kitchen door, studying directions to the Bibb cabin. Flock appeared then, holding a very dead-looking Hershel by the tail, a thin rope of blood swinging from the cat's mouth. Kal fought back tears, as if showing Lipscomb and his goon any more emotion was the most appalling thing she could do.

She watched Lipscomb fold the map and put it in his pocket. Without looking at her again, he turned to Flock.

"Don't leave her like that."

Outside Lipscomb lit a cigarette. He lifted his head to acknowledge a flicker of lightning, followed closely by a roll of thunder from an approaching summer storm. Chimes hanging from a porch beam began to sing a tune of warning. He heard Flock fire twice, each gunshot a commanding boom. And to Lipscomb that sound seemed as natural as the soft rain beginning to fall or the whistle of crickets from the field beyond the house.

Charlie guessed five days had passed since the robbery.

Earlier Hicklin had counted the cash from the score, bundling the bills in straps of five hundred. He'd dried the money from the aquarium over the bathroom sink, the crinkled fifties and hundreds hanging from clothespins. The new-style bills were almost comical in appearance. Like hi-tech Monopoly money with their displaced, oversized presidential portraits, the watermarks, micro-printing and security threads just a few opening moves in the latest game against counterfeiters.

Charlie thought about the life he'd had prior to the robbery—his job at the bank, the apartment, school, exams, car payments, rent, Momma—a life both normal and insulated. A narrow path he'd carved by design.

Maybe the police would find him? They had to be looking.

One morning he had trouble remembering anything before Hummingbird and Hicklin.

That afternoon Hicklin untied him. No words were spoken, no pronouncements made. Charlie tested his freedom by going to the bathroom by himself. Hicklin began his exercise routine in the living room. Sit-ups. Push-ups. Knee bends. Charlie noticed the cooler had been restocked. He helped himself to a bottle of water, feeling strangely welcome in the cottage.

Later Hummingbird shaved him and washed his hair.

And she came in the night as a matter of routine. He'd wake to her pulling at him. When he was hard she'd plant herself, reaching for his hands, but he refused to hold them. She whispered to him about making love, but Charlie wouldn't call it that. He didn't know what to call it. Hours later he could smell her on his fingers like a smoker smells nicotine.

They'd lie atop the mattress like lovers afterward, she telling Charlie stories from her aimless life. Teaching second grade. Vocabulary and grammar and simple math. How seven was her favorite age, that's from when all her best memories came. Then she'd jump to recent history. How the school board found out that she'd lied about almost everything on her résumé. How she was fired and could never work as a teacher again. The sporadic employment after that. Got to the point where she couldn't even get a job. The methamphetamines made her feel better. Helped her forget. She did whatever it took to get them. She met Hicklin a long time ago and her life was never the same again.

I knew he was the one.

Charlie tried to follow her rapid-fire ramblings. Hummingbird's mind pinballing, tongue-tied in a tweeker's stutter. Sentences splintered into shards, but it didn't matter because she was always three or four words ahead of herself.

One time she offered the pipe to Charlie. Put it to his lips, but he batted it away. He saw the euphoria in Hummingbird's eyes. Up for days, she'd crash in a heavy, wheezing sleep.

At night Charlie found Hicklin on the threadbare couch. Empty beer cans on the coffee table. The radio tuned to a classic rock station, the volume low. Something about the disc jockey's voice reminded Charlie of the world beyond that safe house. That ordinary life where it was business as usual. It occurred to him that the world hadn't stopped for him and wouldn't. A voice in his head suggested: *Then why go back?*

He helped himself to a beer from the cooler. Sat down in the chair across from Hicklin, noting the shotgun within arm's reach. The ropes were gone. It was almost as if Charlie could walk out the door anytime he chose. But he didn't want to. He wanted to talk.

"What are we going to do?"

"What do you mean, *we?*" Hicklin said.

"I mean, *us*. How long are you going to keep me here?"

"I fucked up."

"How?"

"They'll come lookin'. But here is safe as anywhere, I reckon."

"Why didn't you kill me?" Charlie said.

"I don't know."

"Did you want to?"

"Yes."

Hicklin's answer came straight as an unsheathed knife. No hesitation.

A lump rose in Charlie's throat. "Who's going to come looking? You mean the police?"

Hicklin laughed. He turned the beer up to his mouth, draining the whole can at once.

"Get me 'nother beer, *Coma*."

Charlie reached for a tall boy in the cooler. Tossed it across the room. Hicklin winked in appreciation.

"Nah, son. The police ain't who worry me."

"Why'd you call me son?"

Hicklin put the beer down and rose. He reached out and touched the boy's face. Charlie withdrew, eyeing the pistol holstered at Hicklin's hip, thinking recklessly to grab it.

"When were you born?" Hicklin said.

"W-what?"

"When were you born?"

Charlie told him.

"Ain't no boy. You're a man! You ever thought of yourself as a man?"

"I d-don't know. Please, sir. Please," he said, recoiling.

"*Sir?* Haven't been called that in a while."

Hicklin let go of Charlie's chin. He lit another cigarette and began to pace. Charlie didn't understand why people lit sticks packed with tobacco and sucked on them. Just breathed in smoke and blew it out. He sipped his beer instead. Tried to shake off the feeling he got when Hicklin touched him. Minutes passed. They heard treehoppers outside. An owl hooting lethargically.

"Why did you ask me when I was born?" Charlie finally asked.

"I don't know."

"You don't?"

"Tell me 'bout your momma?"

"My mother?"

Hicklin nodded.

"I don't want to talk about her."

"She 'bout forty year old?"

Charlie didn't answer. He was fidgeting, broadcasting his nervousness.

Hicklin looked into his eyes. "She got a fake eye, don't she?"

Again Charlie said nothing. He took a long pull from his beer. *How did he know that?*

"I'll be goddamned," Hicklin said after a ponderous beat.

Without a word Charlie gulped down his beer. He was really developing a taste for the stuff, thinking of it as liquid aspirin. The buzz came quickly and his aches subsided, along with the anxiety. He fished around in the cooler and found the blue-and-white label. Popped the top.

Hicklin sat there smoking, watching his hostage.

"Tell me 'bout your daddy," he said.

"I never knew my father," Charlie said. "My momma said he died a long time ago."

"He may have well did."

"Why are you asking me this?"

" 'Cause we just a bunch of bastards in this here house."

"Why don't you let me go then? I won't say anything."

"You won't say nothin'?"

"I swear."

"There's the door," Hicklin said, pointing.

Charlie eased off the edge of the chair as if to leave, but Hicklin eyed him dispiritedly. Apparently the offer of freedom had been rescinded. Charlie settled back in the chair.

"Here," Hicklin said, holding a cigarette toward him.

"I don't want to," Charlie said.

"I'll show you how."

Charlie shook his head.

"It's bad for you. Gives you cancer."

"What's cancer?" Hicklin said. "Just another name for the same thing—*death*. Anything that gives you *that* should be given a goddamn award. Take it."

Charlie took the cigarette and the plastic lighter, studying them like a survivalist would tinder and flint. It took him a couple tries, rolling the tip of his thumb across the spark wheel. He lit the cigarette and puffed, smoke filling his cheeks although he was hesitant to inhale. He tried mimicking Hicklin, holding the cigarette between his fingers, but the smoke tasted terrible. Charlie tried again, sucking a drag down deep into his lungs. He coughed instantly, a jag that had his eyes watering and his insides swapping real estate.

He held out the cigarette in a last act of defeat.

Hicklin staggered over and took it. Patted Charlie on the back.

"Not for you, huh?" he said. "Least you can say we tried."

Charlie took a sip of beer, thinking he might vomit. His eyeballs felt like dice on a craps table.

"That's nasty," he said.

Hicklin lit his next cigarette. He took deep drags, smoking with real feeling. He studied the tip, blew on it so it glowed red. Flicked ash on the floor.

"Wonder what the first person who smoked thought to say?"

"Probably the same thing as me," Charlie said right before another round of hacking.

"I mean, who thought to roll up some tobacco in a stick like this?" Hicklin continued. "Light it and suck in the smoke and let it out, over and over like we do? Who thought to do that first? And why?"

"I was just thinking about that."

Hicklin seemed pleased by this.

"They say the Chinese were the first to use rockets," Charlie said, meekly at first, but when Hicklin cocked an interested ear toward him he went on. "Just gunpowder and fireworks, pyrotechnics in the beginning. But they had the idea to use that powder to get stuff up in the air. Someone back in China had to stare at some gunpowder and figure you could launch a cannonball with it. A couple leaps intellectually and technologically and we're putting people on the moon, running satellites around Jupiter, building space stations."

"You some kind of scientist?" Hicklin said.

"I like rockets."

"That what you study in school?"

"Sort of."

Charlie closed his eyes to stifle a wave of nausea. He wondered if his old life was waiting for him out there? Like he could still inhabit it. Find a door in Hicklin's cottage, open it, and there it would be—his old, normal life.

They sat for a while in silence. A manic voice on the radio announced a motorcross event. Next a woman read a weather report for East Tennessee. Hicklin's mood turned solemn, as if an unwelcome memory had suddenly dropped in.

Hummingbird appeared with a flashlight. She

turned it on and off, playing the light across the walls, in the throes of one of her manic episodes, Charlie recognized. There was a stark hunger in her eyes. The nerves in her face two-stepping along to their very own *Danse Macabre*.

Hicklin didn't pay attention at first. Not until she shined the light in his eyes, wanting to antagonize him. Hicklin shot her that look he'd perfected in prison, suggesting a cut throat and an unmarked grave. It seemed as natural to him as a smile or a frown.

When Hummingbird didn't stop, Hicklin got up calmly and snatched the flashlight from her hands, unscrewed the cap and took out the batteries. It was as effortless a motion as unloading the magazine of a handgun. But Hummingbird grabbed a battery from Hicklin's hand and threw it over his head. Then she turned to Charlie.

"I fucking hate you," she shrieked. "I hate both of you sumbitches!"

She turned and ran. The bedroom door slammed. Moments later they heard her crying.

Hicklin got two more beers from the cooler. He was very drunk, a little unsteady on his feet. Charlie eyed the bedroom door, then the front door. *Maybe when he falls asleep?* The cottage smelled sour, mildewed, the air heavy with smoke of all kinds. Hicklin handed him a beer and sat back down.

"Why did she do that?" Charlie said.

"Because she's in love. That's why."

"Is she your girlfriend?"

Hicklin laughed.

"Nah, she ain't *my* girlfriend. I think she's sweet on *you,* Charlie. . . ."

"Me?" Charlie said, incredulous.

"I think she's got a crush on you."

Charlie felt sick to his stomach. His face must have betrayed this, too. Hicklin winked and laughed again, slapping his knee good-naturedly.

"What's the matter? Never been in love before?" Hicklin said.

Charlie was too embarrassed to answer.

"No little girlfriends to play with your rocket, Mr. Scientist? Not like Hummingbird plays with it, huh?"

Hicklin's words were laced with scorn. His demeanor changed, as though a curtain had been pulled apart. A passing cloud obscuring the sun.

"I been in love," Hicklin said, as if he'd been asked. "Loved men *and* women. People who done time, real time, know love better than anyone."

Charlie shook his head.

"I can't imagine murderers and thieves and rapists being very loving."

"You'd be surprised," Hicklin said, his mood still far from agreeable. "Convicts understand love, sex, power, fear, death better than most people. They get distilled within a prison population. Get more intense. I've seen love between two convicts as heavy as any married couple . . . seen fear come off a person like vapor. Watched men die with a big bad look in their eyes. You know what the *panopticon* is, son?"

Charlie could feel Hicklin's eyes on him, gauging him. Hicklin looked as though he were about to burn down the woods. His words seem to form in a pressure cooker.

"Well, do you?" Hicklin demanded.

Charlie shook his head.

"The panopticon is a prison. A prison where they see you, but you don't see them. And they always watchin', or at least that's what you think, because you don't know one way or another if they is watchin' and it just makes you crazy. Do you know what it's like to be watched? I mean really watched. Stared at. *Studied?*

"I'm not just talkin' guards and video cameras and such. I mean jobs, paperwork, receipts, bills, insurance claims, doctor visits, taxes, satellites up in the goddamn sky. The all-encompassing gaze. And someone's always watchin' and you don't know when or where or who, but there is no escaping it. I spent twelve years being watched. By my own friends, my brothers, by the niggers and beaners and screws.

"And maybe, just maybe, somebody's watching us, too, everyone on the planet. Earth like one big panopticon for the aliens or whatever the fuck might be out there. All I knew was stick with my own kind and use my hate liberal-like."

Charlie tried to follow Hicklin's speech, thinking back to the rants of customers at his teller window, lonely people full of opinions with plenty of time to waste. He finished his beer and got another from the cooler. Hicklin gestured for one, too, Charlie noticing that Hicklin's face was beginning to resemble a fogged-up windshield. Charlie was starting to feel pretty good himself.

Sensing the threat had passed, he said, "The banks know a lot about people."

"Yeah?"

"Yeah."

"Like how?"

"They know how much money you have," Charlie said. "They know your credit score. They know where you live. Your telephone and Social Security number. They know who you write checks to and how often and for how much. They know when you use your ATM card. For some people a debit card's all they know how to use. You can follow them day and night, just by their spending habits."

"And you've done it, ain't you?" Hicklin said.

"Done what?"

"Watched 'em."

"Yeah."

"And they didn't know it."

"No."

Hicklin sneered, as if his point had been made. He raised the beer and drank, dribbling a little down the front of his shirt. Didn't notice or care. He leaned back into the recliner, his eyelids beginning to droop.

Charlie left Hicklin in the living room. Stumbling into the bedroom, Charlie had to reach out to the walls for balance. He found the mattress and plopped down in a drunken heap. Later he heard Hicklin talking to himself. A slurred monologue, like that of any derelict under a bridge. Charlie strained to hear what was being said.

He thought he overheard his mother's name once or twice.

Spoken aloud with the most peculiar of emotions.

They spent their nights in the trailer. November in Jubilation County. A hard freeze that lasted for weeks. Lucy tended to the place as best she knew how. Washed and folded his clothes. Kept the kitchen tidy. Not much money to go around. At least he put a stop to her tricking. Guess he couldn't take it anymore, she thought. Made her love him even more. He hit her occasionally, open handed, and she figured that was a sign of respect. If he really wanted to hurt her he could.

He disappeared for days at a time. She didn't dare leave the trailer because he'd told her not to. Sometimes he came home chapped and tired. A reflective vest, jeans and boots caked with mud. He'd show her a couple hundred dollars. Let's go to the store, he'd say. Then they'd shop like real couples do. She tried to be smart with her allowance and buy the things he liked. Sliced ham. Steak and potatoes. Beer. Lucy never bought herself anything without his permission. She ate what he ate and fought the urge to buy a television or some new clothes. One time she heard the expression "pins and needles."

She realized that's how she walked around him.

But it felt like love.

At night his friends would come over. Men she'd

never seen before who became regulars in their trailer. He treated her politely but firmly in front of them. They never so much as looked at her. She was used to it. Lucy figured it was her eye. They drank beer and carried on. She ironed clothes in the bedroom, hummed old hymns to herself. Still hard not to overhear all that talk about race and politics.

But sometimes the conversations turned serious. Talk of guns, amphetamines, cocaine, gas stations, prison. She figured it all for just that—talk.

Sometimes on a Friday night after a case of beer he and his friends would get loud and rowdy. They'd wrestle. Tempers flared. One time Hicklin punched a guy so hard his nose split down the middle. She spent two days sopping up blood from the couch and rug.

Other times Hicklin and his friends would hop in the one man's pickup truck, take off into the night. Lucy might not see Hicklin for three days. She never asked for an explanation. Was never offered one, either. She was often too afraid to talk to him. But her fear melted away when he took her in his arms. Got up inside her.

Then it felt like love.

Christmas. Lucy made him fried ham sandwiches. Canned apples with syrup. Hot coffee. After that he started coming home cleaner and more frequently. He always had money. And one day he surprised her. A brand-new television. A Betamax. A cast-iron teakettle. A brand-new pair of jeans that almost fit her. His friends still came by. Hardy, wired looking, tattooed. Men who drank bad luck and pissed it out.

Every night was the same. Beer cans filling the trash barrel. Talk about a lot of things she tried to cover her ears from. A couple of his friends, new and old, looked like jailbirds. Lucy always wondered if he'd been to prison. She once found a business card for a bail bondsman in the back pocket of Hicklin's jeans. He was reading books now. One day he came home with a bench press. He lifted weights in the backyard, even lifted through a bitter cold winter. He ate more and more. He bulked up, almost unrecognizable, from one winter to the next. She liked the muscles.

He disappeared into the night.

His friends would come by on their Harleys. Pick him up. They looked serious now. Mean as hell. She heard Cullman, Alabama, mentioned. Conyers, Blairsville, Antioch. "Score" and "brothers" became permanent additions to his vocabulary. Three, four, five days gone at a time.

Lucy cleaned. Put his books in order on the shelf. History and politics. Philosophy. Germany. Lucy tried to read excerpts. Didn't have the aptitude for it. But he took to the books, the learning, the discussions with his friends. There came a time when he seemed to be leading the discussions, leading the men.

There was the one older guy. They all called him Preacher. More and more often he came around. She could tell he'd been in prison. Big muscles, tattoos. A thick black goatee striped with gray. Looked like a chipmunk was living on his face but he was always kind to Lucy. Brought her flowers or pumpkin seeds.

Little gifts for the trailer. He'd say, Please call me Leonard. The strongest, meanest-looking man she ever saw. They would leave in the night and she'd pass two or three days alone. Sleepless nights. The trailer like a rock in a dead field.

Then Lucy found the plastic bag from Gas N Go in the closet. It was filled with cash. Some of it was stained pink. She shrieked at the sight of the pistol. And hidden under a pile of his clothes was a sawed-off shotgun. She walked backwards until she hit the bed and started to cry.

That night Lucy ran outside when she saw the lights from the truck. It was cold and damp. One of the headlights was busted. When she saw him she started screaming. Slapping at him. His eye was in-jured. There was blood on his shirt, scratches down his neck. His knuckles looked like blue marbles. He dragged her in the house by her hair. His face burn-ing red as autumn leaves. He swung at her and Lucy felt her jaw pop loose. Her eye dislodged. She couldn't believe this was happening.

She'd known this rage was in him. But it was like living near a fault line. You go on living there hop-ing to survive the inevitable.

He punched her in the stomach. Lucy collapsed. She heard him tearing the place apart. She held her tummy and tried to breathe. Then he was gone.

Forever.

The next day Lucy found out she was pregnant.

And, months later, she found out the baby had lived.

———————

Tommy *Lang's Nissan* Titan came over the hill and down into a big, sweeping curve. A sprawl of loblolly pines off to his left, farms on his right. The thunderstorms had come and gone all afternoon, leaving a mugginess behind, the late-summer weather predictable, as was the beautiful hour of twilight those storms afforded.

He drove past a house with chokeberry and shrubs bordering the property. A swing set in the front yard. Little yellow and red plastic toys scattered across the lawn. Sheets and pillowcases hung from a clothesline.

He slowed the pickup, looking east. A lone cow stood behind ironwood fence posts. The animal stared thoughtfully at Lang as the truck passed by. As if it had something telling to say.

The trees closed in, breaking every so often to reveal a house nestled back into the land. Dogs from one home ran toward his truck and barked. A man threw a football to his son in the yard. Lang waved. He didn't know them. He wasn't wearing his uniform or riding in the cruiser, either. Just felt like waving.

A couple hours away from the case had done him good. He hadn't slept much in the past three days, working twenty straight at one point. But the state and federal folks seemed happy to run the bank investigation without him now. He had a lot of paperwork back at the office. Phone calls to return. Scheduling at the detention center and courthouse, bailiff duties, court summonses, the administration of simple police work. He shuddered at the thought of that uncomfortable chair in his office. The lousy coffee. Other matters begging his attention. Checks for the month signed and mailed, complaints to address, an eviction to serve, requisition of radar trailers for the Traffic Enforcement Unit. There had been a domestic dispute in the parking lot of the Kroger, but Hansbrough had settled it with a handshake.

But the robbery was never far from Lang's mind.

He thought about the voice mail from Sallie Crews.

Lang was more attuned to her voice than the message itself. He liked her accent. It was warm and sophisticated, part English class and part working class. Pure Rockdale County.

There were other messages, including one from his daughter. All calls he didn't return, not yet. Not until a can of beer or seven.

What Lang really wanted was to stare at a wall and think of nothing in particular.

Back at the Sheriff's Department he'd looked harried, unshaven. He nodded to people in the halls.

They smiled as if forgiving him.

Lang *had put* on a nice polo shirt and a clean pair of Carhartt dungarees. A splash of cologne he used maybe once a year. The bottle was purchased at a Woolworth's in Atlanta several Presidents ago. He figured like wine it aged well, smelling of some bygone era. Like the aroma of old newspapers, hay and horseshit in his father's barn, the exhaust of a two-door Biscayne—his first car. Taking pulls from a cold can of Schlitz between his legs, riding around like he was now. He used to get out on the dirt near the old Dumas line, abandoned back then, and race his buddies, of whom all but two were dead now. Make camp along the river and try their luck against the largemouth bass and sunfish.

Never once imagining he'd be where he was now.

Willie Nelson sang "City of New Orleans" on the radio. Lang recognized the old Lee Greenwood hit, hummed along to it. Never been much for singing. Even by himself in the truck.

Bugs and birds dashed across the road, which turned sharply, then sloped under a canopy of Judas trees. There was an abandoned shed slanted to one side, as if it considered lying down for an afternoon nap. A feral home a few yards away, swallowed by sunlight-starved kudzu. He passed a stretch of horse fence and finally saw Kalamity's Dodge parked in the driveway of her home. A big, round sun setting behind it.

Lang was excited after their conversation. He'd apologized first for calling her drunk the week before, a late-night conversation where he'd sworn to quit drinking, bemoaned his estranged family, the job, his life as one with too many wrong turns. Kal didn't say a word. Just listened. Let him vent, anticipating a similar call the next week or next month when Lang hit upon that special combination of whiskey and beer that sent him spiraling with self-pity. Some phone conversations he wouldn't even talk. He'd just listen to her while she read aloud whatever it was she was reading, a magazine or one of those mysteries she loved. Maybe turn up the television so he could hear it. Put the phone down near her head if she'd been sleeping.

They had—as damaged human beings—an understanding.

For years she took him in. Cooked for him. Drank with him. They'd make love. By morning any sense of commitment would have worn off. Weeks passed before they wanted or sought each other's company again. Off-duty he'd slip into her bar and drink all night. Then Kalamity would take him home. Never been quick to judge. Years like this and not one word from her about it. Yet Lang knew early on that he was being used as much as she was.

He wanted to tell her things, too. About the robbery. About the bank teller, Charlie Colquitt. Probably dead. Visions of that feral child behind a cage, barking at him, walking on all fours down busy sidewalks in town. Nightmares where he woke up screaming at the top of his lungs. He wanted to tell Kal how he was starting to lose his grip. Not caring if he lived or died. Tell her about the loneliness and the binges that temporarily cured it.

Eating a bullet.

Lang often imagined who would find him if he did such a thing. Hunters, maybe, stumbling upon a gnarled mummy in the woods. A hole in the top of his skull, obscured by rotten leaves and rags of clothing. A picture of his family in one hand.

A gun in the other.

A *sudden sense* of caution struck Lang. From the driveway he could tell the kitchen door was open. Flies buzzed in the front yard. A hummingbird hovered near a feeder. Other things perched and observing. Lang ran a hand across his sweaty nape. He eyed the front door again, the windows to either side. No lights on. Nothing.

Near the kitchen door Lang could see dimly inside. A glass had shattered on the floor. He craned his neck and looked into the living room. He saw Kalamity.

He ran back to the truck, retrieved his personal firearm from a holster mounted under the steering column. A Kimber Warrior .45 ACP. He checked the chamber. Satisfied, he faced the house again.

The living room came into focus, a familiar setting now off-kilter. Kalamity had a bullet hole in her sternum and one under her right eye. The image of her burned like a nuclear shadow on his brain.

Where all the bad shit of his life was stockpiled.

The freezer door was open. Someone had thrown Kalamity's cat inside. Hershel's fur was matted with ice. An eye hung from a tether. Water leaked down the front of the refrigerator and pooled on the floor.

He scanned the kitchen. A brass shell casing lay where the linoleum ended and the carpet began. Foolish to leave it, unless the cartridge had been wiped down. Lang looked at her body again, at her smashed and swollen feet, at the slack death mask that was her face. That empty stare he'd never grown used to.

He inched down the hallway, peering down the length of his thumb that was parallel to the muzzle, should he have to point and shoot. He listened for any sound that was out of place, any creaking board or muffled breath a portent for violence.

The bathroom was clear, as were the hall closet and sewing room. Lang entered the bedroom. The bed was made. But the bookshelf and dresser had been rifled through, ransacked, books and picture frames littering the floor. Same with the closet and nightstand. Socks, underwear, jewelry, broken glass, papers and envelopes. All thrown about.

Her killer or killers, he speculated, were sloppy and probably hopped up. Kalamity brutalized and executed. It just didn't make sense.

Lang thought about *they*, assuming there had been more than one.

They hadn't stolen anything. Nothing was missing as far as he could tell. Her purse was left neglected on the kitchen table. So they threw her around the living room, and onto the coffee table. They tied her up and worked her over. Even drank one of his beers, because Kalamity didn't drink beer. *They* didn't want her; they thought she knew something they wanted to know. And whether she did or didn't give it up they shot her anyway.

Lang remembered Kalamity's sister, known among the county gossipers as a family embarrassment. She'd been a schoolteacher once. Developed a bad taste for drugs and worse taste in men. These facts moved in Lang's mind. Thoughts set free like catfish in a pond.

He left the house as carefully as he entered and called Dispatch on his cell phone.

While he waited, Lang walked the property and kept an eye on the road. His heart and gut and throat swollen with a feeling beyond rage. Beyond sadness for Kalamity. By the time Deputy Bower arrived in a shower of gravel Lang still had no proper name for all he felt.

Charlie *woke from* a nightmare soaked with sweat. He rolled over. Hummingbird sighed softly in her sleep.

"Untie me, Hummingbird. I've got to pee."

"I cain't. It's against the rules," she mumbled.

"Please, Hummingbird. I won't tell. Please."

She rubbed a hand down his chest to his boxers, grabbed him with a moan of pleasure. When she finished she sat up drowsily and untied Charlie's wrists.

He got to his feet, the need to piss returning so bad he thought he might go on the floor.

In the bathroom he raised the lid on the toilet bowl, surprised to find excrement in it. His vision was fuzzy. He squinted down into the bowl.

When he saw the heads of tiny white worms Charlie backed away. His need suddenly replaced by a sudden revulsion. He ran from the bathroom. Out of the cottage. Into the darkness.

Charlie *struggled barefoot* down a rocky path. He turned his ankle and yelped but kept limping along until the path got easier. Creekside the soil was moist and soft under his feet. He looked up. A quarter moon in the sky moved in and out of sight above the understory of redbuds and dogwoods. He stopped to catch his breath and vomited.

Charlie surveyed the trees ahead. Sixty-foot plumed pines. Spruces. Ghoulish shadows in every direction. In his state of mind the forest seemed to swallow him.

He thought he heard the footfall of an animal. Deer? A fox? A bear? *Jesus, help me*, he prayed, thinking himself a deathbed believer, not sure what good it would do anyway. For a moment he was certain he'd cry, but no tears came.

He hid behind a tree, gripping the trunk, his hands moving through a silken web of bark lice. There were little white eggs snug within the crevices of tree bark, the lice cool and stringy.

The woods were far from quiet. The whines and pulsations of night creatures everywhere, above and around him. Charlie felt victimized by the sound. *Got to keep going,* he told himself. *There'll be a road. And roads lead to other roads.*

The trees opened on a stream lined with ferns and black birch, the water trickling over slabs of limestone. The swath cut between rocky banks ten feet high. Charlie climbed down the bank, his feet sinking into silt three inches deep. The water glowed a blue-black in the moonlight. He crouched on the bank, wrapping his arms around himself, absorbed by fantasy. He imagined a news crew rushing to interview him. A blanket was thrown around his shoulders. A hot cup of soup offered. His rescuers wore windbreakers, earbuds, the cords disappearing beneath their collars.

What would I say?

Where would I begin?

He got to his feet and crossed the stream, pausing for a moment at the sight of a moccasin in flight. The cool water came up to his shins. Polished stones and mud underfoot. He reached the opposite bank, shivering and tired. Found a ledge he could climb, another gateway to a slope of thick woods. He tried to negotiate the steep terrain with caution but lost his balance, rebounding from tree to tree, finally tripping and falling at the feet of an ancient-looking cottonwood.

Clawing through a leafy detritus, Charlie cried out and rolled onto his back. He looked up at a tree split by lightning, a charred V forking the length of a great oak. He closed his eyes and rested.

Prompted by the patter of rain, he dragged himself into the nook of the split tree trunk. Lightning flickered. It began to rain harder. Something rattled from deep within the oak.

This will be as g-good a place to die as any, he thought.

Exhaustion pulled Charlie into a coffin-sized sleep. In his dreams leathery things slid over him, but they meant no harm. They welcomed him as one of their own. He felt cool air, cavernous air. The rattle persisted. As did the sensation of being overrun, his body negotiated like an obstacle.

REM sleep and *rockets . . . those were always the best dreams . . . in this one he held a competition model, balsa nose and fins with a standard payload packed inside. Next the separation joint, followed by the parachute, the wadding packed tight. Body tube feeling smooth to his fingertips. The thrust ring just above the motor. The specs of the nose base and nose tip appeared. Diagrams he would draw himself in the glorious light from his desk lamp. Protractor in hand, along with his favorite graphite pencil . . .*

. . . jumping as dreams are wont to do . . . where a detailed scale of the tail floated in space, turning to allow a side view of the Tomahawk model. Scrolling like a movie's end credits . . . first the law of tangents . . . the triple-track tracker . . . the law of sines stating $c \div sin(angle)C = b \div sin(angle)B = a \div sin(angle)A$. *All followed by vertical triangles that appeared on his dream screen like a psychedelic after-school special, dancing, spinning in place . . . jump-cutting . . . the apogee of a rocket against a blue sky, a bright yellow sun.*

But then the sun turned black, as if it'd been flushed with ink.

H*e was dragged* by his ankles from the nook of that tree, a familiar voice cursing him. Charlie sensed sunlight behind him and desperately wanted to fall back asleep, to feel protected again. But those hands gripped him tighter. When he looked back at the split trunk he thought he saw the eyes of a snake, a tongue that flickered at him.

Like an old friend waving good-bye.

Hicklin lifted Charlie to his feet and cinched a rope around his neck.

It was dawn, the forest alive with *chacks* and whistles.

Hicklin yanked on the rope, causing Charlie to trip, his feet catching on the exposed roots of a box elder. They crossed another stream, sinking again into the silt, mucky water splashing with every step. Hicklin was mad as hell. That Charlie could tell.

They hiked in silence.

The cottage appeared ahead of them like a woodland mirage. Seventy, eighty yards away. That's all the ground he'd covered. *Swore it felt like ten miles last night.* Charlie's feet hurt terribly. The toes stubbed and stinging, the skin from nail to heel cracked.

The failure to escape depressed him the most. His temples throbbed. He tasted blood on his tongue. He reached behind him and felt a fresh bruise on his tailbone. Hicklin didn't look back once, pulling Charlie as though he were an afterthought, a chore to be carried out. There were a few moments where Charlie thought his head would come clean off.

As they neared the cottage Hicklin took off at a boot-camp trot. Despite Charlie's aching feet, he had no choice but to pick up his own pace. They stopped only once so he could vomit.

He ran a hand across his mouth, dropping to a knee so as to catch his breath among the tall, noble-looking pines. He glanced up. In the distance there was a plane. Maybe a 747, he thought. Boeing.

Cruising at high altitude. Thin and flat against a blue canvas. Charlie wished he could say, *Hello.*

Help.

Anything to attract their attention.

H*e knew how* to get to the plane. If only he had the means.

H*icklin tied him* to the chair again, the rope tight enough to chafe the skin. He smacked Charlie across the face, not speaking. As if an explanation for the beating would have been a waste of time.

Charlie heard Hummingbird whimpering behind him. There was a clatter of dishes. Moments later she offered Charlie a plate of ham and beans and a soda with a straw. He worked his jaw, wincing from the pain as, more blood collected in his mouth.

Hummingbird let him rinse his mouth out before she fed him with a plastic fork. He chewed quickly, painfully, chasing the food with big gulps of soda. Afterward she offered him two aspirin.

When he was finished eating she patted Charlie on the head, leaning in to kiss his cheek. The gesture had a mother's tenderness. He noticed how poor she looked, her skin blotchy, eyes dimly focused. She lit a cigarette and paced for a while, stopping every now and then to read something off the yellowing newspaper tacked over the windows.

Hicklin appeared later that afternoon. The living room floor had been swept, the cans and wrappers tossed, ashtrays emptied. His weapons were neatly arranged on the couch. Action open on the hand-gun, magazines loaded. The shotgun Charlie recognized from the robbery. Black. Oiled. Menacing. Hummingbird turned on the radio and sat down on the couch with her pipe.

Charlie fell asleep, mumbling to himself like a lunatic.

"I'm sorry. I'm sorry. I'm sorry."

They were married in the month of July.
It was a shotgun wedding.
They bought everything that the Lord ever sold.
Except the happy ending.

EIGHT

Sallie Crews walked down a short hallway, nodding politely to two uncomfortable-looking detectives stirring sugar into their coffees. Police headquarters of a metro county. The air-conditioning broke overnight and the whole building filled with an oppressive mugginess by noon. Fans had been plugged into every available socket and succeeded only in circulating warm air around the Robbery-Homicide unit, the entire second floor humming noisily like the tarmac of a busy airport.

Crews paused outside the interrogation room. Took a breath and flipped a sign next to the door. It read: *Interview in Progress.*

Inside, Izuarita Sandoval sat at a wooden table. They regarded each other for a moment. Crews handed Sandoval a Diet Coke, which the girl accepted gratefully. She rolled the cold soda can along her forehead and glanced toward the two-way mirror.

Crews sat down across from her, the chair creaking as she settled in. A fan in the corner made a grating metallic noise as it pivoted back and forth. Izuarita thought the room smelled steamy. It was transient, anonymous, like a doctor's office in a third-world country. She noticed a wire running along the edge of the mirror frame but didn't see a tape recorder or closed-circuit camera. Figured there had to be one somewhere.

Her skin glistened with sweat. There was acne faintly clustered around her cheekbones and chin, probably the reason for all the concealer. Despite the blemishes, Izuarita was a beautiful young woman, with dark Latin eyes and exotic features that wouldn't be out of place at the Copacabana. A space between her teeth was small enough to be considered cute.

She also had a decent helping of barrio attitude but was playing this one nice and sweet at the moment.

Izuarita took two sips from the Diet Coke. Said something in Spanish. Crews pretended not to understand.

"What's that, honey?"

"Nothing."

"Thirsty, huh?"

"Yeah."

"Izuarita. It's a beautiful name," Crews said.

"Thanks."

"Friends call you Izzy?"

She shrugged.

"You know why you're here?"

"I'm not arrested."

"That's right. You're not under arrest."

"Then why?"

"You're a travel teller for the North Georgia Savings and Loan?"

"Yes."

"What's a travel teller?"

"You don't know?"

"I'd like you to tell me."

Izuarita shuffled in her seat. She'd taken off a baggy hooded sweatshirt on arrival, a revealing purple tank top underneath that left little to the imagination. Sweaty cleavage and tight jeans. Hoop earrings. Elegant fingers with lots of rings, purple nail polish. A male detective would have been secretly drooling over Izuarita. Crews smiled softly at her.

"It's like a temp for a certain region, you know. Regular tellers call in sick or take—*este*—*vacaciones*. You know? Vacation," she said.

"So you bounce around all over?"

She nodded.

"At what branch did you fill in most recently?"

"You don't know?"

"Tell me."

"The J-Jubilation County office."

"Off Route Twenty?"

Another nod.

"The one that was robbed six days ago?"

"I didn't know it was robbed."

Crews looked past the girl at the wall. Izuarita wanted to turn around. She tried hard not to shift her eyes or chew her nails. A progression of lies formed in her head.

"How long have you lived in Georgia?" Crews asked.

"A year next month."

"An apartment downtown."

Izuarita thought this was a question, then realized it wasn't. Phlegm caught in her throat, made her cough. She didn't cover her mouth.

A manila folder lay on the table, but Crews hadn't opened it yet. Izuarita wondered what was inside. The more surprised and bewildered she looked, the better. She sniffed, wiping her nose with the back of a hand.

"Want a tissue?" Crews said.

She shook her head, offering Crews a distrustful half smile.

"Where did you live before coming here?"

"Southern California."

"Where in Southern California did you live?"

"El Sereno."

"Where's that?"

"East LA."

"And why'd you move here?"

"I met a guy."

"A guy? Come all the way out here for some boy?"

"Yes."

"Where did you meet him?"

"In a bar."

"In El Sereno?"

"No. In Marietta."

"What were *you* doing in Marietta?"

"Visiting a friend."

"Honey, you're only twenty. Making you nineteen or maybe eighteen when you met this guy. What on earth were you doing in a bar?"

"I have a fake ID, okay? Is that what *this* is about?"

Crews took the manila folder and left without a word. The fluorescent light from the hallway brightened the room for a moment before the door closed. Izuarita looked at her reflection in the mirror, at the wire that seemed to go nowhere. She ran a hand across her forehead. Sipped her soda, staving off a nicotine craving by chewing on a cuticle.

She couldn't believe this was happening. Someone from the bank waking her on a day off, saying a cop wanted to ask her some questions. About the bank robbery and other tellers she knew. Everybody at work had been talking about it. Figured she'd just play it dumb.

Earlier a cop had brought her potato chips and ice water. An hour went by. She thought she might pass out from the humidity. A male detective came in first, asking about her work schedule. Current address. What kind of car she drove. Izuarita just went along with it. She even gave the guy one of her famous winks, thinking it might help. Then Crews walked in and Izuarita knew right away this woman wasn't ordinary police.

Izuarita's eyes wandered. She drummed her fingers against the empty can. Someone had scribbled *God Help Me* into the tabletop with a ballpoint pen.

Concern replaced boredom. Izuarita began to wonder if she might need a lawyer. *Can they do this?* she thought. *Just have me sitting around for hours?* Finally the door opened, offering that phony light again and a blast of chatter and ringing phones. Sallie Crews shut the door behind her. Sat down with the manila folder and a box of tissue.

"And who's Joey Da Silva?" she said.

"*Como?*"

"Joey Da Silva?"

"Oh, that's my brother."

"You didn't recognize your own brother's name?"

"I never called him by that name. He's Jorge to me. Jorge Sandoval."

"Da Silva?"

"Guess he took my father's name."

"Doesn't sound Chicano."

"It's Portuguese. His father was from Brazil."

"And where's Jorge now?"

"Out west."

"That's an interesting way of putting it."

"What you mean?"

Crews didn't explain.

"You talk to him lately?"

"Not since my sixteenth birthday."

"It's been four years?"

"Something like that."

"You don't know where he is?"

She shrugged.

"I do, sweetie . . . he's in prison."

Izuarita put a hand to her face, wrinkling her mouth dramatically. She muttered something in Spanish, a lament of some sort. Crews found it a lousy performance but pretended to buy it anyway. The amateur theater between them might be the only way to gain important information. She handed the girl a tissue.

"*Ay Dios mio,*" Izuarita whispered. She wiped a tear from her eye. Sweat dripped freely from a line of beads near her hairline.

"*No te preocupes.*"

She looked up at Crews, truly surprised. "You speak Spanish?" she said.

"*Seguro que si. Hablo cuatro lenguas.*"

Izuarita looked away again and buried her face in her hands, sobbing. Crews waited patiently.

"What did Jorge *do*?" Izuarita said.

"He is a well-traveled young man. Made a good living selling scores. Terminal Island. Then Victorville. Now he's in Pelican Bay on an armed robbery beef. A pretty impressive résumé. He earned his way inside, that's for sure."

Izuarita reached for the box of tissues, her breathing a little erratic after the forced cry. She dabbed at the corners of each eye and blew her nose.

"And you completely lost track of him?" Crews said.

"I had no idea."

Crews opened the manila folder. Inside was a facsimile of a crudely drawn layout of the North Georgia Savings & Loan. A girly script identified the sketch: *Branch #26044.* She'd used colored pencils to highlight the camera positions, the location of the vault, coin lockers and cash drawers. Notes were scribbled at the bottom of the diagram. Details of cash limits and paint packs, recorded money and shipment schedules.

Crews gave Izuarita a minute.

"Recognize that?" she said.

The girl shook her head, her eyes shifting nervously back and forth.

"It was found in Joey Da Silva's—excuse me—Jorge Sandoval's cell during a random toss. Pieces of the copy your brother made were found in the excrement of another inmate, Brann Kelliher, about five hundred miles away. Some unfortunate CO had to pick through the shit with a pair of tweezers. Kelliher . . . that name ring a bell?"

"No."

Crews slapped several mug shots down on the table, causing Izuarita to jump in her chair. One man had porcine features, large, round eyes, an unkempt beard. There was a tattoo below the Adam's apple. The other man was younger, white, his mouth largely hidden behind a wad of goatee. Same tattoo of a lightning bolt on his neck.

Izuarita studied the mug shots with a glassy expression. She seemed apprehensive, as if fearing the photos were about to grunt and squeal. Crews pointed at the younger of the two men.

"How about a man named Hicklin?"

"No," Izuarita said.

"Leonard Lipscomb?"

"No."

"That's the first time you've told the fucking truth today," Crews said.

Izuarita looked like the firstborn at a puppy mill.

"*What* is going on?"

"Your brother is mixed up with some bad, bad men. And now he's mixed *you* up in the scheme.

You know about La Eme? Know about the Aryan Brotherhood?"

Izuarita kept shaking her head, but not in denial.

"I think I need a lawyer now," she said, in a voice barely above a whimper.

"*Por supuesto, mija.* For goddamn sure."

According to Kalamity Bibb's map the path they wanted was off to the left. The road was dusty, a never-ending series of switchbacks as they headed up the mountain. Flock tooled the pickup between growths of sumac as the beginnings of a great forest took shape. The path narrowed, littered with rocks, fallen limbs, the Chevy bouncing and skidding, Flock hooting at every big bump in the road.

Lipscomb exited the truck first and eyed the terrain, a vista of valleys, the big river and beyond, a soft blue haze on rounded peaks of a supernal green. Dusk was upon them. Flock half-expected Lipscomb to produce a bow and arrow and disappear into the brush. Instead they had sidearms and shotguns. He felt something crawl behind an ear and flicked a finger at it.

Lipscomb studied the old map, part of a brochure for a company that sold custom-built cabins, and looked up toward a thick wooded path to the north. Without a word he started walking. Flock shrugged and followed.

Thirty yards in he turned for a look back. The pickup was barely visible. Far off Flock heard the echoing crack of a rifle, followed by the flutter of birds spooked from their nests. He looked up at the treetops as if he were under siege.

A little later they came upon a deer's carcass. A doe, dead maybe three days, lay on its side, a ghost of gnats marking the spot. Beetles crawled from the doe's puffy belly. Maggots pulsated in the swollen anus. Lipscomb knelt to inspect the animal, swatting at flies. Flock kept his distance, preferring the sharp citric odor of the pine needles to that of decay.

"Don't see an entry wound," Lipscomb said. "Damn thing just might have died."

He said this as if it pleased him greatly. He favored Flock with a quick smile.

"People don't think deer die unless some fat ass up in a stand hammers them with a Winchester."

"Bet that cat didn't think it was gon' die the way it did," Flock said.

"Had eight lives prior to consider that."

Flock covered his nose and nodded at the deer carcass, said, "Damn thing stinks, Preacher."

"You think?"

"Well, Christ, yeah, I think so."

Lipscomb only grinned, shaking his head as if he couldn't disagree more.

Ten minutes later they came upon a granite monolith covered with fungus. Hairy cocoons peppered the crevices. Lipscomb and Flock skirted the rock, into more woods beyond as the land climbed steeply.

Lipscomb paused to reference Kalamity's directions. The sun flickered through the latticework canopy. Fireflies were alight in all directions. For a while Flock walked with his hand on the grip of his holstered weapon.

They continued up the mountain.

The sun was setting. The air grew cooler, easier to breathe. They negotiated rocky ledges, decaying windfalls, hiking in silence. Watching where he walked, Flock almost ran into Lipscomb, surprised to find he had suddenly stopped, his attention twenty yards west where a path revealed itself. Just off the path a camouflage tarp lay on the ground. Tire tracks.

"What about it?" Flock said.

"Could be where our brother parked his vehicle."

"Don't look like that path goes nowhere," Flock said, dropping his hand to the butt of his gun again.

"Looks like it winds down to the other side."

"Hicklin?"

Lipscomb only shook his head.

They walked parallel to a clearing, stopping after a moment to catch their breath. Lipscomb asked for a cigarette. The light was hazy, waning, its replacement a quarter moon rising in the east. Long shadows made it difficult to see. The woods became more animated with nocturnal insects and small animals. Flock watched Lipscomb finger the safety near the trigger guard of his shotgun.

"What we gon' do, Preacher?"

"You just follow my lead."

"You think he's alone way up here?"

"He ain't alone. It's him and a hundred fifty thousand of our friends."

"We gonna kill him or just try and talk to him?"

"His call," Lipscomb said.

Two shadows moved a quarter mile away where a ridge leveled off. Lipscomb knelt behind a windfall, pulling Flock down with him. Flock wasn't sure what his partner had seen.

But after a moment two figures appeared and disappeared between the trunks of twin hickory trees. Lipscomb rose slowly and signaled with hand motions for Flock to flank him at twenty paces. They crept up the slope. A rickety roofline came into view. The barest outline of a cottage, the clapboard illuminated by the moon.

Nightfall.

The only sound apparitions converging on each other.

The hunted unaware of the hunters.

With the rope still around his neck Charlie slept on the couch, dreaming that he walked across a field with a homemade ignition system, one he'd designed from scratch.

Sunset. Rose-colored light. He turned at the sound of singing. There was a choir engaged in a hypnotic cadence, the members swaying in their robes as if moved by a breeze. An all-black choir no less, like the ones he sometimes saw on Sunday morning television. Big churches in Atlanta or Harlem. They looked upon Charlie kindly. The light intensified and he stared up at the sky at a cascade of shroud lines. The canopies of a thousand parachutes pulled earthward by gravity.

The fever dream intensified. The setting sun was blanketed by the parachutes. Hundreds, if not thousands, of payloads. They struck the dusty field in a crashing wave, the parachutes undulating like jellyfish. The voices of the choir soared. They began to clap a downbeat in unison, singing: "When my soul needs manna from above but where do I go . . . ?"

Charlie's eyelids fluttered. A forceful tug woke him from the dream.

"Wake up, Coma."

He opened his eyes. Hummingbird sat next to him, holding the end of the rope. Her breasts were visible through a thin, sweat-stained cotton tank top. A look of sardonic amusement on her face.

He looked around groggily, wiping crust from his eyes. Hicklin was gone, along with the guns and duffel bags.

Hummingbird answered Charlie's question before he could speak.

"He done left," she said. "Not sure when he'll be back. Be honest with you, I don't know if he'll be back at all."

"Where are we going?"

"I don't know, honey. Just somewheres that ain't here."

She offered him an RC Cola with a straw. Charlie sucked the soda down. When he finished, Hummingbird removed the rope from around his neck. She'd wet a paper towel and took to wiping his face.

They sat for a moment in silence. Hummingbird looked around the empty cottage, her eyes lighting up as if a notion had just struck.

She went to the nearest window and tore down the newspaper. Late-afternoon light poured into the living room. She was so excited she clapped her hands and motioned for Charlie to help her with the rest of the windows. It wasn't long before the once gloomy, smoke-filled room was flush with amber sunlight.

"I know what we can do."

She held out a hand. Charlie hesitated.

"Where are we going?" he said.

"Watch the sunset."

"I could just go."

"Just watch the sunset with me *first*," she said, a sadness in her eyes.

She helped Charlie off the couch. He touched two fingertips to his hairline where his skin felt tender as a ripe plum.

"My, my, Coma. My handsome man."

She ran a hand through his hair, grooming him as if there could be a hairstyle somewhere in Charlie's shock of blond hair—now the color of bread crust from dirt and grease. An urge struck to grab her own frail neck, but Hummingbird turned and graced him with a smile, then raised the palm of her hand and blew him a kiss.

Charlie's expression didn't change, as if the muscles in his face were too fatigued to react. But the gesture sparked some strange warmth within him.

They *walked by* a patch of stunted, twisted pitch pines. Red wasps cruised nearby.

"My daddy used to take me and my big sister up here," she told him. "You got any family, Coma?"

"Just my mom."

"Just a momma? But ain't we your family, too?"

Charlie said nothing. There were bats on the wing above them, flitting from tree to tree. Somewhere a hairy woodpecker drummed on a dead limb. He looked at his bare feet, dirty and spotted with bites. One pinky toe had bled badly. The nail not attached anymore.

Hummingbird stopped in shadow. The air there was cool and sweet, earthy. She hustled a cigarette from a pack and lit it, then offered it to Charlie. He shook his head.

"What about Hicklin?" he said.

"Let's not worry 'bout that now."

About a half mile from the cottage they reached a stream guarded by steep banks. Hummingbird eventually stopped to rest on a slab of granite, take in the view. Charlie sat down next to her. He could hear the sound of a nearby waterfall. Far below them there was a river the color of old pennies, a bluish haze on the mountains to the east.

After a while she reached for his hand and brought it to her lips. Charlie pretended not to notice. He'd sighted what looked like a hiking path, slashing through the hollow down the mountain. Darkness was almost upon them. He planned to run. *Thirty more seconds,* he calculated. Hummingbird leaned over and kissed him on the cheek.

"We friends, ain't we, Coma?" she said.

He pulled back to look at her. She only smiled, her eyes welling with tears. She pushed him gently away.

"You go on now."

He focused on the stream below, glimmering with the last light of dusk. A lizard in repose on a rock suddenly darted away.

By then two men were upon them, pulling them apart.

Hummingbird shouted Charlie's name.

He shouted hers.

And they both screamed for Hicklin.

Lucy felt it start like some gradual rising from her insides. The screws tightening. An upheaval. She felt the tautness of her muscles down there. With her belly as big as it was she knew it was starting. But she didn't cry or holler. She ambled down the hall and rapped on the door of the bedroom. Her aunt appeared, wearing a bathrobe, smoking a cigarette, her hair still wet from the shower. Lucy's aunt smiled. Rubbed her hands over her niece's tummy.

Lucy's water broke. The contractions came long and hard. As if a bear were trying to break free from between her legs. By then she was at the clinic with her aunt. The doctor wore wire-rim eyeglasses. Had a bushy mustache. He held Lucy's hand and told her she was doing a fine job. She could feel her teeth grinding together and could do nothing to stop it.

Her aunt smoked one cigarette after another. Nurses tried to shoo her off, but she wouldn't budge. It started to rain outside. Summer storm. A soft patter against the roof of the clinic. Percussive. Like brushes on a jazz snare. The baby roiled the parts between Lucy's legs. She howled in pain.

Lucy knew if it was a boy she'd name him Charles. But she didn't expect Charlie to live. She had moved in with her aunt. Six months pregnant. Broke. A stiff back. Lousy mood. Her aunt had been the first to say the word "deformed." Lucy cursed him then. The father. She was sure he was the father. She swore to never say his name again.

Lucy smoked half a cigarette with her aunt while they picked out hand-me-down clothes from the attic.

Asleep in her aunt's spare room she dreamed about Hicklin. Other men, too. But his memory was strongest. His smell. Muscles in his forearms. The blackheads behind his ears. Lucy loved to squeeze them. When he was in a good mood he'd flip over on his side so she could dig in with her nails. Like a pair of monkeys grooming each other. Memories of him clung to Lucy like pricklers to a pair of socks.

The rest of that afternoon was a blur. A pain like she never felt. Charlie came out headfirst. First thing he felt was the waiting hands of the doctor. At first the doctor studied the newborn as if something was amiss. The baby didn't make a sound. Lucy felt her throat close up. Felt like an eternity, waiting, hoping, fearing the worst.

But then Charlie cried. Lucy raised her head and

stared. She'd never forget the expression on her baby boy's face, so peculiar. Charlie seemed disappointed in his surroundings. Expecting something different. Like a vacationer disillusioned with his accommodations.

Later Lucy held Charlie for the first time. She took deep breaths. Looked with her one good eye into his healthy two.

And tried real hard not to see the face of Charlie's father.

Charlie's lungs felt pinched in his chest. He fought for air. A pair of meaty hands grabbed him by the ears and dragged him backwards. He watched as another man as big as Hicklin scooped up Hummingbird with one arm. The man wore a ski mask. Charlie noticed his eyes—dull as livestock—peering back at him.

The man curled a thick bicep around Hummingbird's neck and yanked her to her feet, choking off a scream.

They reached the front door of the cottage.

Charlie was shoved through the threshold. The other man carried Hummingbird inside. She kicked, her legs cycling and scissoring in the air. She spit and cursed at the men, but neither said a word.

Charlie turned around. Raised his hands in submission.

Please, sir. Please . . .

The polymer stock of a shotgun was the last thing he saw for a while.

Charlie opened his eyes, although his throbbing head told him not to.

They had tied Hummingbird to the chair. The older man reached back and slapped her. He looked at his hand and, disgusted by what he saw, wiped it on a pant leg. He turned his head and glared at Charlie. The ski mask was rolled up revealing a beefy face, a thick goatee like a skunk tail pointing due south.

"What you looking at, boy?" Lispcomb said.

Charlie craned his neck, averting his gaze to the other man. Nathan Flock returned his look with a pointed, level stare, the shotgun at rest in the crook of an arm.

"What's a matter? You a goddamned pussy?" Hummingbird said, directing their attention away from Charlie.

Lipscomb slapped her again with an open hand. A gummy tooth flew from her mouth.

"One of you bitches know something!" he said, his face twisting with accusation.

Hummingbird raised her chin defiantly and said, "I'll go round and round with you all night."

Her tank top hung off the shoulders in shreds, her rib cage breathing through the skin. Charlie realized his right leg was slick with urine.

Lipscomb ran a hand across her forehead. With the other hand he grabbed her mouth and squeezed it open.

He shook his head, clucking his tongue a few times, said, "Jesus. Look at them teeth."

"Never seen meth mouth like that," Flock said.

"You get *kissy kissy* with this right here?" Lipscomb said to Charlie.

"Look at them sores on her legs," Flock added.

Hummingbird shrunk into the chair, a wild guess of a woman breathing in teaspoons. She looked over at Charlie and managed a smile. He whimpered an encouragement. Lipscomb and Flock turned at the sound of his voice.

"What did *he* say?" Lipscomb said.

Flock shrugged, said, "Who is this flabby shit bird anyway?"

"Reckon he might be that bank teller Hicklin took hostage," Lipscomb hazarded. "Stupid mother-fucker shouldn't a took one to begin with."

There was a menacing cast in Lipscomb's eyes. He stood over Charlie. Nudged him with a steel-toe, playfully, as if sizing up his entertainment for the next ten minutes.

"Who are you?" he said.

Charlie scurried to a corner of the cottage. He kept his head down when he spoke.

"Charlie C-Colquitt."

"No, baby!" Hummingbird said. "Don't tell them nothing!"

Lipscomb shot her a look that could stop traffic and without raising his voice said, "I'm going to break every bone in your right arm if you don't shut that fucking mouth of yours."

The calm delivery was enough to give Humming-bird pause. She scowled at him but remained silent.

"So he that bank teller then?" Flock said.

Lipscomb nodded. He turned and knelt next to Charlie.

"You know where Hicklin is, bank teller? Know what he done with the money?"

Charlie shook his head, turning stoic as sun-bleached wood. He jumped at the sound of Hummingbird's voice.

"You ain't never gonna find that money, pecker-wood!" she screamed. "He done left us all!"

Lipscomb pursed his lips in disappointment. He hopped up, spun around and charged her. Charlie struggled to his feet, but Flock knocked him to the floor with a swift kick. He watched as Humming-bird seemed to shrink in Lipscomb's shadow.

Managing to work a hand free, she lunged off the floor—chair and all—and raked her nails down Lipscomb's cheek. Little rivulets of blood appeared in their wake.

He picked her up, hoisting her into the air like a bale of hay. She was airborne. Thrown with stagger-ing force, and if it hadn't been for the wall she might have sailed on off into space. She struck the wall of the cottage and slumped to the floor.

The sound of her breathing only enraged Lipscomb more. Charlie cried out, pleading with his captors, but neither listened. Flock popped him with the butt of the shotgun, then pinned his face against the floor with a muddy boot.

An image of Hicklin appeared, a hallucination, merely a figment of Charlie's traumatized brain. But oddly comforting all the same. Charlie saw Hicklin's shotgun. An iris-in on smoke from the muzzle. The Technicolor homicide about to play out again.

Charlie opened his mouth but could only muster a hoarse cry, his vocal cords shredded, spent like a motor not turning over. Flock watched Lipscomb and Hummingbird with a manic enthusiasm, laughing like people do on a roller coaster.

Lipscomb had become unhinged.

Charlie closed his eyes before that steel-toe boot came down on Hummingbird's head.

Wishing there were a way to cover his ears.

Hicklin spent the afternoon scouting. He stumbled upon a creek surrounded by blackjack oaks and tall spruce, the air along the banks buzzing with wasps and mosquitoes. He gauged where he left the truck, parked just before a covered bridge that didn't seem fit to accommodate a tricycle. Always had a good sense of direction, just like his own father. There were few good memories of him and all of them involved those woods and a rifle. Hicklin had the cash from the robbery on him, rubber-banded in rolls of two thousand and stuffed into a duffel bag. He needed a place to stash it. A place only he might know.

He knew he could make that money last for a good long goddamn time.

And maybe the boy would come with him.

Hicklin crossed a field of broom sedge rank from rainfall, a low ceiling, clouds floating by as if browsing for the perfect place to drop their cargo. He arrived at an old hunting cabin he remembered from his youth—the place he'd been looking for, popular as a rendezvous for trappers of black bear or fox. Built by a Wright or a Donaldson, he couldn't be certain. The cabin belonged to everybody, and for local folks like his daddy and his pals from the mill it had served as a refuge from the responsibilities of married life. He never went a day without drinking and had a talent for cruelty. But something about hunting those woods brought him a peace he couldn't find elsewhere. Brief moments, Hicklin remembered, when his daddy had approached the kindness children expected from their parents yet so randomly received.

Foundation stones were all that remained of the cabin, however. A few rusted traps in the weeds, who knew how many more out in those woods just waiting to be sprung. A chimney had toppled, as if pushed over in some long-forgotten act of desperation.

Must be a hundred years old, he figured, eyeing the crumbled stones and bricks.

There was a box stove on its side, partly concealed by ivy bush. *Could work?* Hicklin passed a hand between pink flower clusters, right across the edge of the stove, its finely cast iron deluded of its luster from years of exposure. He counted six plates. Looked inside at a large orb of web that stretched the width of the oven's interior. The work of a barn spider, the web was peppered with the wings and legs of luckless insects who'd stumbled upon it. An egg the size of his big toe trembled at the center of the oven.

Don't see momma spider anywhere.

Hicklin lit a cigarette, considering the stove. He could smell a big summer rain approaching. Persistent thunder. Flickers of lightning. Without delaying further he stuffed the duffel bag inside the oven. *Sorry for your loss, momma spider.* He looked intently back to the northeast, the placement of his truck to the clearing, the stream and covered bridge, up the narrow switchbacks to the safe house illuminating itself in his mind, as did a trickle of memories.

Know where you stand in relation to things, Lipscomb once told him as they walked the yard.

Hicklin remembered hunting with his own father, on land to the west of where he stood now. He was instilled with a fine sense of direction (and a propensity to drink) if nothing else from the man. More than a decade of incarceration had sharpened that skill to a point, an intuition, a sense of where you were in relation to the dark corners of a prison yard, to the predators stalking the tiers. The phantom paths of the world.

And the beasts who lurked among them.

When Hicklin made for the pickup, he did so through the wind and rain.

H*e drove fast,* dragging a tail of dust behind him. The road became paved. Raindrops dotted the windshield. In the rearview he saw storm clouds. Lightning like the prongs of a trident horizontal across the sky.

At the lower altitude his ears popped. The asphalt was smoother now. The road level and straight. Hicklin felt as though he'd arrived back on a map. Entered the land of public record. Territory thoroughly explored and charted. He made a left at an intersection, then drove for four miles down Highway 9, passing a barn, an old town of tin roofs. Past a feed store, abandoned lots and lonely-looking homes with junk piled up in the front yards. Another left turn brought him to a convenience store.

Where he waited in the truck.

The lone customer walked back to the gas pump and started his car. Drove away.

Hicklin had the place to himself.

The man behind the counter raised his head and nodded when Hicklin walked in, his attention returning to the book in his hands. It was a worn paperback called *A Deadly Shade of Gold*. Fluorescent lights illuminated rows of potato chips and energy drinks. Day-old coffee, a microwave next to the warmer, brown stains splattered across the glass. Hicklin already had an idea where the safe was. Lone surveillance camera behind the cashier. Probably for show. One exit between the restrooms and stacked crates of two-liter soda bottles. Maybe a couple hundred bucks in the place if he really pushed his luck.

He checked out the snack food. Energy bars, beef jerky, crackers, roasted peanuts. He placed items on the counter. The man didn't look up but once. Probably about Hicklin's age. Country and weathered, the cashier's face had the features of a lapdog that preferred to be left alone. A bookworm still living with Ma. He wore a polo shirt with an oil company logo. Chewed on a toothpick as he read.

Hicklin grabbed two Gatorades and a case of beer. Three calling cards. "I get a carton of Spirit Lights, too?" he said.

"The yellow box?"

"Yeah."

The cashier surveyed the goods.

"You going on a trip, huh?" he asked nonchalantly.

"Heading down to Florida to visit my brother and his kids," Hicklin replied.

The cashier turned and looked out the windows. A tractor-trailer loaded with treated wood drove by.

"Looks like we gon' get some rain here shortly."

The small talk went unanswered. The cashier keyed in the items on the register, glancing at the lightning bolts tattooed on Hicklin's neck. He'd worn a sweatshirt to conceal most of the ink, but even with his hair growing out, Hicklin had a face that told people: *Yeah, I've been there and places far worse.*

The register's display read fifty-four dollars and change. Hicklin thought to break a hundred, but the bill was too crisp and new. He handed the cashier three crinkled twenties instead.

"Have a safe trip, now," the man said in parting.

Hicklin paused at the door. There was a tape measure tacked up for the clerk's benefit. When some junky waving a revolver burst in for the fifty bucks in the cash register and a lottery ticket. The tape measure topped out at six-foot-six, the top of Hicklin's head passing just under that mark. A bell jingled against the door as he exited. He walked silently past the pay phone and trash can, the icebox with a cartoon polar bear painted on the side. The locked-up propane tanks.

As Hicklin was pulling out, a man driving a year-old Nissan Titan turned into the gas station. The driver gave him more than a passing glance.

The convenience store disappeared behind Hicklin. He checked his rearview.

He ascended a winding road that led up into the mountains. A moment later he passed a church that looked abandoned. No lights.

It seemed to Hicklin that night had originated there and was spreading outward.

Lang *parked his* Nissan Titan with a notion to fill up the tank. He got out of the pickup, stretched his sore legs against the nagging pains of middle age that followed him like a chaperone. The two days since Kalamity Bibb's murder had been hard to bear. He'd taken a leave of absence at a time when he couldn't afford to.

But everyone knew why.

Other investigators and agencies had involved themselves with Kalamity's case, including the FBI gang infiltration unit. Lang didn't feel like a member

of their fraternity, the investigation now well beyond his expertise. The Jube County Sheriff's Department had kindly but firmly been handed its hat.

Sallie Crews had been in touch with the Federal
Bureau of Prisons and task forces from across the
Southeast. Reports of bank robberies from Bakers-
field, California, to Danbury, Connecticut. More
than a dozen cities. Similar MOs.

Big news from Atlanta P.D. as Mexican gangs
from California were chopping each other to pieces
with machetes on the city's Southside. Mexican Mafia franchises—originating from prisons in Atwater
and Pelican Bay—had set up shop in nearly every
metro county. One house in the city of Smyrna had
five hundred pounds of crystal meth stacked like pillows in a back room. Automatic weapons by the
crateful.

Having started in South Florida, Nazi Low Riders
from Arizona and Texas had traveled farther north
into the Tennessee Valley, killing everyone on a
twenty-name list. Snitches, rival black and Hispanic
gang leaders, even the wife and daughter of a state
witness. The hit squad, pure street muscle and following mandates from the top brass of the Aryan
Brotherhood, was also suspected in a slew of robberies and assaults spanning five states.

Lang could only shake his head after reading the
reports. Lawless men roaming the country. Savages
without morals or restraint. And a couple of them
had shown up in Jubilation County.

Crews had found Lang slightly crazed at Kalamity's house. He'd been sitting on the back porch, hid-

den in shadow, smoking his way through a pack of Marlboros. When they carted Kalamity's body out on a stretcher he got in his truck and left. Kal had been wrapped in a black bag, like raked leaves left out on the curb for collection.

He'd recalled the excitement he'd felt on his way to Kalamity's house. Lang never slept so good as he did there. With her.

Later that night he'd wrestled with memories of her. He drank a bottle of bourbon to forget.

Lang had ignored phone calls, including one from his daughter. When he heard Diane's voice on the answering machine he began to cry. Filled with self-loathing, he couldn't even pick up the phone and talk to the only one of his children who still cared. Beside him, Lady studied her owner as if the hound understood something of the human condition.

And found it exhausting.

T*he little bell* rang when the door opened. Harvey Ballew looked up from his paperback.

"Harvey."

"Well, Sheriff Lang. What's your pleasure?" he said.

Ballew watched Lang make for the red-and-blue cases of beer.

He brought a case of Budweiser to the counter. Harvey offered him a cigarette from a Vantage soft pack.

"I heard about Kalamity," the cashier said, a streak of sympathy in his eyes.

"Yeah."

"My sister was over to KB's place earlier. Lots of people shook up about it. Seems there's some bad folks floating around up here."

"Get me a pack of Mediums, would you?" Lang said.

"Sure thing, Sheriff."

Lang looked outside. Vacant pumps. Orange light under the canopy. The old highway beyond. He caught a glimpse of the Chevy step-side catching a green light before it disappeared from sight.

"Who was that in here just now? Man drivin' that old step-side," Lang said.

"Reckon he's the meanest-lookin' son of a bitch I've seen lately. Wouldn't want to cross him."

"Seen him before?" Lang said.

"No, sir."

"What was so mean about him?"

"You can always tell the ones done some jail time. Them tattoos, you know?"

"Tattoos?"

"Lightning bolts on his neck," Harvey said, pointing to just below his Adam's apple. "Like something from a comic book. But the scary thing—which I don't think he saw me having a look at—was the swastika on his wrist."

"Swastika?"

"Yeah, Nazi shit. Also, he was wearing a sweatshirt. Why in this damn heat anyone would want to wear a sweatshirt is beyond me!"

"How did he pay? Credit card?"

"Nah, he had cash. Fifty-four dollars."

"Drop a name?"

"Said hardly a word. By the way, oddest thing about him was his smell."

"Yeah?" Lang said.

"You know that gamey smell, like you been up in the woods three weeks and bathed maybe twice? It settles in your clothes."

Lang nodded in agreement.

"And the dude was a heavy smoker. Nicotine stains on his right forefinger."

"Good eye, Harvey."

"Why you askin' about that guy?"

"No reason. Thanks. How much do I—?"

"Beer and smokes is on the house tonight, Sheriff."

"You don't have to do that, Harvey," Lang said.

"My treat. I'm just awful sorry about Kalamity. We all spent our time bowed up to her bar and knowed her for a good woman."

Lang nodded gratefully, even though he felt a twinge of shame that so many people knew of his business. He still left a twenty-dollar bill on the counter. Walked quickly to his truck, then tore ass out of the parking lot, heading down SR 9. At Osbourne Road, the mountain road, he turned left, accelerating uphill past the dark church, Lang knowing the country folk who worshiped there in their strange fashion. He drove higher into the mountains.

Reminded of something, he reached under the steering column and touched the .45.

Hicklin was naked. From beyond the bars they told him to squat and cough. He did. The first time he had to strip in front of grown men it had disturbed him. Like a kid in a high school locker room. Now it was routine. A big cock swung between his legs. He was the alpha male with size to match, the pack leader.

The correctional officer stood three feet from the bars, as if he were prepared for Hicklin to run right through them.

He worked his shoulders and chest hard that summer until the muscles were sharply defined. His shoulders were as broad as anybody's in the yard. Much of the tattoo ink had settled in. His face was longer and leaner with goatee. Five years inside and nothing in his eyes had dimmed. He roamed in a perpetual state of retribution, knowing he could take on any nigger or spic or screw in the place.

And they all knew it, too.

Inmates in his vicinity walked as if the lion were planning his evening meal.

The games and daily hustles of prison life were played. Now and then someone got killed. Some fish or scoundrel doing dips on the parallel bars one moment. A toothbrush fashioned into a blunt tip was puncturing his neck the next. The guards got nervous when prisoners wore all their clothing, a big tip-off that something was about to go down. The yard full of Michelin Men, sleeves and tops, pant legs stuffed with newspaper and magazines. The more layers the better. Could save you a trip to the infirmary or, better yet, the big black nowhere.

From the whites-only corner of the yard Hicklin acknowledged violence and its ever-present threat as a stabilizing force. Convicts would attack each other like animals and there was always a reason. Sometimes just two men, other times dozens of convicts from rival gangs, would produce weapons and charge each other. Then the tear gas would launch from the guard towers. Hicklin would clasp his hands behind his head and drop to his knees, per the CO's commands. An amused grin on his face.

He found there was a beauty to a prison riot, an unintentional choreography. As if it were all entertainment to begin with.

He was muscle and brains. White convicts looked to him for guidance. It wasn't long before Hicklin was taking counsel with hard timers. He'd been lucky, too. If it wasn't for a blind spot on one of the surveillance cameras—video that would have been damning evidence of his murder of a black inmate—Hicklin might be on death row. But the investigators had nothing on him. Life went on.

Hicklin took orders and did as he was asked. Satisfied, the Brotherhood let him in.

Blood in. Blood out.

It was a mantra among the gangs. Black, brown, white. Only way to stay alive unless you were a queer or Jesus freak.

The games continued. Drugs were king. Hicklin helped the Brothers get their slice of the profits, the Georgia chapter being their most recent and clandestine outpost. Coded communications with AB in other prisons revealed a vast network of criminal *enterprises within state and federal facilities. A chess match played since the 1960s between the Brand and rival gangs, law enforcement, wardens and guards. In places like Marion, Lewisburg, Tamms and Atlanta. Out west to Folsom, Chino, Atwater and Pelican Bay.*

The fun even trickled into the state pens. Texas, Louisiana, Tennessee, the Carolinas. One or two Brothers blessed by the council would show up and set up a franchise. It was that easy.

They'd x out the poseurs and wannabes before last call. The imitators had their balls handed to them. The AB reinvented itself.

An exclusive circle of the hardened.

The Brotherhood's aspirations surprised and enticed Hicklin. Domestic terrorism, robberies, drugs and weapons trafficking, killing police officers and judges. Men locked in a cell for twenty-three hours a day. Brooding on ways to expel their hatred.

Some of them even got college degrees along the way.

Outright war at Hays erupted with the blacks one winter. But everyone knew that, although outnumbered, Preacher and Hicklin's crew was the fiercest and most ruthless. It all started with a slight made against a convict. Escalated into a hostile struggle for power. Control of the heroin trade.

That's because everything meant something inside. Using the wrong toilet could and did ignite the conflict. Boundaries were set long ago, like ancestral overlords drawing up a battlefield. For a few months the violence seemed incalculable and as reliable to occur as the sun was to rise.

Hicklin earned an extra year inside for chewing a man's ear off. He ate it in front of a howling pack of onlookers. An African was set on fire and ran screaming down the tier like some Hollywood stunt-man, a trail of cooked flesh dripping off his arms and back.

At one point the guards took to spraying them with liquid tear gas. If there had been a hole big enough for the two thousand convicts, the prison staff would have thrown them all in and wiped their hands of the whole business.

It was a tense existence. Living day to day at such a heightened alertness was hard on the nerves. It physically transformed Hicklin.

When he looked in the mirror one day he no longer recognized himself.

Charlie tucked his knees and rocked quietly.

Thinking about death.

What is it going to be like? How will they do it? Will it hurt? Will my mind keep going? Thoughts just drift off into space like a wayward radio signal? . . .

Hummingbird was dead. He tried not to look at her body.

Now Flock stood over him, talking to Lipscomb in the other room. Flock braced the shotgun across his left forearm, the weapon like some sleeping python. The muzzle dipped periodically and Charlie recoiled as the big black hole pointed at his head. He figured Flock was doing it on purpose.

Lipscomb grew angry during their conversation, a hostility directed at himself that filled the cottage like smoke from a blocked chimney.

"It ain't here!" Lipscomb said, clearing off a counter of dish plates to emphasize his point.

"You shouldn't a killed her," Flock said. Off Lipscomb's look he knew to explain his comment with as much deference as possible. "I mean . . . bet a bean she knew. Maybe just had to give her some time?"

Both men stared at Hummingbird for a moment, her body as discarded as wrapping paper on Christmas morning.

"Probably right," Lipscomb agreed. "But I wasn't interested no more. I didn't want to hear it from her lips."

He turned and looked down his nose at Charlie.

"I'd rather hear it from him," he said.

As if on cue, Flock scooped Charlie up, righted him on the sofa. Charlie felt his face go all funny. He fainted briefly.

Regaining consciousness, he struggled to meet Lipscomb's eyes, fearful that the man might grab something and start hammering at his feet. A realization struck him. *No one was coming to his rescue.*

"Shut that door," Lipscomb said to Flock, before turning to Charlie again.

Lipscomb sat down and put a suggestive hand on Charlie's knee, turning his head with his other hand as if to kiss him.

Charlie retracted, frightened, batting at Lipscomb's advancing hands.

"You know where he is, don't you, bank teller?"

"No, sir," Charlie said. "He comes and goes. I've been here—"

"—more than a week I reckon."

"Feels like longer."

"Where is he?"

Charlie shook his head. "I don't know."

Lipscomb sighed, letting a well-timed beat pass before slapping Charlie across the cheek. It was meant to be playful, but hard enough to rattle his teeth.

"Where did the motherfucker go, bank teller?"

"I told you I don't know! He leaves. He comes back," Charlie said, smarting from the pain. "They had me tied up like a dog most the time. I think he had a truck."

"A truck?"

"Yes, s-sir."

"Well, Jesus, bank teller. You're just full of revelation tonight."

Charlie refused to look at Lipscomb anymore, as if his nervous system wouldn't allow it.

"Seriously," Lipscomb continued, "a fucking revelation. That is my goddamn pickup truck. A C-ten. Bought it in '80. Replaced the ball joints and brakes myself. Got a crate three-fifty under the hood and ten thousand miles on it. Know why there's so few miles on it?"

Charlie shuddered. Shook his head.

"Because I was in a place called *prison*."

"I don't want anything to do with all this," Charlie said, his whisper as much a protest as it was a plea.

But Lipscomb didn't hear him. Charlie got the impression the man didn't hear a lot, except for the sound of his own voice.

"Now what does that tell you, bank teller? Hicklin driving my truck and all?"

"That you all were friends?"

"My gawd, Nathan, you hear that?"

"I did hear it. The boy is puttin' *two* and *two* together like a regular crackerjack."

"Well, bank teller?" Lipscomb said.

"I don't understand."

"That's okay, bank teller," he said. "We'll just wait right here for our *friend,* Hicklin. A hunch tells me he'll be back. And if not, well, I'm sure there's things we could do to kill time."

Lipscomb ran a calloused hand through Charlie's hair. His palms hardened like the sole of a shoe.

F*lock peered past* shreds of newspaper that still covered one of the windows. Darkness. Not even a flood lamp to illuminate the cottage's immediate vicinity. He settled into a chair across from the couch, spitting on the floor, the shotgun resting across his lap. Lipscomb lit a cigarette. Ran another calculated hand through Charlie's hair.

The smell of slow ruin was all around them. Charlie couldn't keep from trembling. He stared at his feet. Then, summoning some resolve, looked up at Lipscomb.

Lipscomb followed Charlie's eyes, too, a malicious smirk appearing, a hand reaching for his sidearm. Charlie shook his head again.

"No—no—"

"I have to admit," Lipscomb interrupted, "those are some ugly feet you got there. Is that a hangnail I see? Toe jam? Them little pieces of lint that find their way up there. You chew on the nails, don't you, bank teller? I can always tell when a man chews on his toenails. The nail grows back all funny. The way *yours* do."

He grabbed Charlie's filthy left foot, inspecting it, running the tip of his thumb along the nail of the big toe like you would the edge of a blade.

"Been hunched over, chewing on 'em, haven't you?" he said, his voice rising to a fervor. "I take good care of my feet," he declared. "Always have. Now yours? I think they could use some improving on."

He raised Charlie's foot up to the light.

"You know how I feel about ugly feet?" he continued, his voice bold and worthy of a pulpit. "Well, do you, bank teller? It's all about the socks. And the shoes. But you obviously inherited some awful feet. Probably your momma, I suspect. And I think they could use some rearranging. A little swelling can do toes some good. Now how 'bout it, bank teller?"

He relinquished his hold on Charlie's foot, removed the magazine from the .45, jacked out the round in the pipe and slammed the clip home again.

He reversed his grip, the muzzle firmly in his left hand, the butt of the handgun taking on the look of a dead blow hammer. Charlie shouted in anticipation, but there was nothing he could do. Lipscomb skirted the coffee table away with his leg, hopped off the couch onto his knees, before he snatched Charlie's quivering foot again. He raised the gun and hollered:

"Tell me, you sorry sack of shit! Where's Hicklin? Where's our fucking money?"

Charlie shrieked, his eyes growing wild with fright.

"No! No! No!"

Lipscomb brought the butt of the pistol down hard on Charlie's left foot, striking the big toe with the force of a blacksmith forging steel. Charlie felt the nail come loose. Blood popped from the wound like a blister bursting. Some notion of self-preservation occurred to him. He turned on his side, kicking his legs as though trying to tread water.

His foot caught Lipscomb square in the face.

But the big man only laughed, playfully swatting away Charlie's bicycling legs like he was toying with an energetic puppy. The two men hooted in laughter. Charlie continued to struggle, swinging his legs back and forth to avoid the blows. Then Lipscomb caught hold of Charlie's right foot, hammered at it twice, let go, only to grab it again. *Is this a game we're playing?* Charlie tired, the pain turning dull and bearable, and for a moment he thought himself human in appearance only.

Desperation churned in him like the paddle wheel

of a sinking steamboat. He hoped that someone would pick up a gun and shoot him in the head. That familiar refrain, said aloud or merely imagined he wasn't sure:

Please stop! Please don't do this! Please stop!

But Charlie couldn't account for the sudden swell of courage. He jabbed both legs at Lipscomb, one foot catching his captor under the chin. Solid as an uppercut. Lipscomb was stunned momentarily. He recovered, lurching forward on his knees with the handgun hammer raised high in the air.

"You li'l sumbitch!"

He swung, catching Charlie's rib cage like a slab of hanging beef. Lipscomb struck a kneecap, a shin, a wrist. Bone and flesh wrought by the flat edge of the magazine. Charlie cried out, his hands in spasm, his fingers rigid and curled like fishhooks. With his last ounce of strength he lunged at Lipscomb's face, gouging his eyes in a final desperate attempt at survival.

He reeled with a painful grunt, but Flock was there with the stock of the shotgun. He struck Charlie in the forehead, knocking him backwards.

"Motherfucker almost took out my eyes!"

That's when Lipscomb unsheathed a knife.

Lipscomb steadied the Randall knife over Charlie's face before running the blade down the bridge of his nose and across his quivering lips. Charlie's heart started to shimmy in his chest like a dryer out of balance.

"Ever had a dick in your ass, bank teller? Know what that *feels* like? It's a pain no man was ever really supposed to experience. But God in his infinite wisdom let us figure these things out for ourselves. And he might not have intended it, but we discovered the human anus and found it worthy of fucking."

Charlie's vision blurred, the main room of the cottage taking on the warped appearance of a fun house. Lipscomb flicked the tip of the knife blade against Charlie's cheek. A nick appeared, producing a sliver of blood. Charlie sensed the end of his life approaching.

And a death he could have never imagined.

It was not until a round of buckshot ripped through the front door with the force of a dozen nail guns that he thought his odds of survival had improved.

A startled Lipscomb and Flock dove for cover.

Charlie knew Hicklin was near.

Charlie's saving might be a possibility. If not a priority.

The Lord has left us now.

NINE

A light came on inside the church. Station wagons and pickup trucks found it like moths to a flood lamp. The church had a gravel drive, a small porch where an attendant lit lanterns and hung them from hooks. The wood structure didn't look like a place of worship. A fresh coat of paint had been applied, as if its tenants decided to put another Band-Aid on the wound. A two-by-four had been tacked above the door. Written in a fluid script, someone long ago had stenciled the words: The Church of the Holy Lamb with Signs Following.

When the gravel drive filled, people parked their vehicles with an instinct for order along the shoulder of the road. The women wore ankle-length dresses. Hair long and uncut. Tennis shoes. Loafers. Soap and water the only cosmetic that touched the skin of their weary faces. They carried platters and butcher paper and clay cookware. Wooden serving spoons and bowls lidded with tinfoil. Men unloaded picnic tables from the flatbed of one of the trucks. Carted them off to the grounds behind the church.

These men wore short-sleeve dress shirts. White cotton or flannel. Pens or cases for their glasses tucked in the breast pockets. Many walked with a leatherbound copy of the King James Bible. A tethered red ribbon marking some passage or other. One man was much older than the others and he walked with the help of a cane. It was hot that night. Sweat stains spread in wide crescents under their arms. Archaic-looking faces, they might have traveled across time to attend service that evening.

A dumpy man with thinning gray hair opened the hatch on his camper bed. He and another man removed a wooden crate. And another. The crates had hinged lids made of mesh. Whatever was inside them responded to their sudden relocation with a series of dry rattles. Another man approached. Lifted a cardboard box full of fruit jars. With an elbow he shut the hatch to the camper and joined the others.

The women chatted behind the church, unseen, their laughter sounded supernatural. There was an occasional breeze. Clouds trekked before a quarter-full moon. Rain to the west. Someone turned on the exterior lights, simply two flood lamps at either end of the porch. Spiderwebs revealed themselves where the roof met the foundation. Stringy webbing like fishing line, insect wings and legs and leftover parts trembling in the light. The spiders welcomed the 65-watt bulbs like a pulsing dinner bell.

The men hauled the crates inside the church. One man carried a guitar case, followed by a primitive PA system. The older man with thin gray hair paused outside to smoke a cigarette. The others gravitated toward him. A hound trotted excitedly around their feet. Sniffing. Wagging its tail. Its owner patted the dog's head. The subject of coon hunting came up. Led to other topics. Conversation nonlinear. Casual. Bill Elliott raced down in Woodstock. A brother of one of the men from Blairsville suffered from the cancer. But when hands were laid on the afflicted areas he was healed with God's holy fire. When the discussion came back to the subject of God they uttered "amens" in succession. Told stories that had been told before but felt right to tell again.

A truck passed them on the road. To the lone driver it might have appeared as some apocalyptic gathering. A séance. Something equally cultish. The church was one of the few structures with a working roof this high up the mountain. Because the road went on. Higher and higher. To a place where the timber was still king.

The men paid the pickup little attention. Conversation dwindled. They all seemed to know it was time. One by one they ushered themselves inside, the old man with the cane leading the way. The pomade in his hair glistened like grease in a frying pan. The women trailed behind, their work setting up the warming trays and covering the food completed.

An old woman the color of parchment carried a wash pan before her. She wore a handspun dress dyed blue from indigo root. Her face was pruned and shrunken, yet her hazel eyes glowed as if she had just been born. Eyes ready to cry for the first time. She hummed delicately to herself, then opened her mouth to speak. Strange words came out, not quite English, punctuated only by a recognizable "hallelujah." No one reacted. It seemed expected.

There were two rows of pine pews inside the church. An altar with a podium where the wooden boxes were placed. Fruit jars filled with a honey-colored liquid. A propane tank. A small amplifier. A guitar in its stand. A man fidgeted with a video camera. He looked through the viewfinder, sliding to one corner of the room where a tripod had been set.

The women filed in, patiently following the men.

They followed their husbands or brothers or cousins. When everyone passed under the door frame it was as if the last page of a book had been read.

And a new one begun.

Lang drove up muddy switchbacks, forced to use his high beams; the twisting snake spine of road revealed numerous slips and ditches. Dirt shoulders. Deteriorating and lacking guardrails. He had a faint recollection as to where he was, a memory of the way, the backbone of the ridge that simply ended and the only way up from there was on foot. In the valley below, the old Dumas line ran out, pockets of abandoned trailers all that remained. Hill people made themselves at home there, squatting, living by their own law. Reaching a point in their lives when no one else wanted them and the feeling was mutual.

Ten years ago you could hear the dogs tearing themselves apart at night. Money exchanging hands. But he had to put a stop to all that shit.

He came upon a downed hickory tree blocking the road. The truck had carried some speed and Lang had to slam on the brakes, causing the back end of the pickup to fishtail into a controlled slide that got his heart rate blast-beating. He hadn't been paying attention, an absence he noticed more often, especially when he was driving. His mind dangerously adrift, minutes of his life vanishing with no recollection of where he'd been.

The lost time added up.

Might come a time I'd want it back. But by then it'd be too late.

Lang secured his sidearm and walked toward the big tree, backlit by the high beams of the pickup. The mountain road beyond slanted upward and narrowed, winding like a wormhole into impenetrable darkness. He ran a hand along the rough, shaggy bark of the hickory. It came away wet. Crud on his fingertips. He wiped his hand on a pant leg and walked back to the truck.

Not understanding what he was about to do.

Like walking in the woods with a flashlight. His hunch to follow the tattooed man from the gas station up into the mountains was foolish, sure. And there was no sign he had been up this way. *Man's long gone,* Lang told himself. *Or if he's still in Jube County he sure as hell ain't up here.*

But that last bit of speculation didn't find traction in Lang's mind. The mountains were full of stands and cabins. Campsites long abandoned.

You'd need a hundred men to comb this mountain alone.

His fingers caressed the butt of the holstered Kimber.

What the fuck are you doin', Tommy?

He hustled a can of beer from the fridge pack. It opened with a hiss. He took a sip. Moths clamored around the headlights, beyond their reach another hairpin turn and then empty space. A sensation of being watched struck him, as if the woods were taking inventory, acknowledging his presence. *Let 'em watch.* He lit a cigarette and turned on the stereo.

The thought did occur to just leave. Drive down until he hit some familiar roads. Put the beers in a cooler he kept in the bed, cruise around for a while in the dark. Eventually go on home. He'd had about enough anyway, and the moments when he was thinking straight seemed few and far between. He could cook some chili. Play with the dog. Watch television. Go on a big drunk. Had enough money put away. Pension. The house paid for. He sure as hell wasn't planning to run for Sheriff again. They could see it in his eyes and he could see it in his own.

He flipped down the visor and looked into the compact mirror.

You got options. Go on a diet. Quit smoking. Sixty coming up awful fast. Get in real good shape. Maybe get one of those consulting-type jobs. Secu-

*rity. Redecorate the house. Put in a swimming pool.
Get that satellite that records programs, what everyone talks about. Call up the ex and ask about the
kids like any responsible man would. Maybe reunite
with them. Bet they'd be shocked by what they saw.
Yes, sir. That's the new Tommy Lang. He done had
himself an awakening. Could even start going to
church again. Put the bottle down once and for all.
Get right with Jesus and all that stuff they talked
about. Could drink vegetable juice and smoothies
and do sit-ups and rub cream on my face. Dye the
gray from my hair. Maybe get a new wardrobe. Go
to the doctor and get a full checkup and really listen.
Do a total inventory. Head down to the city for a
day. Hell, a weekend. Buy some books. Go to a mu-
seum. Something. We got to do something, Tommy.
It done got to start now. Just turn the truck around.
Turn the truck around. Turn the truck around . . .*

. . . who am I fucking kidding?

Lang reached for another beer, putting the empty
in the cup holder. He propped his boots on the dash
and sighed. One more beer. Then he'd turn around.
"Whipping Post" by the Allman Brothers Band
played on the radio. Lang drank the second beer
quickly. Opened another. Figured he would just sit
there a little longer.

Enjoy his beer and music in the quiet darkness.

Until his mind was made up.

Hicklin *got lucky* and he knew it.

He'd intended to hide the Chevy, hike directly up

to the cottage. It was a difficult climb but a straight shot through the woods. Stay long enough to leave Hummingbird enough cash to get by for a little while. Make plans with Charlie for an overnight escape. To where he didn't know, but he had some ideas.

He left the pickup hidden under the camouflage tarp, groceries and beer in the front seat. Halfway up the mountain a hunch told him to circle the safe house, take stock of who was inside.

Hicklin flanked the cottage at dusk, getting within earshot, the faint orange light of the safe house's interior coming into view. He knelt under the shade of a black gum tree, winded and sweating, watching as fireflies lighted in the gloaming. He heard laughter. A familiar voice followed by a short, muzzled scream.

Charlie.

There was a commotion occurring in the main room, thumps and banging and the deranged cackle of Hicklin's old friend Lipscomb.

The lamp in the living room cast a soft halo around the front door. Hicklin crept forward, using the dense trees for cover, the shotgun waist high and steadied on the cottage. He heard the sonorous hoots of a horned owl, a distant rumble of thunder. He fingered the safety back, the button located on top of the receiver tang of the Mossberg. Hicklin hadn't heard Hummingbird and intuition told him she was already dead. He could almost feel Charlie's jackhammer heartbeat from where he hid.

Hicklin knew why those two monsters were there. And he knew what they might do.

Charlie started to scream.

As if the forest had birthed him, Hicklin appeared some fifteen yards from the safe house, the muzzle swinging up to his shoulder as he took aim at the front door. A flame reached out and licked the open air. The front door exploded with buckshot. He saw Flock and Lipscomb dive out of harm's way, their curses loud and vicious. He racked the pump and chambered another round.

Alternating between buckshot and three-inch Magnum slugs, Hicklin fired again, one round ripping through the middle hinge of the front door, all but destroying it. He backpedaled, melting into darkness as a hornet's nest of return fire singed the air around his ears. He took cover behind the trunk of a white oak, feeling a hot prickling in his right shoulder as a scatter of buckshot from a 12-gauge ripped through tree limbs and peppered the ground around his feet. Just a flesh wound, but a reminder for Hicklin of the firepower his former partners were packing.

He could hear the twin *clacking* of the pumps from inside the cottage.

He retreated some thirty yards from the gaping hole that used to be the front door, knowing he had an advantage as darkness fell on the mountain. Lipscomb and Flock wouldn't be able to see three feet past the cottage, although they had smartly killed the lights inside. Hicklin leaned the shotgun against a nearby pine tree. Drew his pistol and took a deep breath.

Gunsmoke hung lazily across the threshold of the

safe house. He crept to his right, his stealth impeded by size 14 steel-toes. But his lateral move went unnoticed, the silence broken only by Lipscomb and Flock's muffled bickering. Hicklin sprinted to another thick cluster of pine, swung around and leveled the Sig Sauer on the western wall of the cottage, locking the night sights on a low window that looked into the living room. He squeezed off two rounds, followed by a single trigger pull, exhausting more than half the magazine a moment later with one last double tap.

Hicklin heard glass break. A few inches of black barrel were offered through an open window. A double-aught olive branch.

He ducked and flattened his back against the largest tree trunk he could find as a chorus of gunfire erupted around him.

"I *didn't hear* no 'Police' or 'Come out with your hands up,' so it must be our old friend Hicklin!" Lipscomb said.

"Old friend, my ass! He done shot me!" Flock objected.

"You hit?"

"Just a graze," Flock said. "Tore my shirt is all." He laughed nervously, fingering the rip in his twill shortsleeve, tender and bloodied skin beneath. Lipscomb responded with a raspy laugh of his own. Leaning against the wall, he pushed the couch toward the south wall of the cottage, taking cover behind it.

"Hey, boy," Lipscomb said, whispering.

"What?"

"Get from that wall. Slugs go right through the clapboard."

Flock shuffled past Charlie, kicking him out of frustration. His nerve seemed to be going, judging by the expression on his face. Lipscomb turned and peeked around an edge of the couch. The trees beyond as dark as a dead television. Rain began to fall.

"We just want to talk, Hick," Lipscomb shouted. " 'Bout the score. Maybe a miscommunication on your part. Done got your days of the week mixed up. You hear me, Hicklin?"

Wind rustled through the treetops. Raindrops clunked against the roof. Lipscomb surveyed the room. Charlie was on his side, curled up like a baby. He had his hands clasped behind his head, protecting it like some trench-bound soldier. Lipscomb counted six magazines. Seven rounds per clip.

What's one or two less?

Dissatisfied by the silence that answered him, he raised the handgun and pumped two rounds at Charlie, missing him by inches. Charlie screamed, covering his head.

"Hear that, Hicklin? We're having a little fun with your bank teller!"

He let Charlie's sobbing sink in for effect, suspecting that Hicklin was tuned in to the hostage or Hummingbird or both. *Otherwise, why would he have come back?*

"First let me say I'm sorry about Hummingbird,"

Lipscomb said. "But she's moved on to tweeker heaven. Now I'm keen to put one in bank teller's gut next!"

Lipscomb was scanning the empty shadows of the surrounding woods when a round ripped through the window just above his head. Two more followed as Lipscomb ducked out of sight, peeking around the doorjamb, trying to zero in on the muzzle flashes. There was a reprieve that lasted a few dozen heartbeats, interrupted by a blast of buckshot with a Magnum slug chaser. Lipscomb and Flock flattened themselves against the baseboards as the cottage came apart around them.

Flock answered first, rolling to his right and firing out the front door with his sidearm. Double taps at twelve o'clock and two o'clock. He caught Hicklin's muzzle flash and popped a few more rounds in its direction. Too dark to get a position on him, though, Hicklin just another shadow within the depths of that thick, unforgiving timber. *Might as well have thrown the bullets out the door.*

A burst of gunfire crackled, a chaotic call-and-response. Both parties pausing for a moment as if to enjoy the noisy echo that followed. If the birds and crickets and frogs could have called 911 they probably would have.

"What the hell is he doing?" Flock said, flustered by their predicament. He righted himself using his elbows, squatting on his heels.

"Saying hello, apparently," Lipscomb mused.

"He's got a funny goddamn way of sayin' it."

Lipscomb smiled and leaned back against the

couch. Realizing his weapon was empty, he dropped
free the exhausted magazine and reached for another from a pouch on his belt, popped it into the
HK's Mag Well and thumbed the release slide.

Meanwhile his partner sucked air, the look on his
face one of pure impatience. It was as though Flock
could no longer contain the frenzy within him. He
rocked on his heels and rose, keeping to the one
wall of the cottage that wasn't decorated with bullet
holes.

"To hell with this," he said.

Lipscomb watched his partner curiously, realizing
a second too late what he was about to do.

"Flock, you dumb asshole! Get your ass back in
here!"

But he wouldn't listen. Flock stepped outside into
a hard rain to face the darkness. He dropped his .45
and raised his arms as if to show he had no other
pistols on his person. Next he produced a hunting
knife, clutching it like some ancient warrior, and
hollered as if he were addressing thousands of enemies at once.

"Come on out, Hicklin, you motherfucker! Let's
quit this Mickey Mouse bullshit once and for all!"

Hicklin hustled just behind the tree line, finding
cover by lying flat within a patch of wild shrubs. He
eyed what was left of the ghostly-looking front
door. Noticed the generator was failing. A shadeless
lamp in one of the interior bedrooms dimmed considerably. There had been no movement for a few

minutes. No sound. Soothing cool rainwater trick-led down his spine. Not keen to talk yet, he couldn't help but think of his own betrayal.

Lipscomb.

A man he'd robbed with. Done almost ten years' time with him. Many moments of friendship and brotherhood, but a camaraderie that was ephemeral by nature when money or drugs or guns were in-volved. Preacher had become like a father to Hick-lin in prison. But what did that word mean anymore?

He mulled over his options, sensing the world had become opaque.

The windows painted black.

Hicklin watched the silent cottage, a multitude of considerations running through his mind.

Charlie.

Maybe if he could save Charlie it would all be worth it. Best bet was to wait Lipscomb and Flock out a little longer. Pretty soon Hicklin knew Lip-scomb would grow impatient and wander out with a gun to Charlie's head, ultimatums in tow.

Things would either happen *to* him or *for* him.

To Hicklin's surprise he heard Lipscomb's voice, raised in objection as Flock appeared, moonlit and hulking before the shattered front door. A driving rain began to fall, a percussive swell filling the forest around them. Flock produced a knife and Hicklin heard him announce a challenge. A raving sociopath on display. Going for that extra gear.

Hard for Hicklin not to admire the balls on the kid.

But there was no time to get cute.

Hicklin rose undetected, stepping laterally into a thicket of mountain laurel that bordered the western edge of the clearing. A moment later a black muzzle appeared among the shrub's poisonous flowers.

Flock had taken a few more steps away from the cottage, nervously scanning the woods ahead but not once bothering to check his nine or three o'clock. Hicklin was twenty-five feet away, cloaked in darkness. He dared not show himself, not mistaking Lipscomb's silence for strategy. No doubt the convict was watching—Flock a piece of peckerwood bait for Hicklin to pounce on.

He was fine right where he was and figured whatever quality of round next in the chamber would do the job. He hazarded the buckshot at that range wouldn't be lethal, but it surely would do a number on Flock's face. Take him out of the equation.

Hicklin focused down the long muzzle at the single dot sight. His target was briefly outlined by a flicker of lightning. Hicklin drew a breath and exhaled slowly. He closed his left eye.

The butt jerked into his shoulder.

He knew instantly what round had been in the chamber.

It was a hell of a shot in such poor conditions. And lucky. Flock's body jumped to its left as if he'd been yanked off his feet by an invisible crook. His leg pancaked and Flock—minus some of his head—fell to the ground.

Hicklin had no time to spare as a double-fisted salvo strafed the thicket of laurel, Lipscomb showing excellent trigger control, even with his weak hand. Hicklin retreated into the forest, head down, bullets whining around him as a tit-for-tat dance of muzzle flashes could be seen from a cottage window.

While Lipscomb reloaded, Hicklin heard the generator sputter and flatline.

Be strong, he wanted to tell Charlie. Not sure of his next move. *Don't do nothin' stupid.*

L*ed by the* beam of his Maglite, Lang stumbled up an incline, negotiating downed trunks and rotten husks. A river of pine straw gave way to rocks slick from the recent rain. He looked back at the Titan, barely able to discern his pickup in the darkness below.

Tall pines and sapling branches served as obstacles to his ascent. At times he had to move laterally ten or twenty feet before he could continue. Every step appeared ominous. He hiked about fifty yards, pausing once when the terrain became more agreeable to smoke a cigarette, every minute that passed reminding him of his foolishness. His thoughts turned dour. An impulse to end it then and there. Against this tree or that.

A sorry-ass life, Tommy.

Here in the woods where it just rains and rains and rains.

The report from a shotgun dopplered down the mountainside. Lang froze. The sound seemed to come at him from all directions, an avalanche of echoes prickling his skin with alarm. Followed by small-arms fire and the boom of that 12-gauge again. An impression of the gunfight formed in his mind, somewhere northeast of his current position. Lang's heart began to gallop. He unholstered the Kimber and continued on, half a step slower, his eyes and ears tuned to the vast forest that surrounded him. He reached the edge of a brook. Slabs of limestone jutted from the ground in a peculiar uniformity. He cocked an ear but heard only the roar of rainwater draining downstream.

Moments later gunfire broke the eerie silence, .40- or .45-caliber handguns punctuated by the blast of a pump shotgun. Sounded like two armies talking across a pasture. Lang grew breathless, but he kept on, squinting at the faint beginnings of a hiking path just ahead. He kept the beam of the flashlight low and tried to ignore the pain in his chest.

The anxiety eventually passed. Replaced by urgency. His senses maxing out. The needle way past red.

He thumbed the safety on the Kimber. Played the flashlight across a carpet of pine needles. There was the sweet smell of kudzu flowers. Wet earth and citrus. Rain whispering down from the canopy.

Lang swore he heard the thrum of a helicopter.

Crews studied the tilted landscape from an array of monitors inside a mobile command post, the static radio communications of two helicopter pilots bouncing back and forth over the intercom.

There was microwave downlink equipment. Night-vision and resonance something-or-others that the techie fooled with. He liked to hum while he worked, tapping his feet, as if the sound track to the evening's activities played in his head.

The FLIR camera systems made everything look flat to Crews. The mountains and thick rolling forests in high-contrast gray scale. But between the weather and deserted terrain it rode her eyes hard. Either too much depth or too little. She felt lost in the images. Hadn't slept much. Spent too much time squinting under inadequate light.

Too many reports and files and memos. Not enough police work.

The wrinkles were coming in at the corner of each eye. She rubbed at them, exasperated, her mind wandering the channels dug by lack of sleep and undue stress. She caught her reflection in the computer monitor. Crow's-feet, bags under the eyes. She'd never bothered with creams or lotions or preserving treatments and didn't figure to start now. Unlike some women, Crews just accepted the face age gave her and got on with the business at hand.

A state trooper brought her coffee. Said it was Exit 149's finest. The kind that cost fifty cents, a little Styrofoam cup plopped down followed by a stream of foul black liquid. Who knew where the coffee came from or how long it'd been in the machine.

Crews didn't care.

She had a pair of helos on loan from the State

Patrol Aviation Unit. They'd taken off from an operations center in Athens. Just ahead of the weather, the helicopters flew north, over the big hydroelectric dams to Tugaloo Lake, veering west at the Chattooga River toward the state parks, land forever protected in its natural state. She followed their progress on the monitors, saw what they saw, mainly Virginia and white pines that covered the earth in black bushy strokes. The occasional car traveled down the road, illuminated like a white mouse in a field after a controlled burn. She saw houses, churches, little specks of heat in all that gray. Some upstart developments near major intersections. A trailer park. Shiny rooftops and antennae.

Winding roads that just seemed to disappear.

The helos had run two by two for more than a week over those same woods. Jubilation County was just too damn big, haystack big, with a couple hard-core ex-cons serving as her needles.

One bird's nest in a forest of thousands.

The bird's nest with the money and guns and maybe even a hostage named Charlie Colquitt.

She broke the monotony of the FLIR flyovers by studying the case file. Leonard Lipscomb's jacket was an inch thick. A life of petty crime that graduated to misdemeanors and eventually a few felonies, armed robbery the crime that warranted a decade-long sentence without parole. God only knew what crimes a man like him had gotten away with. Lipscomb was career all the way.

Good behavior, my ass.

The helicopters made a final pass, dipping into a wild-looking valley, an ocean of tree-soaked mountains that led right to Jubilation County's northern border. A thousand more yards and they would technically be out of her jurisdiction.

The coffee cup was at her lips when Crews dropped it in her lap.

"Command, are you seeing this?"

Everyone in the mobile unit leaned in together, gathering over her shoulder. Crews could feel a collective breath being held.

"Copy, AU-One-Thirteen. Suppose we got some hunters up there?"

"Command, yeah . . . and some deer doing double taps with a .45?"

Specks of light flashed under a dense canopy. What looked like a one-story cabin, partially obscured and as remote as it got for those parts.

The signature of gunfire was unmistakable.

And then it was gone.

Hicklin looked up, surprised to hear the faint whir of a chopper. The rain and wind intensified. If there was a helo in the area it sounded far off and way up, and dealing with some nasty weather conditions.

He heard Lipscomb bark an order at Charlie. Hicklin moved among the trees, practically blind, at times unable to see the hand in front of his face. Nothing to go by but the feel of the polymer pump of the shotgun.

"Hicklin? Hey, Hicklin?"

Lipscomb's voice carried out the front door like that of some cave dweller grunting a warning. A primitive sitting before a fire. Discarded bones in the dust.

"I'm here," Hicklin replied from behind a column of oakwood.

"Show yourself!"

Wind gusts had loosened the branches of a Scotch pine he'd used to thatch the roof. A cover to keep those very helicopters that were in the neighborhood from taking notice. If the helos were even looking in the first place. Lucky bastards might of just stumbled onto the safe house. Hicklin wondered if with all their fancy cameras they could have seen that doozy of a gunfight. Be hard not to notice. At least twenty rounds exchanged direction. Not to mention what if some poor fool was out wandering the woods, even at such a late hour, and turned an ear upslope. Hicklin doubted it, though. Most of the day hikers and granola folks frolicked across ridges and mountains to the east, in the well-advertised parks and on trails where every view was breathtaking and the bears and ticks left you alone. Hicklin figured the only people on *his* mountain were convicts.

But it would not be a safe place for much longer.

"I'm right outside, Preach," he said, right before relocating behind a crooked tree trunk that seemed to corkscrew out of the ground.

"Thanks for clarifying, son," Lipscomb answered. "Got anything else as profound as *that* to say?"

His voice was bold, assured, like Lipscomb knew something Hicklin didn't. He fingered a soft pack from his breast pocket of his shirt, pulled the cigarette out with the filter tip between his teeth.

"I'm listening," he called out.

"Way I see it, son, you have some interest in this here bank teller. Otherwise, I'd be talkin' to pinecones. Why you took him I may never know. Saw in the paper you reorganized that colored manager's head, so I guess you haven't gone completely crazy. But you really had no business engaging us."

Lipscomb paused, as if awaiting an acknowledgment.

"Go on!"

"My guess," he said, "is you stashed the money close by."

An awkward silence followed like the delay on a satellite feed. Hicklin sucked the tip of the cigarette and dropped it on the ground. Mucus tickled his throat. He kept down an urge to cough.

We might as well be talking with string and two tin cups.

"I want my money!" Lipscomb said. "Far as I'm concerned, you can have bank teller here. Clock's ticking on you, Hick. Got some motherfuckers really pissed on this one. All the way to the top of the chain. First big score set up for us and you jump it all for yourself. You know I'm sure there's already a contract out on you? Brothers on both coasts know about you, boy."

Another long silence followed, only broken by

the sound of hundreds of pine trees creaking in protest of a gust of wind. Lipscomb finally spoke, the tone of his voice harsh and bristling.

"And to think I once thought of you like a son."

Lang *was wracked* with sweat, his legs trembling from overexertion.

He skirted a creek, hearing toads and salamanders and other night creatures as he passed. Stones were slick with moss. He negotiated an embankment, reaching for tree trunks to steady him. There hadn't been any gunfire for twenty minutes. The only sounds the far-off trickle of the stream, a rhythmic chant from birds on the wing high above him. Yet Lang thought he could still hear the report from the shotguns, like the battle was still ringing off the tree bark and rocks.

The beam of the flashlight quivered, its strength fading. Just what he needed. *Batteries run out and I'm up shit's creek*. He looked around, but the view was the same. Nothing but heavy timber. Deer droppings and mushrooms and hemlock. A hangnail of moon the color of ice, holding court before a parade of clouds.

The land eventually plateaued, the air cooler at that elevation. He came to a break in the trees where a path appeared. Lang amusingly expected a Cherokee with a war club to walk out from under the dogwoods, introduce himself. The flashlight sputtered. Lang saw faces in the tree bark, perceiving the weight of history in those old woods, the beam of his Maglite casting warped shadows. Forms and impressions.

All the damn people who might have walked this trail over the last thousand years.

And now you can add your name to the list, buddy.

Lang wondered if they had been as deranged as him.

The path gradually steepened, other trails converging at a kind of intersection. One path, the largest, caught his attention. *I'll be damned if you couldn't drive a truck down that one.*

It wasn't long before Lang saw the tread marks.

Moments later, he came upon what looked like a great hunk of rock, parked at an angle. Behind it a narrow alley that wound down the mountain.

Lang held out a hand to touch it. The beam of the flashlight dimmed.

Shit.

He pulled the tarp off the Chevy step-side.

Hicklin *reloaded from* the ammo caddy on the stock of the shotgun, figuring he could punch some rounds through the wall, distract Lipscomb and circle behind the cottage. But the more Hicklin thought about breaking in, the riskier a plan it seemed. Maybe if he could get close to Lipscomb, get him on the ground . . .

Both parties were blind and shooting at shadows. But trying to coax some life from the generator would be a waste of time. Fuck around with the injector in the dark, zero visibility. Making noise when noise was the enemy.

Nothing ever works out like you plan. Not in the real world anyhow.

None of his options sounded appealing or tactically sound. In fact, every consideration seemed stupid as hell. *Preacher don't play games,* Hicklin reminded himself. Lipscomb knew the angles, always thought two or three steps ahead. He played every situation to his advantage, whether it was a heist, a drug run or just convincing you to buy him lunch. Back inside even when Lipscomb fucked up, Hicklin got the feeling it was all part of some plan only he was privy to.

You could always just leave?

The notion gave him pause.

. . . disappear down the mountain. Right now. Cut the distance to the clearing where the old foundation was. Grab the money. Get to the truck and make for the highway . . .

He could see the iron stove in his mind, the hemlocks around it arranged like headstones. If he measured his steps, kept his bearings, he knew he could find it in the darkness.

. . . wasn't that far. Get cleaned up in a bathroom somewhere. Change clothes. Stay the night in some exit-ramp motel where the curtains smell like the fur on a dead dog. Lay low forever and hope you never run across an ex-con hip to an old hit list . . .

Men with ties to the Brotherhood were everywhere. They laid courses for brick and mortar. Worked construction. Repaired motorcycles. Hung around dingy tattoo parlors. They seeped into bars and pool halls, looking for action, looking for scores, looking around. They lived in trailers and run-down apartments. Houses with no mailboxes. In compounds where flags of hate flew.

A few lived in cars, cooking meth in the console.

But ten grand for his head? *Big motherfucker. You'll know 'im when you see him.*

Word would get around. Even the blacks and Hispanic streetside bangers might get in on the hunt.

In his world the grudges and headhunts ran forever. His name would equal blood. He would have to live in the zone for the rest of his life. Because going back inside wasn't even an option. He wasn't a snitch about to rely on protective custody.

You don't need anything inside that cottage anyway.

Walk. Walk away.

Cut and run, you damn fool.

This ain't like you. . . .

He heard Charlie grunt as if he'd been kicked.

Hicklin rose and approached the tree line. He froze in a gasp of hesitation, thinking on what he was about to do.

No, man. No. It ain't right. Ain't smart. You know better than this.

The front door of the cottage looked like an open elevator shaft waiting for someone to fall in. The moon appeared briefly from behind a tanker of white clouds.

He laid down the shotgun and unholstered the

.45, tossing it to the ground. He announced himself and waited for Lipscomb's reply.

It was Charlie who came out first, a gun pressed to the back of his head.

Run down river, river run down, run down river, river run down.
Kneel down brother, brother kneel down, Kneel down brother.
Better kneel on down.

TEN

The guitar player wore suspenders and a cotton dress shirt buttoned to the Adam's apple. He strummed a chord on the cheap electric. An angular riff that seemed to be in search of a tempo. The music filled the church. A subtle shift rippled through them all. Soon the women were raising their hands. A man, the pastor, took the pulpit. Opened the Good Book and without looking began to recite Scripture. The pastor spoke evenly at first. But his tongue soon filled with excitement. Sweat dripped from his forehead and chin. And then the alpha and omega overcame him.

I grew antlers once and it cost me my job, he said.

Cost me my job with the Lord Jesus and to fall out of favor with that boss spells doom any which way ye sell it!

They said amen.

One boss. Any others? Don't wash with the Lord!

They said amen, the word falling from their lips in succession. The pastor punched the Bible with his right hand and shouted that it was the only book *and the only church and the only Son kingdom come and he was only setting the stage for the next witness.*

He read more Scripture. It was in English, but eventually his words slipped into the indecipherable. He stomped his feet and spoke of Jesus and Jesus alone and how the scalded dogs that were the devil's army would find no comfort in their kingdom. And the congregants reacted with more "amens" and "hallelujahs."

It was as though some sweet liquor had been passed among them. He shouted that the Holy Spirit was there and ready to grow antlers for mankind and cast down all the serpents. The holy-rolling ecstasy spread among all the congregants. Sweat pumped from their pores. The pastor's voice filled the room like a firecracker. The guitar player matched his intensity, strumming more chords, an upbeat rendition of "The Holy Ghost Bites the Most." Some women broke out in song. The lyrics strangled and coughed up while others swayed silently in their seats, teeth clenched, hands raised in submission.

The pastor put the Bible down and stepped off the stage. Others rose and approached the pulpit to bear witness. The guitar player strained his fingers along the neck of the instrument. A twangy hymn took form. The next speaker walked past the wooden boxes. He twirled on his toes, hands held high above his head.

Eyes closed and ears deaf to the rattles emanating from within.

"That you, Hicklin?" Lipscomb said from the depths of the cottage.

"Who else might it be?"

He was suddenly blinded by a brilliant beam. A tactical light trained on his face. Hicklin squinted, raising both hands to shield his eyes as if the light were strong enough to knock him over.

"Toss that knife now," Lipscomb said.

Hicklin reached behind his back and produced the knife, holding it up briefly as if for inspection. Then he chucked it.

"Bet you didn't think I had this, huh?" Lipscomb said with a twitch of the tactical light. "Us sittin' in the dark here like a couple of border monkeys."

Lipscomb had made Charlie strip off his clothes. He stood wearing a look of shame, naked and trembling, hands covering his crotch. Hicklin's heart sank. His organs pulling at it with hooks and chains.

"Let the man put on some clothes," he said.

"*Man?* You sure are sweet on this bank teller, ain't ye?"

"You can shoot us both right now," Hicklin said. "I won't move a goddamn muscle."

"We'll see about that."

They sparred eyes, Lipscomb realizing his protégé's threat was far from empty. Lipscomb played the light off Charlie, looking him up and down as if amused by some sculpture he'd chiseled. He kept the HK pointed at Hicklin when he produced a pair of handcuffs from his belt.

"Well, I reckon stripping the man of his clothes *was* a bit much," he conceded. He gestured with the tac light. "But first I want you on the ground. Cuff up. You know the drill."

Hicklin took a step back and lay on the ground as asked. A moth landed on his cheek, fluttered its wings and launched toward the light. Lipscomb turned and kicked Charlie toward the cottage.

"Get you that shirt and pants you was wearing, bank teller," he said, adding, "and hurry it up. I got a low tolerance for boredom."

As *Charlie searched* in the darkness for his pants and shoes, his bare foot kicked something hard on the floor. He knelt, his hand finding a .357 Taurus snub nose, the same revolver Flock had worn in the small of his back. It must have fallen out during all the shooting. Charlie glanced at Lipscomb.

He's not even watching you, Charlie. And he doesn't know what you're capable of. . . .

Lang *was lost.* He played the dying flashlight over twisted roots, disoriented, the woods on that part of the mountain like a city where all the streets appeared the same.

He clicked off the flashlight and stood in absolute darkness. Black as a deep sleep. The forest a pillow smothering his breath.

He shook off a surge of panic and lit another cigarette. Lang smoked quietly, blind to everything but the smoldering tip of his Marlboro. It was exciting to be so still, deprived of half his senses. But a part of him wanted to scream.

Just stay here. Stay here and fossilize. Years would pass. Then the hunters would find you. A petrified man. Meshed with the wood.

Like some rascal born from the trees and eventually reclaimed.

Back near the creek he recognized the odor of decay before coming across a wild boar. A sow no less, dead maybe a week. With the flashlight he could see through the skin, thin as paper, the maggots and beetles undulating beneath the surface. She wasn't a large animal compared to some of the boars he'd heard about in those mountains— sounders with individual boars rumored to be as big as riding mowers. The mother didn't look to have been shot, either. Lang figured the sow died giving birth.

Not far away were the remains of the boar's piglets.

Out here anything could happen.

Sometimes things just died. They don't always need a reason. . . .

He thought about two boys from over in Fannin County. They had been driving back from a night at Kalamity's bar, both drunker than shit. The passenger, a kid about twenty-three years old, stuck his head out the window to puke, just as the car drifted toward the shoulder, passing the solid steel cable of a terminal down guy.

Took his head clean off.

His buddy kept driving. Didn't even notice, as drunk as he was. Went on home without bothering to look over at his pal's corpse. He left the car in the driveway, stumbled inside his house and passed out in his bed. Five quarts of blood leaking all over the passenger seat of his car. A little girl walking her dog found his friend the next morning. Nothing but a giant tongue and some spine where the head used to be. They'd found his head about a mile down the road in a drainage ditch. A murder of crows marking the spot.

Lang dropped the cigarette and stepped on it, suddenly angry at himself and not knowing why. He was trying to remember the name of that decapitated boy.

Lang listened to the rain finding passage down through the canopy. He hoped for a little more gunfire now.

So that he might find a way out.

Lipscomb *watched* *as* Hicklin—following instructions—cuffed his right wrist to Charlie's left. Lipscomb offered a slight gesture, as if honored by their company, and they marched into the woods. Hicklin knew once they walked out into that clearing and saw the spilled chimney, the iron stove, the duffel bag . . .

It would be all over.

Lipscomb would calmly raise his weapon and shoot them both in the head. All the play had gone out of his eyes, Hicklin noticed. His mentor had taken on the look of a man who'd exorcized whatever betrayal and nostalgia he'd felt and was now yearning only for usefulness and results.

He kept the light trained just ahead of Hicklin, hanging back about five yards, the Heckler & Koch he fancied ready to fire from all manner of defensive positions.

Lipscomb had left *almost* nothing to chance.

They trod carefully over pine windfalls and sodden earth, eventually arriving at a stream, *the* stream. Hicklin led them east along the bank. Instead of scaling the rock, which would have taken them to the money, he hiked upslope into the forest again.

He turned once to look back at Lipscomb. The tactical light met Hicklin, blinding as the sun emerging from a total eclipse. He figured he had five more minutes before Lipscomb began to ask questions. If he could just get in close enough, make a move for Lipscomb's knife. Or close the distance and get at the .45 without putting Charlie in danger. Ram his forehead into Lipscomb's mouth and take him to the ground. Crush his nose with the thrust of a palm. With Charlie as deadweight he'd only get one shot.

Lipscomb needed him if he wanted an easy way to the cash. But that wasn't enough leverage to swing a deal. He knew any more stonewalling would result in Lipscomb getting violent. He'd torture and kill them both. And when the heat died down he'd spend a month scouring the woods.

Hicklin trudged forward, Charlie struggling to

keep up. They made eye contact once, Charlie looking sickly and exhausted. He wanted to say something, anything, but the right words never materialized.

Lipscomb holstered his pistol and unslung the shotgun, prodding them in the back with the muzzle as if they needed reminding he was there.

Hicklin *recalled memories* of the time he and Lipscomb served together. They would walk the track of the prison yard, always moving, because when they were walking people knew to leave them alone. The cell houses at the north end of the facility rose up like slabs of chalk, a water tower beyond the wall, what Hicklin thought must have been miles of concertina wire. He remembered the noise from the textile mill, the yard always bustling, convicts moved here and there, penitentiary escorts crossing the yard with their special human cargo. Sharpshooters eyeballed the proceedings from their perches up in the gun towers. But it was Hicklin and Lipscomb's block of the yard. When they hit the end of the track they would turn back and walk it down again, always talking, always moving, always scheming.

Most of the time Lipscomb prattled on about things that mattered to him. Personal loyalty, race as an obsession they all had to succumb to. How he wanted to do more than abuse glue sniffers and peckerwoods. How he could never tolerate a traitor.

His musings ran rampant.

But he captured every convict's attention. Every youngblood. Every fish.

They flocked to him and he either worked them over or signed them on.

But he only confided in Hicklin.

Crystal meth and heroin. The ongoing war with the blacks and Latinos. So-and-so in Marion planning a hit on a federal judge. The home address of that one nigger detective who was constantly rousting some of their mules. The commissary not carrying Dr Pepper and Reese's Pieces. *The yard won't be dry much longer,* Lipscomb was fond of saying after a shipment of OxyContin or dope.

Hicklin remembered dark nights filled with the chorus of white convicts. Honeycombed cell blocks. Voices bouncing off the steel doors and studded rivets.

Sieg Heil!
Sieg Heil!
Sieg Heil!

Many times their nine-by-five cell was the only place much of it made any sense.

Hicklin conjured up a mental photograph of the basketball courts, him and Lipscomb taking turns on the pull-up bars, AB muscle keeping watch. They *could* have been father and son. There had been a power between them, a power to control and define the politics of prison yards.

They prowled. They pranced. They stalked. It was a ruthless form of theater.

Lipscomb used to say that *they* were the forgotten. *No more mothers and fathers, brothers and sisters, sons and daughters. Only the Brand mattered.*

Those memories of family and friends, a normal life on the outside, with its freedoms and rights and luxuries, had been erased.

And that's exactly how they preferred it.

C*harlie tripped and* fell to his knees. He was panting. Hicklin stopped to help him up.

"Son, I'm about tired of this shit," Lipscomb said. "I was curious how it might play out, but I ain't so curious no more. Tell me where we heading or I'm just going to drop y'all right there in that water."

Hicklin raised a hand to the light, to the shadow that held it.

"It's close," he pleaded. "Upstream."

Lipscomb turned the flashlight on Charlie, then back on Hicklin. They appeared pale and featureless, like faces lifted from the knotted trunks of trees.

"I believe there's an old hunting cabin over that way," he said, a vague awareness flickering behind his eyes.

T*he trees grew* bunched like arrows in a quiver. Charlie's breathing intensified. Hicklin put a hand on the back of Charlie's neck, feeling a fever heat, the skin slick with sweat. He thought the boy was on the verge of collapse. When he doubled over and began to heave, Hicklin patted him on the back, rubbing his shoulders in some strange, paternal way. An exasperated voice called from the shadows.

"Okay, I think I've had all I can take of this here bullshit. . . ."

Hicklin turned to Lipscomb and the tactical light, hoping to placate him with news of their proximity to the cash, when they both heard the click of the .357's hammer. Lipscomb cocked his head curiously.

Hicklin closed his eyes. Prepared to die.

Then he was yanked off his feet.

Charlie had sprung to life, like a linebacker charging a tackling dummy. Even more surprising was when he produced Flock's snub nose and fired wildly at Lipscomb. Lipscomb ducked his head, throwing up his arms in surprise. He lost his grip on the tactical light and an eerie backlit shadow fell over them all. Still charging, Charlie fired again, grazing Lipscomb's shoulder. The charge knocked him backwards, the shotgun slipping by its sling off his shoulder. He scurried up the slope, reeling, already drawing the .45.

Charlie squeezed the trigger in succession, exhausting the wheel in less than ten seconds, dry-firing as if he thought the weapon would reload itself. It was random, panicked shooting that scared his target more than harmed him, Hicklin trying to gain an advantage but stumbling, yanked by Charlie to the ground. Lipscomb returned fire, narrowly missing them both. The sloppy, close-quarter firefight illuminated their mad scramble up the hill and the difficult footing to be had on a slope of pine straw and leaf marl.

Lipscomb fired twice more, the muzzle flash providing a brilliant strobe, enough light to glimpse Hicklin and Charlie lunging toward him. He back-pedaled blindly, tripping on the rot of a downed poplar. Before Lipscomb could fire again Hicklin caught him by the wrist. He yanked and twisted, liberating the HK, but Lipscomb proved too strong. They wrestled for a moment, all grimace and wet, chunky breaths—Charlie an accessory—the two old friends writhing like soldiers locked in a game of hand-to-hand.

Lipscomb managed some separation, stunning Hicklin with a kick to the kneecap. He collapsed instantly, snagging Charlie off-balance, eyes searching the forest floor for the .45.

Lipscomb stomped backwards through a mess of leaves and brush, reaching under his shirt for a stainless-steel Ruger he had tucked in a spine holster. He raised the revolver with a clear shot of Hicklin when his leg fell into a depression. His boot tripping a circular paddle.

The sound they heard was a swift, mechanical attack. The bones in Lipscomb's left leg snapped like a broomstick over an angry knee.

He groaned through gritted teeth, firing the Ruger once up into the canopy. He fell sideways, dropping the pistol.

And reached for the bear trap with both hands.

Lang left Hicklin's truck and followed the winding path, not sure where it would lead him. Twenty minutes later Lang came upon a large opening, a ghost road he recognized as the one he'd driven up. He turned left and started to walk, breathing a sigh of relief at the sight of his Nissan up ahead. He'd already tried to call Crews on his cell phone, even text her the license plate number of the Chevy, but there was no signal.

The reports from a barrage of gunshots struck his ears like a crack of thunder. A few moments passed. A fifth and sixth shot from a large-caliber handgun. It was close by, closer than he expected. His trot turned to a sprint. When he got to his pickup he turned and looked up at the wall of trees. Another gunshot—the last—rang out.

He holstered his Kimber in the steering column mount and cranked the truck, wheeling it into a quick three-point turn. With only his running lights on, Lang drove back down the mountain road. Panting like a greyhound. Wondering what those animals might be doing to themselves up in those woods.

The underside of the trap's jaws clamped on Lip-scomb's left leg below the knee, pinching its girth to the width of a beer bottle. The teeth of the trap were enormous, like those of an alligator. Heavy cast iron. Tempered steel springs. A chain disappeared under a blanket of leaf decay, the ring holding the trap in place pinned down deep into the earth.

The sudden pain had punched the air from his lungs. Face depleted, he squinted, studying his leg in disbelief, his upper body rocking in a kind of half-hearted sit-up. Grinding his teeth as if being eaten alive.

Hicklin promptly picked up the tac light and searched for the .38 on the ground, finding it just half a foot from Lipscomb's reach. He played the beam across his old friend's leg, Lipscomb choking a scream off at the sight of his knee. He turned a pale face toward the light, to Hicklin standing over him with the Ruger. Charlie had scooped up the shotgun and was at his side, holding the Mossberg with shaky hands like a caricature of some rural guerilla.

"Keys?" Hicklin said.

Lipscomb wrenched his eyes back and forth between them, a pained look masking the animal ready to fight to its death. He reached in a breast pocket and handed Hicklin the keys to the handcuffs. Lipscomb raised his hands submissively, palms up, every twitch of muscle fiber causing him to wince and strain. Hicklin steadied the revolver, his eyes veiled.

"You win," Lipscomb said. "Just take me to a hospital . . . you can just push me out the door. I don't care. Just don't leave me like this! I won't say nothin' to nobody! I swear it!"

Lipscomb's begging came like a poison chaser. Even with a leg one tug from coming clean off, Hicklin knew Lipscomb could talk his way through anything. A savvy pitch was coming.

You help him and see. He'll roll on you in a heartbeat.

Unless there was a bullet in his head.

Hicklin looked around, dancing the tac light off tree trunks and thick nothingness. As if he half-expected to see a bystander frantically dialing the authorities.

Kill him.
Maybe.
Then what are my options?

Despite *the protests,* Hicklin pressed a muddied boot to Lipscomb's thigh, digging the muzzle of the .38 against his uninjured kneecap.
This is worse than any death. . . .
Charlie looked away.
Hicklin pulled the trigger.

Breathe in the fire, breathe in the fire.
God hates a liar on a Palm Sunday.
Stick in the knife, stick in the knife.
God hates a coward on a Palm Sunday.

ELEVEN

A woman shook a tambourine, accenting the trebly rhythms of the guitar player. The audience was transfixed. The small church proceedings now a hot, sweat-soaked ordeal. The air smelled of camphor and steam. Witness after witness took the pulpit. Some men rubbed the tops of the wooden boxes with the palms of their hands. Yet the boxes remained closed for now.

An improvised hymn was sung, the tune turning grim and erratic. The voices of the congregation meshed and then disconnected. The guitar player carefully selected each note with fingers that strained to find them.

A man took the stage. He flicked his wrists at the audience, then toward the ceiling. He clapped.

Brother Rollins is right, down to the core!

We all grew antlers that almost cost us our jobs!

"But the job is here and now!"

The faithful joined in a concussion of "amens." An ecstasy spread down the aisles. Hands raised, some of the women opened their mouths and spoke in tongues. *Without any warning or apparent plan the man at the pulpit knelt down.*

And opened the lid of the first box.

He lifted a three-foot canebrake rattler from its depths, holding the snake high above his head. It slithered between his fingers and around his wrist and down a forearm. He reached in with his spare hand and pulled out a smaller rattlesnake.

Seven or eight more congregants had stepped forward by now. The tambourine and guitar accompanied the procession, locking into a hypnotic rhythm. Another man reached into the box, his right hand emerging with a four-foot timber rattler. The reptile's broad triangular head sliding between his thumb and forefinger, licking at the air with flicks of its tongue. Dark crossbands the length of the snake's body were oily and smooth-looking in the light.

The man lowered his hand to waist length. The snake turned curiously up toward his shoulder with no obvious intentions. He spoke of being breast-fed from a dirty dog until the one true God took his lips away and set them right.

The man ran a thumb along the brown stripe behind each eye of the snake. The rattler held itself steady as if trying to reciprocate the tenderness of the moment.

More men and women took the stage, opening the remaining wooden crates while others started to dance in the aisle. They shuffled back and forth with peculiar hopping motions. Palms upturned. Wild-eyed, their mouths moving to the revelry. A woman pulled two copperheads from one of the serpent boxes. She dropped one and reached down to pick it up. Handed it to another woman. Like clowns from a car at a circus, the snakes were pulled continuously from the boxes. Twined and twisting. Thick as handfuls of drained pasta.

They prayed and passed the snakes along. One of the women opened a mason jar and took a sip of the strychnine-water mixture. She passed it to a man who was cradling a canebrake rattler as you would a puppy. He took three large gulps from the jar and passed it on. . . .

. . . Hallelujah, there is no throne like God's throne. . . .

One of the believers had lit the rag wick of a glass jar filled with kerosene.

He passed a finger and then a fist and then a wrist over the flame in slow, measured movements.

The room filled with the hysteria of the spirit, the Holy Ghost coming down on its supplicants in waves of tornadic power. The plank floor quaked a little underfoot like some divine tremor.

The snakes writhed. They slipped through the fingers of the devout.

Studying their handlers like you would the occupants of an asylum.

Or an emergency room.

Hicklin and Charlie ran through the woods, barreling behind the scattered beam of the tactical light.

They crossed the creek and climbed the limestone bank. Eventually the trees gave way to shrubs and grass. The grove appeared under a faint detail of moonlight. Charlie tried to keep up but struggled to get his wind back. He watched as Hicklin made for the hemlock that marked the old stone lodging. He disappeared from view for a moment when he reached inside the stove and pulled out the duffel bag. He took off at a dead run but soon stopped.

Hicklin turned to look back at Charlie. The boy stood frozen in place, hands on his knees, his expression a mixture of dejection and fatigue. Hicklin favored him with a soft smile. Realizing himself what was occurring between them.

Charlie was joining him in whatever happened next. Willingly. As if there were no choice now, no words to speak, no deliberations. But as they stood in the grove, the rain clouds having parted to allow a clear view of the night sky, Charlie realized for better or for worse he cared about his captor.

Hicklin's smile turned to a hardened scowl. He nodded.

But there was meaning to be found in his eyes.

They backtracked, finding the Chevy step-side after two wrong turns. Hicklin intuited that the tarp had been disturbed. It troubled him, but there wasn't time to fret. He rolled up the tarp, covered the shotgun with it behind the front seats. He stuck the key in the ignition. Gave Charlie some instructions and climbed out. Charlie slid over and tapped the brake with his left foot. Flicked the turn signals.

Tail- and brake lights worked.

One less reason to get pulled over.

Hicklin tucked the pistol under his right leg and eased the pickup down the path that led to the nameless mountain road. After a fifteen-minute descent they were on pavement.

Hicklin drove carefully down a set of switchbacks, his and Charlie's ears unplugging at the lower altitude. A fog settled across the road, stretching out beyond the ridge to the east and hovering above the valley like some mannered, watchful relative. Hicklin rolled down the window, lit a cigarette from a pack he kept on the dash. Charlie watched him.

The thought of getting Charlie something to eat occurred to Hicklin. A hot shower for them both.

And when he looked over at Charlie, he was met by a consenting grin.

The road ran adjacent to a wall of granite. A yellow sign warned of falling rock. Hicklin slowed the pickup for a hairpin turn. Another set of switchbacks followed, the headlights occasionally catching reflectors on a mailbox, the spooked face of a possum. Charlie glimpsed a single distant porch light hovering in the darkness.

Hicklin knew they were approaching the flats, his mind already planning a side-road route across state lines when they passed Tommy Lang's Nissan Titan, the pickup hidden in a drive obscured by rotted fence posts.

Hicklin punched the gas, chirping the tires. A

sickening jolt hit him in the gut. He checked the rearview mirror. The lights of Lang's truck came to life.

In pursuit.

Lang *had parked* under a bower, a little recess just off the mountain road where a series of fence posts stood slanted and age bent, as if to remind passersby of the long-dead hands that had planted them. He smoked a cigarette and was considering a beer when the lights of the Chevy appeared through the fog at the top of the ridge only to disappear again. Lang held his breath, waiting. A minute later the old pickup rumbled past him.

Lang glimpsed the driver and a young man in the passenger seat. He watched. The road eased against an embankment. The driver tapped his brake lights once.

Then the Chevy gunned it down the hill.

Lang flicked the cigarette out the window, cranked the truck and pulled out onto the road. He turned on the high beams and punched it through the fog, taking a long curve bordered by half-grown pines a little too fast, his tires digging for grip. He saw the silhouette of Blood Mountain off in the distance, and the taillights of the step-side before they disappeared into a blanket of mist.

He hit sixty before he let off the gas, rolling dangerously through a corner. The tires screeched and spun against the slick layer of chert, finally sticking before Lang could play demolition derby with a cliff. There was a hundred-foot drop past the guardrails. And another hundred feet of granite outcroppings.

That sumbitch is flying. . . .

After five minutes Lang considered them all but lost. The road narrowed, cutting back and forth between walls of pine, splitting here and there like bronchial stems. He slowed to a crawl, passing the old rickety church like some lost tourist.

The road turned to blacktop. Lang stopped at an intersection, rolling down the windows, looking right and left before U-turning back up the mountain. He had hoped to hear something. A car horn or chirping tires. The rev of an engine. The clank of a railroad crossing. Anything.

There was nothing but the wind passing through the trees. Humidity with an undercurrent of coolness, the sweet aroma of muscadines on the air.

Unnatural. Dismaying.

Lang returned to the church. There was a front yard but no driveway, a dozen vehicles parked at angles. He glimpsed more cars behind the church. No sign of the step-side.

Shouting and singing met his ears when he opened the truck door, accompanied by a jangling, cultish music. Lang slid his Kimber into its holster, tucking it inside his waistband along with two spare magazines.

He heard foot stomping. Loud, incoherent voices. But there was something else, a kind of a sub-rhythm beneath the manic worshiping. Lang cocked his head and listened.

The collective rattling of deadly snakes.

He had been out to this church once before, fifteen years back for a fatality. A man from North Carolina had been bitten by a cottonmouth. His hand swelled to the size of a catcher's mitt and when he fell to the floor three more snakes bit him. Lang remembered walking inside the church, a small crowd of believers standing over the poor son of a bitch, praying and moaning. Struck Lang that he had walked into another universe, a place as alien as he could imagine. The man was vomiting when Lang arrived, the victim's eyes looking as though they'd been sketched in with a charcoal pencil.

A now-retired deputy named Creston had been first on the scene. Told Lang that when he entered the church there were about ten snakes slithering around, hiding under benches, searching for nooks and corners. One of the wranglers had already gone to work with a hook, snagging rattlesnakes and dropping them into a burlap sack. Old Creston turned right around and called the jail and Animal Control. It took a good hour for EMTs to find the place. Another thirty minutes for the county coroner.

Lang recalled the crates. The persistent buzz. A distinctive noise, that rattle you never wanted to hear when out hiking or hunting. When they brought the man outside on a gurney everyone relocated to the porch and continued praying, some distraught, but most seemed disappointed more than anything else. As if the cable had gone out during the Super Bowl. *The victim had failed them all,* one man had remarked. Not the snakes, not God, but the bitten man.

And all Lang could think was, *How?*

Lang tried to look through a window. Condensation was as thick as a layer of paint. A gutter, rusted over and clotted with pine needles, hung partially detached from the roofline. He peeked around the corner to the backyard. There was a brush arbor with picnic tables. Cars and trucks clustered on either side.

He stepped off the porch and turned a corner, following a set of tire tracks to the far side of the church property. Lang's eyes adjusted to the vague glow of a tin-shaded flood lamp. He stared down a long row of cars, using the brightness of his cell phone screen to discern one vehicle from the next.

The Chevy step-side was parked between two station wagons.

The service inside the church was peaking in intensity. A preacher shouted to the rhythm of stomping feet, the voices that answered elegiac and possessed. Lang tried to maintain some situational awareness, prowling, studying the entrance.

One way in and one way out, buddy.

He thought to call for backup. *Hell, you'd have to drive three miles just to get a signal.* Could just sit in his truck and wait them out?

Or drive on home. Forget about the whole thing.

Get drunk. Quit. His specialty. Behavior that had defined him for more than a decade.

Walk into the woods then. Straight to hell or oblivion, whichever's got a vacancy.

Lang drew his sidearm and put a hand on the doorknob. Took a deep breath.

He was smarter than this and he knew it.

He met with a swelling of heat and violent sound. Lang scanned the church's one room, seeing nothing but the backs of people's heads. All of the worshipers too caught up to notice or acknowledge him. He looked down the aisle at the pulpit, at the people on the stage, mostly men in sweat-soaked shirtsleeves. Maybe twenty of them swaying and singing.

You're in a goddamn nuthouse now, Tommy.

One man had several rattlesnakes in his hand. He danced around, holding the snakes above his head as if hoisting a trophy. The serpents hung vine-like, flat heads turning as if they waited for a cue. Their eyes were bold and black. Little tongues tested the air. Lang heard the rattles even above the hand claps and possessed babbling.

A fiery preacher bellowed from the pulpit as a canebrake rattler slithered from one hand to the other.

"I once grew antlers and it cost me my job!"

"Our Host!"

"The Ghost!"

"He bites the most!"

Lang tried to follow the preacher, but his words

descended into gibberish. The room smelled of melted wax and hair tonic, sweat and sawdust stomped from the old floorboards. Lang surveyed the room again, the Kimber casually hidden behind his right buttock.

A young man, five pews down, turned as if hearing some phantom noise in his head. Lang studied his profile for a moment. The gaunt, dirty face. A pitiful white shirt.

Looking like a stray dog that had survived a kennel fire.

Charlie Colquitt.

The music and voices were pounding Lang's brain to jelly. He couldn't think. Charlie turned to see Lang better, his lips forming a word of warning.

. . . Don't!

The man standing next to Charlie had a back and shoulders broad enough to fireman's carry an Appaloosa mule. He twitched, glancing over his shoulder like a pitcher checking a fleet-footed base runner. Then he and Lang made eye contact. Time elongated, Lang's brain rimshotting as his body instinctively adjusted into a shooting stance.

I've seen that look in a man's eye a couple times.
That look.
Mean enough to kill Jesus.
And then ask for Mary and Joseph.
Gun!

The first round whistled past his ear.

Lang instinctively returned fire.

He squeezed two rounds and ducked to his left below a pew. A window shattered behind him. The burst of gunfire had the congregation in a frenzy of a different kind. Lang raised up, aimed and fired once, a point and shoot he wished had been quicker. Too many bodies rioting to lock in on the big, broad-shouldered gunslinger—who apparently didn't care who he killed besides Lang.

He showed too much of himself trying to locate the gunman and a heavy round took out his left shoulder. Lang saw red and hit the floor hard, the injured shoulder going loose and wet. He sat up, breathless from the pain, glad to see his arm still attached. Most of the panic inside the church was stampeding past him and out the front door. He had a glimpse of the preacher behind the pulpit, pointing a long finger as if directing traffic, hollering nonsensically.

"Satan is here and now and this is the time of the satinback!

"Grow antlers or bow to the endless tunnel!"

Screams and more gunfire. Lang somehow reloaded, in spite of a near-useless left shoulder. Bullets blew apart the pinewood pew in front of him. People pinballed down the aisle.

More shots rang out. Lang hunched against the pew as a salvo of hollow points chunked it to pieces. Holes opened in the front wall. Lang watched men and women fall, shot in the back.

The gunman emptied his magazine.

He's reloading.

Lang turned, checked his background and sighted

on the shooter. He fired one-handed, three trigger pulls that sent unbearable pain up his arm to a shattered collarbone. A woman near the pulpit dropped from sight. The gunman disappeared down an aisle, using an old man in a checkered shirt as a human shield. The congregation continued to pile up, dead or alive, following instinct at the threshold of their church.

Lang slumped back behind the pew, starbursts of pain clogging his vision.

Wondering what it was like to pray and really mean it.

Hicklin *had driven* around the church to the backyard where there were more vehicles parked. Picnic tables were set up along a thicket bordered by yellow daisies. A hollow of darkness beyond. Charlie looked out the window toward a morbid black sky, snapping from his daze when Hicklin got out of the truck and quietly shut the driver's side door.

He tucked Lipscomb's HK into his waistband. Two clips in each pocket, the lips of the magazine facing up for an easy grasp. He pulled his sweatshirt down to cover the grip of the handgun and nodded to Charlie.

They walked around to the front of the church. Hicklin paused before a fogged-over window, hearing some feverish proclamation followed by a round of applause. A guitar resonated through the clapboard. The structure itself seemed poised to crumble at every wallop.

Hicklin hesitated at the door. He eyed the road in both directions, studying the cars parked where the front yard met the shoulder.

"There's somebody followin' us," he said. "We needed to get off this here road."

"Are you sure?" Charlie said, whispering, a lip quivering with uncertainty. "Could we keep driving? I'm scared of this place."

"You ever been to church?"

Charlie nodded.

"We'll go in here like we belong. Ever wanna belong to a church?"

Charlie shook his head.

"Might even talk to some folks," Hicklin warned him. "But not if I can help it. Don't you make eye contact with nobody. Look straight ahead. Like you're real interested. In a li'l while we'll head back out. I'm gonna buy us some breakfast, get you new clothes. I promise. You believe me, right?"

Charlie nodded again that he did.

Hicklin opened the door.

Naked bulbs hung from the ceiling of the church, providing a sickly yellow nimbus. A man in the corner videotaped the action with an old shoulder-mounted Beta. Another man leaning on a walker for balance turned and smiled at Hicklin and Charlie, gesturing in welcome to some available seating. Hicklin took Charlie by the wrist and led him to a pew in the middle of the room.

Feeling beads of sweat lining his brow, Hicklin wiped his face with a sleeve and studied the commotion. On the altar platform a dozen people were handling snakes. Others held mason jars, sipping a liquid Hicklin damn sure knew wasn't corn whiskey. The pastor ranted, his voice demanding and powerful.

"Want and need two different things, come the remission of sins! Best we put our house in order. Put it in order right now before the Lord does! 'Cause when the Lord put your house in order, ain't no turnin' back!"

Charlie tried to focus straight ahead, watching a woman with waxy, sickly-looking skin swaying from side to side in the first pew. Next to her were two children in their teens, their clothes shabby and homespun, boiling in their own sweat. A man Charlie assumed to be their father stood next to them, his hands clenched and held head high as if he was trying to fend off an imaginary blow. Charlie listened to the English being spoken around him, but the words were incoherent, a holy babble with just enough vowels to sound familiar.

"Halejebawidnusaliyababelajohavacripdonnawajasteyamannalaweya!"

Charlie had heard about these people, too, even recognizing a few faces up on the stage as customers from the bank. There was the man who owned a maintenance company. Another who managed a tire depot. They were holding snakes in their bare hands, clucking their tongues, eyes rolled back to reveal nothing but sclera. It all struck Charlie as pornography—to witness these secret, obscene lives—yet he found himself entranced by the fervor of the worshipers.

He perceived a change in the atmosphere of the church, like the barometer dropping before a thunderstorm. He turned and locked eyes with a man at the front door. Caught a glimpse of a silver-and-black pistol in the man's hand. Charlie tried to speak.

Sensing something as well, Hicklin looked over his shoulder at the front door. The man from the gas station had stepped inside, a hand on the grip of a 1911-model pistol.

Hicklin shoved Charlie to the floor, drew and fired twice before taking cover himself. Charlie fell hard on his elbow and stayed down, shocked by the gunfire.

And the screams.

He watched from under the pew as men and women scrambled like dancers over a hot bed of coals, their steps prompting bits of sawdust into the air. A woman fell in the aisle; the mason jar in her hand broke, a clear liquid splashing into her eyes. Charlie heard a man still shouting from the pulpit. Hicklin had hardly moved, standing brazenly and firing toward the church's front door.

Charlie watched a rattlesnake drop to the floor and slither away. Panic gripped him.

Because there were a lot of snakes.

And they had started to bite.

*T*he pastor was holding four snakes in one hand when the men opened fire on each other.
. . . the age of antlers is upon us! he shouted.

As if some hypnotic hold on the rattlers had been broken, one whipped at his neck, the fangs unfolding from the roof of the snake's mouth, catching cotton and skin. The snake struck again. Quick as a car wreck, the fangs hooked onto the pastor's jawline, the snake hanging there like a necktie. The pastor opened his mouth and groaned. His knees buckled.

The snakes lashed out, recoiled, reloaded. The congregation fled, a mass of colliding bodies. The timber rattlers—usually reluctant to bite—had followed some cue peculiar to serpents, striking indiscriminately. A woman had gathered more than a dozen in both hands. She held them high above her head, even as the snakes bit into her wrists and forearms. She didn't or couldn't let go.

The gunshots were deafening. People spilled over the pews. Some simply cowered and screamed as though shell-shocked. Shot in the neck, a man spun on his feet and fell on a cream-bellied snake more than five feet long. The eastern diamondback, smothered, struck him near the wound in his throat.

The camera man dropped his gear and escaped through the front door. Others dodged the reptiles by hopping, dancing, a clumsy clubfooted shuffle to the church's lone exit. But the snakes were animated. Achilles tendons and calf muscles their targets.

The guitar player wielded his instrument like an axe, bringing the Fender down on a knot of serpents. His amp erupted in a wail of feedback.

Rattlesnakes hung from his arms like the long leather fringe of a frontier jacket.

————

Sallie Crews scrolled through e-mails on her mobile from the backseat of a sport-utility. A convoy of Bureau vehicles headed north into the mountains, escorted by Georgia State Patrol units, the desolate road they traveled illuminated by a bevy of blue emergency lights. All the resources of the GSP, GBI and federal agents were at her disposal, as were the Aviation Unit, Field Operations and a local SWAT. The commander of Troop B had pledged officers from six different posts. Sheriff's Deputies from four neighboring counties pitched in, establishing roadblocks and checkpoints along targeted routes. The logistics of a tri-state manhunt were being sorted through.

The photos of three men had been released to the media.

She couldn't get Sheriff Lang on his cell phone.

The convoy slowed before taking a turn. The road they were on uneven and in need of repaving. The driver cracked a window. The air smelled untainted and earthy.

"Pardon me, Agent Crews?"

Jesse Moye, a detective on loan from a metro county's Crimes Against Persons Unit, clicked off his phone and signaled to Crews in the backseat. She looked up from a pile of paperwork in her lap with a cop's natural anticipation for bad news.

"What is it, Detective?"

"A Jube County nine-one-one dispatcher received a call about thirty minutes ago. Report of shots fired at the Church of the Holy Lamb. Apparently two men just started shooting at each other during the service."

"Sounds like somebody didn't like the sermon."

"Or gunfight at the Jesus Christ Corral."

"Where the hell is that church?" Crews said.

"Not far from where y'all picked up those thermals," Moye said, already punching in an address on a dash-mounted GPS screen. "By the time you get to the church the road doesn't have a name anymore. Deputy Hansbrough from Jube County will lead us up there. You get ahold of Sheriff Lang?"

Crews shook her head, trying to quell a wave of dread and apprehension.

At the intersection of State Route 29 Hansbrough's patrol car flashed its lights and took off, leading the convoy up a long, winding switchback that cut through an enormous pine forest. The mountain they were climbing struck Crews as massive. And sparsely settled.

Crews felt a cramp of inevitability.

There was big trouble ahead in the darkness.

Lang slumped, the slug in his left shoulder having taken his breath away, rendering him temporarily immobile. He could barely raise the Kimber with his right hand. Pinned behind a pew, he tried to count how many rounds he had left in the clip.

One? Two?

The panic inside the church was unbelievable. Screams of agony from more than a dozen snakebite victims.

So this is what hellfire eternal sounds like. . . .

He tried to put pressure on the wound. He struggled to sit up, thinking of the seconds he had to spare.

Wound 'em if you have to. Center mass. Even if it costs you your life.

He peeked over the edge of the pew. The gunman drew a bead on Lang but was suddenly distracted by a man with a guitar. Instead the gunman pivoted and shot the axe-slinger point-blank, then snapped two shots back in the Sheriff's direction. Lang scrambled the length of the pew, staying low as wood splintered around his head. A few people desperate to escape tripped over him. He glimpsed a bloody face. A swollen hand. A serpent loose on the floor.

The gunman pulled Charlie Colquitt up and proceeded to shoot anyone—man or snake—in his way. He kept an eye out for Lang, too, suspecting he was the only other pistol in the house.

Know your background, Lang reminded himself. He could hear a child crying from the far end of the church. A woman yelling. A man praying loudly for forgiveness. The warning rattles from a dozen snakes.

And kill him.

But kill that boy and I'll hand deliver you to Hell myself.

Before he could come up shooting, a timber rattler jerked through the air and bit him on the wrist of his injured arm. The snake struck him again, near the kneecap, its fangs snagging on the denim upon release. Lang wouldn't have thought something could move so fast.

He kicked the snake away and crawled to the far wall. He tried to raise the Kimber, but Hicklin had him covered. They regarded each other for a moment, standoff-style, until Hicklin shook his head, a gesture of mercy or merely a suggestion Lang would never know.

He dropped the Kimber. The localized pain of the snakebites was spreading body-wide. Lang was going into shock.

At the door Hicklin kicked a woman out of his way, pulling Charlie across the threshold and into the night.

Lang's vision dimmed. Outside, several more gunshots could be heard. A man screamed. Lang felt the dry scales of a snake brush past a dangling finger. The world went numb and cold.

Hicklin drove back up the mountain, slowing only to study a break in the trees or an outcrop. He finally turned onto a path just wide enough for the pickup, paved with pine straw and tunneling through the woodlands. With the trail unmarked and unpaved, the truck's suspension suffered mightily before Hicklin hit asphalt again near the state line. The land dipped and climbed, as if the countryside couldn't make up its mind. They followed a stream for a while, the road sweeping back and forth, always descending, a feral home or farmhouse dotting the foothills around them. Charlie saw a sign that read: *Tennessee Welcomes You,* but Hicklin had nothing to say. He noticed telephone poles and road signs, fleeting moonlit views of houses sitting well off the land, properties bordered by cattle fencing or barbwire.

They crossed over railroad tracks that looked long in disuse.

Thirty minutes later Hicklin merged onto the interstate, still in shock, the pain in his back and left shoulder a dull throb. He drove hunched over, one hand on the wheel, the other reaching back to feel the wound.

"Should've known one of them poison-drinking assholes would have a piece in their car," he finally said.

Hicklin replayed the scene in his mind, hearing Lipscomb's voice: *You're slipping, son.* Charlie had turned a corner and was sprinting toward the pickup. But Hicklin lagged behind, almost strutting like some cocksure action movie star. Didn't know if it was arrogance or showmanship, but for a moment it was as though he were back on the yard and all eyes were on him.

He'd felt the big sting of the bullet first and *then* heard the pop. When he turned, a shaky teenager with an old .22 stood there, wide-eyed confusion on his face, as if the boy thought there was only one bullet in the handgun or an unspoken courtesy which allowed Hicklin to return fire. Hicklin raised the HK and blew most of the kid's ear off. Then

Hicklin gut-shot him twice. The boy dropped the pistol and fell to the ground, clutching his stomach.

Hicklin's thoughts drifted to his mentor and friend again, up in the woods, Lipscomb praying his fearful prayers. Making promises. Offering to reverse the hit ordered by the AB leadership inside. If Lipscomb could see Hicklin now he'd be laughing.

"Why didn't you kill that man back there?" Charlie said.

"Which one? I think I killed a couple."

"The man who came in behind us. The man you shot at first."

"Johnny Law?" *Good question. How did he stumble on us? Thought I lost him at the gas station.*

Hicklin watched three highway patrol units racing northbound, followed by an ambulance and an unmarked cruiser with dashboard LEDs strobing. He eased off the gas. Red and blue lights disappeared in the rearview mirror.

Hicklin adjusted himself in the driver's seat, wincing from pain. He lit a cigarette, aware that Charlie was watching him. He could feel the back of his bloodstained shirt sticking to the skin.

"Can I get one of those?" Charlie said, nodding to the pack of cigarettes on the dash.

"No. You can't."

"Why not?"

"Because they're bad for you."

Hicklin winked. Not wanting Charlie to worry. Hicklin was doing enough worrying for the two of them.

He drove south for an hour. Plentiful signs for hotels, fast food and gas stations at every exit. Charlie had nodded off. He mumbled something in his sleep. Hicklin turned on the radio, hoping a little music would take his mind off the bullet in his back. Classic Country Gold, Ray Price singing "I Can't Go Home Like This."

Charlie woke with a start, grasping at some imaginary projectile from his dream. He yawned. Rubbed sleep from his eyes. For a while he watched Hicklin, noticing how he was flexing the fingers on his right hand.

"I used to live up here," Charlie said, acknowledging the signs for an upcoming exit.

"Where?"

"By the university."

"What makes you think you don't live there no more?"

"I just don't," Charlie said after a long pause.

When he looked over at Hicklin Charlie was concerned by what he saw. All the color in Hicklin's face had gone. He shifted in his seat again, every breath costing him.

"Is there a drugstore? Maybe a Walmart?" he said.

"Next exit. It's open twenty-four hours."

"We need food. Some clean clothes. I need—"

Hicklin held his breath at the sight of a police cruiser with its light bar flashing, parked on the shoulder of the exit ramp. He signaled, falling in behind a tractor-trailer. Charlie slumped in his seat. The police officer appeared to be studying a laptop.

Didn't even look up. Hicklin made a left turn at the stoplight. Checked the rearview mirror. The Crown Vic started rolling but went the other direction.

It was a busy strip, restaurants and shopping centers on either side of the parkway. A lot of people still out that time of night. The whole situation made Hicklin nervous. He clenched his jaw. No matter what he did, he couldn't get comfortable. The pain was getting worse.

A towering sign indicated where the Walmart was.

"I need a first-aid kit," he said, admitted, and it was then Hicklin realized he was still holding his breath.

H*e handed Charlie* a hundred-dollar bill and nodded to the duffel bag in the backseat.

"Go on change that shirt. Put them sneakers on. Can't go in there looking the way you do."

"You're not going with me?" Charlie said.

"I can't."

Hicklin looked away. There were more than a dozen cars and RVs parked in the lot. A few people trickled out through brightly lit sliding glass doors, pushing shopping carts or carrying grocery bags. Hicklin knew the tremendous risk he faced by letting Charlie go in by himself. He shifted in his seat, felt the pain of a hundred sharp teeth chomping on his shoulder blade.

"I don't know if I can do it," Charlie said.

"I trust you'll do whatever your heart tells you. Now go on . . . and keep your head down in there."

He kept the engine running, watching Charlie limp across the parking lot. Hicklin relaxed against the headrest. A weak hand found the grip of the .45. His stamina depleted, he tried to keep his eyes open, but it was no use.

And Hicklin for once was scared. He had a vision of a parallel life, one where he took Charlie to Little League or showed him how to dress a deer. Hicklin saw himself in a house on a quiet street, looking out the window at Charlie while he played with friends in a modest front yard. The aroma of a sumptuous meal wafting from the kitchen. A hand on Hicklin's shoulder, Lucy's maybe, but when he looked up her face was blurred as if it'd been wrapped in Visqueen. He couldn't summon the details. Then in the dream a megaphone voice barked commands. Police sirens wailed in the distance. He seized from a terrible pain, as if someone had taken a can opener to his rib cage, only to watch as Lucy pulled a steak knife from his back, showed it to him. His blood running the length of the blade, down to the handle, across the knuckles of her pale, fragile-looking hand. Looking at her, he somehow understood her intentions.

Hicklin smiled.

Then he tilted his head back and let Lucy run the blade across his Adam's apple.

Charlie turned right toward the men's room. No one so much as looked in his direction. There were two checkout lanes open. An overnight crew busy pulling pallet after pallet of plastic-wrapped goods out onto the floor. He splashed water on his face, washed his hands, wiped his neck and behind his ears with a paper towel. He looked as though he'd been mistakenly buried alive. Despite the clean white T-shirt, it would have been hard for someone not to notice his filthy slacks or sour odor.

He grabbed a shopping cart and made for the clothing first. Socks, boxer shorts, a pair of khaki work pants, a three-pack of undershirts. He heard two college-aged girls drunkenly giggle behind him, but Charlie didn't pay them any attention. Near the pharmacy he found the first-aid kits, gauze and bandages. Tweezers. Peroxide. A big bottle of Advil. Then he grabbed some much-needed toiletries. Deodorant, toothpaste, toothbrushes.

He pushed the cart across the store to the grocery aisles. Bread, sandwich meat, bottled water, potato chips. Charlie didn't waste time, but the thrill was there . . . as if he and Hicklin were on an adventure, on the run together like outlaws. He could have escaped by now, called the police and by sunrise been sleeping in his own bed again. But ever since attacking Lipscomb, Charlie had felt a charge like no other.

Maybe the way we are now's the way it's supposed to be?

He was one of three people in line. A young black girl, seven months pregnant and counting the minutes till her shift ended, gave Charlie a cursory glance, sniffled, then ran all his items across the scanner. She checked the hundred-dollar bill with a counterfeit pen and handed him his change without a word.

In forty-eight hours she'd see Charlie's face on television.

And the flicker of recognition would almost induce labor.

Hicklin heard a knock on the passenger side window. He opened his eyes and saw Charlie standing beside the pickup with the shopping cart. Hicklin's throat tightened. After a moment he leaned over and opened the door. The pain had subsided temporarily, but he knew it would return. Charlie hurried, loading all the shopping bags into the backseat of the truck.

"Just leave the cart there," Hicklin muttered.

Charlie got in. Hicklin put the pickup in gear.

"Why are you crying?" Charlie said.

"I ain't."

But a tear had squeezed from the corner of an eye. Hicklin wiped his cheek, surprised when his fingers came away wet. He didn't say anything and neither did Charlie. They got back on the interstate and drove south until a sign for a cheap motel caught Hicklin's attention.

It was well after midnight. A light rain began to fall. The motor lodge was poorly lit, the lot mostly empty. Hicklin noticed they could park behind the long row of rooms and out of sight. He gave Charlie cash to pay for three nights, not sure if they'd even be staying more than six hours. As the boy walked away, Hicklin waited with the engine running. A hand on the .45 tucked under his right leg.

And he closed his eyes again and held his breath against the pain.

And the flowers died, on the northbound side.
And I could care less.
This branded man's headed west.

TWELVE

Hicklin *sat naked* at the edge of the bathtub, watching the warm water mingle with his own blood. He'd never felt so vulnerable in his life, not even when he was forced to strip for some screw. But he really didn't have a choice.

"I just can't get it. It's too deep."

Charlie was attempting to extract the bullet from Hicklin's back. He needled and gouged with a pair of tweezers, the black hole near Hicklin's shoulder blade oozing blood like a stopped-up garden hose. Hicklin wore a sustained grimace on his face. He reached with his good arm for the can of beer resting on the rim of the tub.

"I don't think I can do it. So close, but . . . I'm sorry," Charlie said, unable to hide the disappointment in his voice.

After another particularly painful minute of digging with the tweezers, Hicklin realized Charlie was probably doing more harm than good.

"You tried, Charlie," he said. "All you can do. Go on clean it real good and hand me that bottle of Advil."

Hicklin turned the bottle up. Five or six little flesh-colored pills dropped into his palm. He downed them with a High Life chaser and stretched his neck until something popped. He pivoted and winked at Charlie.

"Damn," Charlie said.

He cleaned and dressed Hicklin's wound as best he could, his patient sipping beer, staring at the pink water swirling around his feet and down the drain. Finished, Charlie draped a towel over Hicklin's shoulders. Then Charlie took a step back, as if a sudden idea could have knocked him off-balance if he wasn't careful.

"You know I bet my mother could help you," he said.

Hicklin didn't move, but his mood turned a shade darker.

"She's a nurse," Charlie clarified. "She would know what to do."

"Her name's Lucy? Lucy Colquitt?" Hicklin said.

They were silent for a while, both waiting to see who would speak first.

"So it's true? About you and my mother?"

"She sounds real familiar." Hicklin let out a nervous laugh.

"So what are we supposed to do?"

Hicklin didn't answer. He gestured for Charlie to leave him alone.

He shaved. It took almost twenty minutes to get dressed, but Hicklin managed without asking for any more help. The boy had done enough as far as Hicklin was concerned. But the beer and pills could mask only so much. His right arm tingled and he couldn't stand straight up. Over the years he'd been punched and kicked and bitten, sliced and stabbed, gouged and choked.

This pain was different.

Charlie turned on the showerhead, testing the water with his hand. Hot. Hotter. Hottest. He pulled off the soiled clothes and eased into the tub. The stream of warm water felt good. He sank to his knees. Sat Indian-style, a week's worth of sweat and crud washing off him.

There was a new toothbrush, paste, mouthwash and deodorant waiting for him on the bathroom counter. He used a third of the tube of toothpaste, brushing his teeth for nearly ten minutes.

He opened the door and found Hicklin sitting back against the headboard of one of the twin beds, smoking a cigarette, watching a muted television. A cable news ticker scrolled across the bottom of the screen. The Pope. An earthquake. A flood. The economy. The President. Hicklin opened a bag of chips and offered it to Charlie while he dressed.

"How you feel?" Hicklin said.

"Better. You shaved your mustache."

Hicklin waved a hand, as if to ward off the reminder of his new look.

"Get you somethin' to eat," he said. "I already made me a sandwich."

It *was midnight* when Sallie Crews arrived at the Church of the Holy Lamb.

A frantic scene outside. Bodies haphazardly lying on the ground, some newly dragged from the church, many in distress. Pockets of people comforting one another, tending to the wounded, restraining the hysterical.

Emergency lights lit the faces of the living and the dead. Agents and state troopers set up a perimeter. EMTs established triage. Crews left her vehicle and crossed over to Deputy Bower. She could tell Bower was badly shaken. A man bleeding behind one ear walked slowly past her as if she weren't there. He held a snake hook in one hand, a burlap sack in the other.

"Don't go in there," Crews said sharply, and to Bower, "Have you seen Sheriff Lang?"

The deputy looked blankly at her.

"Bower?" she said again.

Bower turned to the church. "I ain't never seen nothin' like that."

The man with the hook was just outside the door, silhouetted like a spectral exterminator. Light came through bullet holes in the front wall. Crews walked up to the threshold and looked inside. At least five dead bodies in the aisle leading to the altar. She asked the man in the doorway what happened. He didn't answer. His grip on the snake hook tensed. Crews inched forward, cautiously watching the wrangler.

He picked up a five-foot timber rattler and dropped it into the sack. The homely church smelled of blood and wholesale carnage. She heard someone moan. Lang was lying on his side beneath an over-turned pew, a snake coiled against a knee. She heard those same warning sounds elsewhere in the church, the rattles like crickets in a pasture.

Can I get to him?

The wrangler methodically made his way through the church, stopping often to hook snakes, lifting them carelessly into the sack. At Crews' urgent request he coaxed the snake away from the Sheriff's body, pinching it behind the head.

Lang was in big trouble, breathing badly. He opened an eye for Crews.

She ran for help.

Hicklin made his bones with the Brotherhood by killing an inmate to prove himself. Two weeks later he stared up at bedsprings, listening to his bunk mate. A folded newspaper was laid across the toilet. Two guards patrolled their tier, doing their counts with an old-fashioned hand clicker.

Hicklin heard them click off each cell in pairs. Then the cell door locked automatically. The guard in the central control booth had tucked them in for the night.

You did good, son, Preacher said.

Don't call me son.

I figure you to have no daddy. Breast-fed from a damn dog, did ye?

Hicklin locked his fingers behind his head.

You hear me? Preacher said.

I hear you.

The Brand started out west. Long time ago. But it's here. Right here between these walls. The hacks don't know the extent of it.

I think they do.

Nah, son. Trust me.

What do I do now?

Well, tomorrow we gonna play cards and lift.

I prefer chess.

Thinking man's game, Preacher said, chuckling. You're so sophisticated.

Anything to pass the time.

What you know about time, son?

One day. Then another. Another after that, Hicklin replied.

One hour. One minute. Ever live like that? I break my day into twenty-second blocks. A couple of breaths.

I don't follow.

Oh, you will. There's an art to it. Livin' minute to minute. I call it the increment rule.

Yeah?

Yeah. Start hearing different. Start seeing different. Living like that becomes a drug. You walk around in the goddamn zone all day, every day.

I like that.

So how'd it feel?

How'd what feel?

Don't be coy, Preacher said.

Stuck 'im in his ribs. I've had harder times filletin' a catfish. Dragged his body all around the damn floor to get the message across. My ten will be life soon as they find out.

They ain't gonna find out.

How you know that?

Didn't I tell you to trust me? We run this show. This is our playground.

I don't see how. Browns and blacks. Sheer numbers. The yard here it's like twenty to one.

But they all know.

Know what?

How goddamn sick and crazy we are. Five of us counts for plenty. And fear go a long ways, Preacher said.

Fear?

Yeah.

What 'bout me?

You're one of us now.

Don't have a choice, do I?

Not really.

Yeah?

Yeah. What about Lucy?

She's dead to me. As I am to her.

Sweet girl.

I don't care anymore. Haven't cared for a while.

You know what this is, right? Preacher said.

The Brand?

Yeah.

I think so.

Well, what is it?

Lookin' out for our own. Us against them.

Lipscomb chuckled.

What's so funny?

Heroin. Meth. OxyContin. Cough syrup. Cell phones. Cigarettes. Addresses. Bank accounts. Contracts. Protection. Prostitution. Politics. We play the game because the game is there to be played.

So it ain't just 'bout us.

No, niggers and spics useful to us sometimes.

So it's all about power, huh?

That is a special word, Preacher said.

Yeah?

Say it again.

What?

"Power."

Power, Hicklin said.

You done good today, son. That faggot was a snitch and had to be taken care of anyway. You know that, right?

Yeah.

Sieg Heil, *Lipscomb said.*

White power.

Now come up here and give me a kiss.

Go fuck yourself.

If only I could, Preacher said, chuckling again. If only I could.

They didn't leave the motel room. Hicklin watched television, paying close attention to the local news out of Atlanta, doing his best to hide his discomfort.

Charlie slept well into the afternoon. He woke up to find Hicklin watching television in the same position he'd maintained most of the night. The window drapes were drawn, the room nice and cool. If he had slept, Charlie didn't know.

"How's your back?"

Hicklin ignored the question. "You were having one helluva nightmare last night."

"I used to never have nightmares," Charlie said.

"Don't lay no guilt trip on me, now."

"I wasn't."

Charlie stretched his arms above his head. Arched his back like a cat waking from a lazy afternoon's nap. A weatherman on television was pointing to a tropical storm gaining strength in the gulf.

Lulled by a couple cold beers that night, Charlie fell into a peaceful sleep. Hicklin slowly got up and turned off the lamp. He left the television on, a gray blank screen. His last cigarette smoldered in the ashtray, wreaths of smoke hovering above the twin beds.

He watched Charlie and considered leaving. It had been foolish to stay that long anyway. Quietly, Hicklin packed the duffel bag and grabbed the keys to the truck. Tucked the handgun inside the waistband of his jeans. Every movement proved difficult, the wound below his shoulder blade having a paralyzing effect.

Hicklin had a hand on the doorknob. He turned for a last look at Charlie. The boy slept soundly, no nightmares now. Living up to his nickname again, Hicklin thought, sleeping as though he lay in a coffin.

Hicklin hooked the curtain aside and studied the half-full parking lot. Their room faced a wooded lot, but he could still faintly hear the hum of traffic on the interstate.

Go. Just go.

After a few moments he set the duffel bag down, wincing as he did so.

And like Charlie, Hicklin didn't know where to go.

"What time *is* it?" Charlie asked.

"About six."

Hicklin got up from bed. Made a pot of coffee, poured a cup and walked past Charlie back to the twin bed. Hicklin fingered the TV remote, mindlessly channel-surfing. The dressing for his wound needed changing. Charlie couldn't help noticing how uncomfortable Hicklin looked.

"You can go, I figure."

"*Go?*"

"Yeah. I guess that's the only thing to do now."

"Just *go?*" Charlie said, his voice cracking with indignation. "I don't know where to go."

"Go back to your own life. Your momma. Finish school."

"Could *you* go back? After all this? I'm not sure I can."

"Course you can. You're a bright boy."

"Look at me," Charlie demanded.

His tone gave Hicklin pause. He raised an eyebrow, regarding Charlie's cheekbones and ears, the crease between the boy's eyes just above the nose. Hicklin knew he saw himself, as if in a mirror from childhood. Or back during his first stint, when the fear came at night, just a fish staring beyond the bars, at the darkness of the cell block. The smell of concrete and iron. Waking every morning with the knowledge he might have to kill someone to stay alive.

"Tell me it's not true," Charlie said.

"What?"

"Tell me you don't think it's true."

Hicklin stamped his cigarette out. Both his hands were trembling.

"I think it's true if that's the truth we want," he said.

The *prison-issue pillow came wrapped in plastic. Hicklin melted the bag down. When it was cool and pliable he rolled it between his palms until it took on the shape of a railroad spike. He put it in his hiding place. When he took it out the following night it was hard enough to sharpen an edge against the rim of his bedpost. Didn't take long. An hour here and there, working in secret.*

When Hicklin had fashioned the plastic into a workable point, he wrapped the bottom edge in duct tape. Worked the grip in his hand until it was comfortable. For two weeks the shank stayed hidden until Hicklin was ready to use it.

Everything went according to his plan on the stairwell. He brought the shank down onto the base

of his target's neck. Going deep. Hicklin felt the ver-
tebrae part and his victim's legs buckled.

Hicklin walked away from the scene thinking
about what was for breakfast.

Charlie watched the light fade around the edge of
the motel room curtains. An artificial orange glow
replacing the daylight. Hicklin fidgeted with the air
conditioner. His mood a little brighter, he smiled and
told Charlie how in prison they never had the luxury
of AC. How much he was going to enjoy freezing near
to death that night. They shared a laugh and maybe
to their ears that laughter sounded similar.

Charlie spoke of the plans he'd made in what
now seemed to him his *other* life. What he would
like to have in his workshop one day. He explained—
because Hicklin expressed interest—that a good scientist or engineer always kept a log of his progress.
Charlie favored a notebook, although it could be
considered quaint, but eventually wanted a really
powerful desktop computer to design custom models. He outlined for Hicklin the basics, like tools:
pliers, screwdrivers and a good stock of sandpaper
of varying grits. Cradle stands and spike rows and
an assembly jig for the rocket fins and side cutters.
Plastic cement.

The details gave Hicklin some pleasure. He en-
joyed hearing Charlie describe what obviously was
a great passion, although Hicklin understood nothing about model rocketry. Charlie rambled on about

different construction methods, how he'd once made an ogive nose from balsa wood, a design so impressive the president of the rocket club had said it was as fine a piece of craftsmanship as he'd ever seen. Charlie smiled, remembering this unaccustomed pride in himself.

He told Hicklin about the parasite drag he encountered on one particular model. "It had been the launch lug all along," Charlie explained, but that happened before he'd built his first tower launcher. By eliminating the drag he'd discovered a more stable trajectory for the rocket. "When you watched a rocket rise like that," he said, "the sky seemed to grab it and pull it higher."

Hicklin smoked, nodding here and there, asking Charlie what this word or that word meant. He tried to picture a tiny rocket launched from a field. Tried to follow its trajectory.

He popped Advil and drank bottled water from the mini-fridge, switching to beer when Charlie offered one to him. The black Mossberg was on the bed, by his side. When Charlie reached for his pack of cigarettes on the nightstand Hicklin didn't say anything. Twenty-four hours had passed. Only a few reports on the church shoot-out. Very few details. Just crazy people in a rural county shooting at each other. Hardly news when there were plenty of crazy people in the big city doing the exact same thing.

No headlines about Charlie—or a murdered cop—yet.

———

"You okay? Hey? Can you hear me?"

Charlie's voice sounded distant, almost a whisper. Hicklin had been sealed in a dream, the same one he'd often had for the past twelve years.

The room was seven by ten feet, the walls painted white. One window with a metal frame. He could never see anything from the window. . . .

In his dream he lay on the lower bunk. Water was bubbling up from a drain in the floor. It was this sound that made him sit up. He hopped down, bare feet splashing in a few inches of water. He reached up to wake his celly on the top bunk, but Lipscomb was gone . . .

And the water continued to rise. Began to fill the cell.

It was hot enough to steam the window inset. Hicklin numbly watched as the water rose to his knees. He waded to the door, but the hatch was sealed. Climbed to the top bunk and tried to wipe off the condensation from the window in the wall. Too far to reach, and nothing to see outside. He looked down at the floor. The water was at the boiling point. The heat was suffocating.

He could only watch.

The water lapped at the top bunk.

He clawed at the ceiling, the paint compacting under his nails. Underneath was solid steel. Hicklin knew he would drown.

That's when the lights of his cell went out.

———

"**W**hy did you kill Niesha?" Charlie said.

Hicklin looked for his cigarettes on the night-stand.

"Who the hell is Niesha?"

"My manager at the bank."

"Oh. I didn't know," he said, shrugging. "She gave me a reason, that's all."

"Like your friend?"

"Who?"

"The big guy in the woods."

"Lipscomb? I didn't kill him."

"You shot him."

"Well, I just wanted to make his life difficult."

"You double-crossed him, didn't you?"

Hicklin lit a cigarette, mulling the question for a minute.

"Okay. Yeah. Guess I did."

"Why?"

"You talk too goddamn much in the morning." He strained to sit up, grimacing, his pillow sticky and damp from night sweats. The dressing for his bullet wound was bloody and needed changing. He stood restlessly, looking around the motel room. Half-expecting bars to have been added to the windows while he slept. He glared at Charlie.

"What?" Charlie said.

"Suppose you quit askin' me questions. I can't stand no gabby—" Hicklin blew smoke and finished the thought.

"—cell mate."

Charlie gave him a look.

"Were you dreaming about being back there? In prison?"

"No," Hicklin lied.

"What was prison like?"

"You really want to know? Lock yourself in a closet for twenty-three hours. Eat a rotten apple and stale bread. Piss in a bucket. Shit in that bucket. Then repeat it every day for a year."

Charlie considered the description, not speaking for a while.

"That mean you were in some kind of isolation?"

"Nah. Not for all of it I wasn't."

"What's your dream like?"

"I swear I don't know why I ain't shot you and be done with it."

"Because you can't," Charlie said wisely. "Because you're bad, but not crazy. And you're hurt. You need me."

Hicklin could sense the boy's satisfaction. He turned on the lamp, disgusted by the sight of the ashtray next to his bed. He lit a cigarette, fluffed a pillow and leaned back.

"Prison is just its own little world inside this here one," said Hicklin. "Only way for us to make sense of what there is, what we are. Some people just wander, yeah. Some don't fit nowhere. Some are just straight fucking sociopaths. They wind up where I was at. Shit, some wind up as politicians and CEOs. What matters is we all got to find a little world to belong to. We go searching for it; other times it finds us.

"Prison world got its own ecology. Its own politics, its social violence." He smiled cynically. "Close to *Heaven* as I could find. I figure if I don't make a move real soon I might go back to Heaven, or just go down."

"If *we* don't make a move?" Charlie echoed.

"Yeah. *We.*"

Charlie frowned thoughtfully.

"Did you like my mother?"

"Suppose I liked her," Hicklin said, a concession he was willing to offer.

"Did you love her?" Charlie pressed him.

"I don't quite get that word," Hicklin said.

"'Love'?"

"Yeah."

"Me, neither," Charlie said.

"Why's that?"

"I think it's like, uh, a neurological mousetrap."

Hicklin looked puzzled. "Why not just say you don't believe in no such thing as love. Like a *she-done-him-wrong* country song."

Charlie rolled his eyes, Hicklin taking some enjoyment in needling the boy. Hicklin had known Charlie chiefly in expressions of panic, terror, pain, trauma. *Nice change to see this other side of him,* he thought.

Taking fresh notice of the terrible bruise on Charlie's neck, another beside his left eye, Hicklin detected a feeling not unlike sympathy. *Must of looked like hell in that Walmart.* He shrugged it away. Found the bottle of Advil and took three pills followed by a big gulp of water.

"Was my mother in your gang? Was she a Nazi?"

"Fuck no, boy," he said. "She wanted what poor women like her always wants."

"What's that?"

"A husband who works. Pays the mortgage. An ironing board. Big ol' television. Homeowners insurance. A decent car and nice dresses. All regular stuff for regular people, least I suppose."

"You didn't want that?" Charlie said.

"I wanted to make money the quickest way with a gun, and when I went to prison I wanted to make money there, too, and protect my white brothers. You talked about sandpaper for your rocket kits and such. I wanted to *be* the sandpaper. As coarse as it came."

"You care a lot about being white."

"It's everything." Hicklin paused to consider his words. "*Was* everything."

"Uh-huh. Who made you white?"

"Now don't be startin' this silly shit," he warned.

"Come on. Who made you white?" Charlie pressed him.

"Reckon God did," Hicklin said almost inaudibly.

"You believe in God?"

"I do."

"Even when you were in prison?"

"More so."

"Why?"

"I knew God was real when I saw the walls and walked the yard of a state penitentiary for the first time. God is just another security system."

"I'm not a believer," Charlie said. "I'm an existentialist."

"A *what*?"

"The universe is a big place and it had to come from somewhere. That question is the one we should ask. But we won't ever have an answer. Our brains hit a wall that's too high to scale. So that's, uh, existentialism?"

Charlie couldn't settle on an answer. It just sounded right to him.

"Well, what about the soul?" Hicklin suggested.

"Don't have one. We're just animals."

Hicklin stubbed out his cigarette. Turned his attention to the television. But he wasn't done.

"Animals, huh? Then I roamed with the worst of 'em. I lived like one. Focused on nothing but this body of mine. But listen here, I saw more in men's eyes I could deal with sometimes. We weren't just no pride of lions because . . . more to our lives than kill or be killed."

"Not the way you've acted so far," Charlie murmured.

Hicklin's expression soured, eyes opaque and dismissive. He cocked his head awkwardly to one side, as if fighting off a surge of pain. He squinted.

"Sayin' I ain't got no soul?" Hicklin said.

"We're both going to die, and it'll be like we were never born."

"Know what? Fuck you," Hicklin said. "I'm tired of listening to you."

"Fuck you," Charlie shouted back.

Hicklin looked astonished. His first reaction was anger, but eventually he relaxed, almost to the point of laughing.

"Now where'd *that* come from?" he said to Charlie. "You tell a man to fuck himself, be prepared to back it up."

"I did back it up. I took on your buddy in the woods. And I cleaned that bullet hole and patched you up," Charlie said, his bravado sounding tinny. But he didn't look away.

Hicklin nodded thoughtfully.

The kid had shown more concern in the last twelve hours than anyone had Hicklin's entire life.

"So *what was* my mother like?"

"Like me I guess," Hicklin said. "Young. Poor. Naïve. That's the holy trinity of trouble right there."

"Why did you leave her then? Leave . . . us?"

A sudden jolt of pain saved Hicklin from answering.

"Go on get us a couple cold ones," he said with a grunt, trying to raise his arm.

"Are you okay?" There was a great show of great concern on Charlie's face.

But Hicklin shook him off. He took a sip of water and lay back against the headboard, a mountain of pillows supporting him. Eyelids at half-mast, he took on the appearance of a tranquilized grizzly bear.

"You ever play Lowball, Charlie?"

"*Lowball?* Is that some kind of Nazi game?"

"No, Son. It's a game . . . a game for intellectuals," Hicklin said, his eyes suddenly twinkling with amusement.

They played cards into the night, with no real sense of time, like a member of a touring rock band or a gang of long riders. Charlie figured that's exactly what it must be like, running on fumes and loving every minute.

It has been ten days, he reminded himself.

Felt longer to him, time elongating to the point where his life before the robbery seemed trivial by comparison. He had begun to understand why criminals and vagabonds, restless spirits, wanted to live like this. He thought about his hero, Robert Goddard. Pioneer and father of modern rocketry. Sickly and fragile, hollow chested, braving nor'easters on his parents' front porch. Wrapped in blankets, learning to be ill as if illness was a natural state for his body to be in. Routine as hunger. Knowing that the trauma of perpetual sickliness would result in greatness.

Charlie—thinking of Goddard—hoped, deep down, for a similar transformation.

He sensed it happening like a sputtering fuse to dynamite. Something that would remake his own life.

Or result in madness.

Hicklin studied his cards. He had lost the first couple hands to Charlie on purpose. The impulse struck Hicklin again, to get up and walk out the door. A need to be free and clear. There was nothing to prevent him from bailing. Not even the pain.

Except for Charlie.

Hicklin liked how Charlie didn't gloat or boast of his beginner's luck. Like so many jailhouse poseurs and wannabes. Charlie played cautiously, but he played like a man.

The game of Lowball as Hicklin taught it was a standard version, where the wheel was the lowest possible hand. Ace-to-five low. You ignored the straights and flushes. Hicklin studied Charlie as he drew his cards. Pondered what came naturally to him, finding the lowest, poorest hand.

He told Charlie how Lowball was a game popular with convicts. A challenging game that worked against what most people considered logical.

Hicklin once knew a guy named David Jay, but everyone called him Bad Hat. A big Nazi fuck from Orange County who followed an ex-girlfriend all the way to Powder Springs, Georgia, just to beat the shit out of her with a football helmet. Did a dime for that and similar acts of violence at places like Hancock, where Hicklin met him, before being sent off to Reidsville, where he was never heard from again. Hicklin told Charlie how Bad Hat was the best bluffer he'd ever seen. A great actor like all good criminals.

Charlie nodded. Hicklin couldn't tell if Charlie understood what he was trying to tell him . . . but at least he was listening.

Hicklin *woke up* to debilitating pain. He called out Charlie's name. Gritted his teeth and sat up.

"I can't feel my arm. It's gone numb."

Charlie turned on the bedside lamp. The motel room was ice-cold. The curtains swayed above the air conditioner's vents.

"You need to see a doctor."

"It's out of the question."

"You could see my mother. I could drive us to her house."

Hicklin considered the alternative. Charlie dumps him at a hospital and he goes back to prison? A place where he'd surely have to face the constant threat of assassination for the rest of his life. Or maybe he ditches Charlie? Stays on the run only to die of infection . . . or be crippled by nerve damage?

"Do you think she can help me?" Hicklin finally said.

"She's got medicine, antibiotics. She can get that bullet out of you. I just know she can."

Charlie told him where Lucy Colquitt lived.

Not so far away, Hicklin realized.

You're a stupid fuck, you know that?

Yeah, I do, Hicklin told himself.

Well, you're just talkin' to yourself anyway. Like some medical in the loony bin. This is a one-way ticket to the laughing factory. Droolin' on yourself ain't far off.

I ain't interested right now.

Look at you. Let Charlie drive you to his mother's

house? Are you fucking crazy? The kid looks like a slug begging for salt after a day in the sun. Just coastin' down the highway with your alleged long-lost son. Might as well be goin' to a goddamn Little League game.

Just go away.

I can't figure out for the life of me what the hell happened to you. I really can't.

Maybe I finally grew up.

Grew up? And did what? Decided to rob a bank to commemorate your graduation into adulthood?

I told you, shut up.

You're goddamn forty-one years old. Spent half of it as a resident in the Georgia Penal System. But that stint in the panhandle was nice. Lasted three days in Pensacola before they picked you up. Couldn't get enough, could you? But neither could I. I wanted to go back as bad as you. But as smart as you were, for the life of me I can't figure out why you jumped the goddamn score.

Thought you was better than your brothers, huh? Thought you was smarter? A perfect plan in place. Could of come out with what, sixty? Eighty thousand? And think how much clout you would've earned. Boys out west would've been singin' your praises. Hell, they already were! You were in the perfect spot. Six months from now you would've been phased in somewhere. Run a crew. Oakland. Nashville. Phoenix. Denver. A lead soldier on the streets. Know those Arizona cats made 'bout twenty million pure profit just distributin' meth.

Of course you knew that. You're me.

*But no, you had one of your damn impulses, huh?
Wanna move out to Montana with one big chunk of
money that ain't yours to begin with? Start fresh
and settle down? I swear it's that damn Jubilation
County. Somethin' in the goddamn water. Just breeds
foolishness. And just when I thought I had you under control. We was workin' so good together.*

*Thought a guy like Lipscomb wouldn't find you,
but he did and then you wronged him.*

*You should be in an orange GDC jumpsuit pickin'
up cans off I-20. Should have just stayed in prison.
It wouldn't have been hard to do. But you and
Preacher hit the streets round the same time. And he
offered you a sweet deal. The score set up out west.
Safe houses, transpo, guns, intel. Another score three
months down the road. And you fucked it up!*

*But then you take ol' Coma here hostage, too.
Like you needed a buddy or somethin'. Already
convinced yourself he's your own flesh and blood.
Ever stop to consider maybe he isn't, you stupid
sumbitch? Did you ever consider the pure coinci-
dence of it all?*

*What are you gonna do? Send the kid to Har-
vard? Catch up over beers and a couple Westerns?
Gonna bond over a viewing of* Shane? *You lost that
battle long ago.*

I wish you would just finally go to hell.

*Tell that kid to keep it under seventy. And no, this
person inside you, this extra goddamn gear, ain't
going nowhere.*

*Maybe the kid is right. Ain't no soul. You're just
the sum of chemicals interacting.*

Oh, just go on thinkin' that. Who kept you alive when you got out of Segregation? Who built you into something fierce? They knew your name from Sandersville to Rome. Hell, you know they talked about you at San Quentin. Pelican Bay. Marion. They knew of you. That Hicklin cat, he's smart and lean. Last of the Georgia Boys. The real deal. Big badass cowboy.

And why? Because of me. I cut you from wood.

Most people wish they had a voice like me.

When they threw you in that open bay tent unit, who saved you? In the recreation hall when that big Salvadoran nigger wanted to fuck you sideways. Who bowed up and showed everyone that you were hard and the last to be fucked with? Who tore out his fucking tongue? Who does that? You could have been a lot of things in life. But the last thing you are is a daddy.

Just stop. I got to concentrate.

What's a matter? In a little bit of pain?

You know it.

How about ol' Lucy? I'm sure this reunion will be right nice and emotional. Now you think this Charlie belongs to you? God knows how many men that woman might've fucked. I remember the letter you got from her. Committed to your fucking memory. Told you to flush it down the toilet. I had a son and I think it's yours, but you're no good so wah, wah, wah. . . . You might have ten kids for all we know. Want to go pick them up, too? You're making a huge mistake, but we can fix this. First you off the kid. Boost another car and head west as fast as you can. It's a risk, but we got friends in Muscle Shoals.

No.

This morning they'll no doubt have you and Preacher and Flock's face on the news. Statewide manhunt. Wasn't like you stumbled on that bank on your way for a morning cup of coffee. Someone sold you the guns and someone inside laid out the floor plans and security cameras and delivery schedule and where the cash lockers was and all the weak spots in that podunk bank. Plus think if they pinch Cueva and you get the Mexian Mafia involved? Holy shit! Pray you've practiced breathing through a gaping hole in your throat. It won't take the law much longer. They crossing t's and dotting the i's as we speak. Let's not forget you pulled a Wild Bunch inside a goddamn church, killed a cop probably. But I can't blame you for that move. I was the one in charge then. Like the good ol' days. Now I'm just some second-class citizen. And don't think those fine men max-locked in concrete shoe boxes out Florence way don't know. They might have twenty or fifty plans in various stages of design. Heists. Hits. Kidnappings. So they know. White nigger in Jubilation County fucked it up. Smell the blood from here.

What's the move, then?

Take that .22 in the glove compartment and bury a round in the kid's head. Then dump him and the truck at a gas station car wash.

I think I need a doctor.

I'll find you one. Now do what I say. We're running out of time.

———

Lang *looked out* through sticky eyelids. Whatever was being done to him hurt. He didn't like it. Ventilator down his windpipe. Breathing short and shallow. When they touched the edema in his right hand and forearm, pain and nausea flared up.

He'd been immobilized. The ambulance was moving. Somebody repeated his name, called out vital signs. He heard the words "hypotension" and "severe envenomation." Sound of tires rolling over gravel, crackle of a CB radio, emergency codes he recognized.

This is goddamn serious.

He tried to envision all his considerable pain being dumped into a steel drum. Mentally pushing the swollen kneecap down into the barrel, then piling on the shrapnel torching his shoulder, the ember that was his palm.

Sometimes the effort to stifle pain worked. But not this time.

I need more goddamn drums.

Lang found it nearly impossible to concentrate. He wasn't sedated enough not to feel panic. The urgency in the voices of the paramedics suggested that death was a possibility. No dream this time, the one in which he needed to pull the trigger on his sidearm but couldn't—typical nightmare for law officers.

The ambulance moaned to a stop. A paramedic popped the release and Lang's gurney was lifted from the rear of the bus. He heard the pneumatic *swish* of the sliding glass doors, wincing from the strong lights overhead as they rolled him down a hallway.

He couldn't see much of the faces looking down at him. He felt cold. Smelled the plastic of the ventilator mask, the hands in latex gloves tending to him.

There was a commotion of which he was dimly aware, doctors and nurses in the emergency room of some hospital working around his limp body. A trauma surgeon waited. There were problems around the multiple bite wounds. Except for these places, Lang's body had turned the color of discarded snakeskin.

That dream again. *Throw down the useless gun. Anywhere. And run.*

Lang kept on trying to dump all his pain in the barrel, but his hand felt like it'd been dipped in lava. And he wondered, with all that pain spilling over the edges of the drum, if Charlie Colquitt had lived.

C*rews watched the* sunrise, hands in her jacket pockets because they were trembling from too much caffeine and no sleep. She was used to exhaustion, but this was a special type of fatigue. She suppressed the urge to bum a cigarette from a deputy smoking along the perimeter of the crime scene.

They found two bodies on the mountain. One on an old logging road, half a leg missing, bled out—the other kneecap blown out—blood still viscous in the early light. It led to the rest of the leg, still caught in a bear trap and pecked at by crows.

The cottage was three hundred yards away, hidden amid thick timber. On her walk up she'd noticed a few paths leading to God knew where, some of them wide enough for a pickup or sport-utility to pass. They had an unidentified near-headless male, the remains crackling with dung beetles. Inside the cottage was an unidentified female. Badly beaten, her head kicked in like a rotten pumpkin. At least two dozen bullet holes in the walls.

Last night's rain had softened the ground. A spiderweb anchored beneath one corner of the roof glistened with dew. Crews walked carefully around Flock's corpse, trying to reconstruct events while she craved a smoke.

Birds soared in sunlight. Squirrels were everywhere, chasing one another through the hemlocks at top speed. A helicopter circled, blades whipping the treetops. She turned and watched men in windbreakers on the wooded slope.

A good square mile of mountainside began to swarm with federal and state agents as it became light enough to see well. A lot of experienced personnel, but Crews thought it for everyone.

This is one huge fucking mess.

They soon identified the bleed-out as one Leonard Lipscomb, otherwise known as Preacher or LB in hard-core state pens like Hays and Calhoun. The deceased had worked at his leg for a good hour before breaking both his tibia and fibia in half. Cutting through the tendons and muscle with a Gerber multitool. Crews couldn't begin to imagine the man's agony, or his will to be free. He'd finished the job with a pretty decent tourniquet, using the sleeve of his twill shirt, and crawled on his belly leaking blood like a beer tap before finally passing out.

The Medical Examiner agreed it was the toughest thing he'd ever seen a man do to himself.

One huge fucking mess, Crews thought again.

From witnesses who had been in the church she got a make on the pickup, partial plates, positive ID on the perp and probable hostage. The camcorder had been smashed, but there was a good chance they could salvage the tape. Someone had pulled a piece on the fleeing suspects, got off a round, but had little to say from the morgue. This break had come to Crews as a game changer. Hicklin had a two-, maybe three-hour head start. And he or Charlie might be injured.

The call was made.

Crews gave in to her weakness and bummed a Marlboro Light from the first person in uniform she found with a pack of smokes. Her old brand. The first drag tasted the same as it had ten years ago. The nicotine shot straight to her head. She studied the layout of the cottage, noting the generator and water pump, linkages forming.

This Hicklin must have planned to hide out for a month, maybe more, wait till the heat died down and drive off with all that loot.

Then what was the point in taking a hostage? Why piss off your convict buddies in the process?

Crews knew that Charlie Colquitt was still alive and being kept alive when he and Hicklin had left the church. Still alive yet for unknown reasons. The teller couldn't be leverage or collateral. This Hicklin character could have done him in the bank, or five minutes later or—hell—five *days* later. This was

Hicklin's safe house. Flock and Lipscomb either knew just where it was or found out about it from Kalamity Bibb. And the dead woman inside the cottage with her head smashed in? Probably killed for not giving up Hicklin right away. Possibly Hicklin's point person on the outside. A lot of hard-core bangers in the joints had one or more women checking things out, making moves for them on the streets. Smuggling drugs, laundering money, relaying messages, mailing care packages.

Crews studied .45-caliber shell casings scattered about like loose change as ERT techs set up shop at their newly discovered crime scene. They used digital cameras, covering Flock's body from a dozen angles. Crews mashed her cigarette against her heel and pocketed the butt. An image came into focus in her mind like a photograph in a chemical bath.

Charlie and his captor. On their way to . . . where?

A *rookie patrolman named* Terrence Malloy was still on call for another six hours. It didn't stop him from taking a Code Five-M at his mother's place on Tulip Street. He picked up coffee and a fried-egg sandwich, his breakfast greasing its way through a brown paper bag.

The sun showered the street with orange light, oaks and alders shading the path behind the old frame house. The Stars and Stripes hung from pole brackets on the front porch. His mother had left the garage door open, expecting his arrival. Malloy parked inside and cut the engine of his cruiser. The police band went dead. A night and morning of misdemeanors and DUIs in Zone Seven silenced for a little while at least.

"Hey, Momma," he said.

Althea Malloy opened the screen door and shuffled aside to let her son pass. She wore her favorite bathrobe, slippers, wide awake and cheery eyed even at such an early hour. He followed her to the kitchen, noticing her arthritic movements as she pulled out a chair and turned to the stove. Still a couple good years before Malloy expected her diabetes to start calling the shots. She had tea brewing.

"How's work, sweetheart?" she said.

Malloy sat down at the kitchen table. Opened the lid on his coffee. On cue his mother was there with a spoon and a napkin. He poured some sugar and stirred it. Put the lid back on. He unwrapped the sandwich from the wax paper and ate.

"Six more hours on call and then forty-eight off. Been one damn thing after another this week," he answered between bites.

"I pray every night," his mother said, her voice almost theatrically weary.

"I know. It's okay. They gave me a gun and everything." Malloy winked at her. He took a bite from the sandwich, savoring it for a moment before chomping it to bits.

"So much wickedness out there."

"True," he said with a shrug. "But most times it's fender benders and kittens stuck in trees. The occasional homicide. Domestic dispute."

Malloy's mother gave him that *look* only a retired schoolteacher could give. Thirty years in the Georgia Public School System. Won every award an English teacher could win. *You are a smart butt.*

"Your brother called. Got the interest of some agent for one of his scripts. A school buddy and he already had meetings, pitching this idea and that."

"Yeah, well, when Knucklehead sells one he can pay off that student loan."

"When your younger brother is accepting his Oscar we'll see who comes asking for a loan."

Malloy knew the next question was going to be about his love life. He was working on a quip when he heard the rumbling from an old Chevrolet 350 motor next door. He looked out the kitchen window at the step-side, mud caked on the fenders and door panels, watching as the pickup backed into the driveway of Lucy Colquitt's home. Two men got out of the truck and disappeared inside the carport. The younger of the two caught Malloy's attention.

"Is Miss Colquitt home, Momma?"

"Lucy Colquitt? Probably. But I haven't spoken to *that* woman in fifteen years."

Instinct told him that that was the kid. Malloy had already seen the All Points Bulletin on the mobile laptop inside his cruiser.

He radioed Dispatch.

Then he undid the strap on his holster, peeking between the blinds at their neighbor's house. There were neat rows of a vegetable garden in the side yard, begonias blooming along the walkway. Lucy Colquitt was a woman he barely knew. Always kept to herself. Never very friendly, either. He often wondered if the color of his skin had anything to do with it.

"I need for you to go into your room and lock the door," he told his mother. "Did Uncle Kertus set up that flat-screen TV for you?"

"He sure did. Got that *dee-vee-dee* player hooked up, too."

"Go in there and put it on and I'll bring you some breakfast. On a tray just like Daddy did."

"Whatever you say, Terry. Since you won't hang out with your dear old mother, I'll just go see my friend *Mr. Poitier.*"

"You do that, Momma. And lock the door."

I'm running out of roads to ride.

THIRTEEN

Lucy Colquitt gently touched her forehead, rolling her eyes from the pain of a metronomic ache. She was terribly hungover, her mind thickened by alcohol. Sunlight slashed through the windows. The house was half-dark and all quiet. Could have been the next evening for all she knew. Most of the previous days had been spent in front of the television, sipping peppermint schnapps and Wild Turkey, watching *The View* and Court TV. Soap operas. The local news. The phone rang periodically, but no friends or family came calling.

Local newspeople had tried to reach her, leaving messages. Coax her into giving an interview.

She'd spoken to Sallie Crews a few times.

Lucy vaguely remembered having conversations with the woman. She might have told Crews about the day Charlie was born. About how Lucy had never felt pain like that, squeezing him out that little space between her legs. How it rained real bad that afternoon. Crews assured her she was going to find Charlie. She asked Lucy if anyone had contacted her. Charlie? A man or men? Lucy told her no.

Three days morphed into one long bender. Lucy made a drink an hour, started around ten in the morning. She recalled eating once or twice, a grilled cheese and baked potato. But the food made her sick to her stomach. She showered. Put some clothes in the wash. Made the bed. Floating through her home like a ghost with no one to haunt. There was a phone call made to Charlie's apartment complex. Spoke to someone in the office and reached an agreement for management to accept a personal check for his next month's rent. She didn't want Charlie's life to have gone to hell when he came back.

Even though Lucy secretly believed her son to be dead.

She watched the five o'clock news, reasonably sober and alert. When there were no updates on Charlie she changed the channel to a classic movie station. Humphrey Bogart on the screen, playing a bad guy in *The Desperate Hours*. *The Night of the Hunter* was next. She had always had a big crush on Robert Mitchum growing up, still captivated after all these years by that sinister, seductive-looking face of his. She picked up her novelty table lighter—a rooster where you pushed down on the wings and a flame shot out from between the beak—and lit a cigarette.

Charlie hated that lighter. Hated her smoking, too. *You'd be amazed how many nurses and doctors smoked,* she'd say, trying to reason with him.

But she didn't care if the whole house smelled of stale smoke. She wanted that odor on everything, between her fingertips, in the curtains and pillow-cases, on the upholstery.

Let it stink, she thought furiously.

Her attention returned to the television, to Shelley Winters and those cute kids, trying to reconnect moments from her own childhood.

Nothing came.

She went to the kitchen, returning to the couch with a glass, ice and a bottle of bourbon.

Lucy maintained a steady drunken buzz through the rest of the film, in awe of Mitchum and his scary tattoos and—even scarier—the songs he sang as he stalked the children.

Her good eye glazed, a memory of a man she once knew creeping into her mind.

She hummed a remembered tune and watched through the windows as the sun went down.

. . . safe and secure from all alarms, leaning, leaning, leaning on the everlasting arms. . . .

Lucy often wondered if she was a good person. She would take inventory of all the bad things she did, like when she worked at the bank she took fifty bucks every day for two months and forced balances, but they never caught on and she quit just in time.

Never cared for foreigners or minorities. With those people her step definitely slowed a bit back at her old job at the Jube County probate court. It wasn't until she finished nursing school and started taking care of people that Lucy achieved some sort

*of fulfillment. As if she'd righted herself from crash-
ing into rocks. Redeemed herself a little in the eyes
of the Lord or karma or whoever was keeping score.*

*But the worst was when she wanted to kill Char-
lie before he was born. Her aunt told her to flush it
out with Coca-Cola, but then they got to talking
and there were a couple of other ways. Like taking a
needle up there or pulling it out with a coat hanger.*

*Her aunt said the baby at that stage would be real
small.*

*Wouldn't look like nothin', Lucy's auntie had told
her. After the fight with Hicklin, she thought for
sure Charlie would be retarded or damaged, but she
went through with it. Glad she did, too. He was
such a joy to raise. A quiet, precious little thing who
looked like her in some places, in some places . . .*

Lucy's *false eye* floated in a bowl by the bathroom
sink. When she moved the bowl, the glass orb would
bob in the soapy water. The pupil and iris of the
acrylic twin would roll one way, then the other, cant-
ing to the motion of the water. At times the eye seemed
to be looking at her, as if it had something to say.

Before bed she washed and dried her face. The
empty socket was gray and puffy, the eyelid droop-
ing like a broken awning. She was proud of her in-
jury, as a ravaged victim of conflict would be proud
to have survived. A haggard sister of the Civil War, a
whore routinely beaten and whipped.

"What have I to dread, what have I to fear, leaning on the everlasting arms . . ."

She was up before the sun, having gone to bed with the chickens, a pint of whiskey in her bloodstream. She decided on grits.

Lucy dropped a teaspoon of salt into the briskly boiling water. Added the grits and a raw egg, some butter. She stirred.

The first cup of coffee had restored her balance. The sun was just starting to peek over the hills to the northwest. Her garden desperately needed tending, having gone neglected most of the month. Tomato and squash she rarely ate. She had tried okra, but it never took. At least the baby beets and carrots always came out great. Lucy canned them, brought the vegetables to the girls at the hospital. Of course, she always had some for Charlie. Lord knew what he did with them. Probably blew them up with his rockets.

She ate at the kitchen table. Chased her breakfast with two aspirin. Her hand shook when she poured a second cup of coffee. She gripped the mug tightly, easing it to her lips. Both hands shaking now, white-knuckled. The mug stinging her palms.

Moments later a coughing fit sent Lucy into a tailspin. She reached for a box of tissues, just in time to hack a gob of phlegm. She wadded the tissue, put it in the pocket of her robe. She lit a cigarette without thinking. Too accustomed to the way her body ached. That general, imprecise awfulness. She turned on the television and caught an early-morning traffic report.

Commercials.

She changed the channel. Another affiliate. A news ticker scrolled along the bottom of the screen, the anchor reading breaking news. "The suspect is considered armed and dangerous . . . authorities believe . . . to be in North Carolina . . . national forest . . ."

Lucy brought a hand to her mouth. It was a picture of Charlie she'd given Sallie Crews. Up on the screen. Along with another picture of a man Lucy no longer recognized.

Lucy phoned every number from every business card, leaving a dozen messages for Sallie Crews to call her. She watched the morning news programs for another hour, desperate for information, but apparently there were more important things happening in the world. Anxiety and tension gave way to fatigue. She lay down on the couch and closed her eyes, dozing with her cell phone clutched in one hand.

In her dream they had found Charlie and the man who took him. Her son was coming home a hero, they said. She walked toward him. Charlie wore a flak jacket and looked unharmed, escorted by two police officers. She called out his name, raising her arms to him as if to squeeze the life from his body.

Just a couple more feet . . .

But Charlie and the officers ignored her, walking by, Charlie not even blinking. She pleaded with her stone-faced son, unable to comprehend the blankness in his eyes.

They helped him into a police cruiser and closed the door.

She charged the car but was restrained by unseen arms. She could only watch as Charlie was driven away.

In the dream there were so many things she wanted to say.

But words jammed in her throat, her mind like a mailbox stuffed with returned letters.

H*er head snapped* at the sound of an engine in the driveway. She got up quickly, tying her robe and watching the screen door at the end of the hallway. A pickup truck backed into the carport.

Her heart beat faster. She tilted an ear to the rumbling sound of a muffler going bad.

They gawd.

Charlie appeared. He carried two duffel bags and supported a distressed-looking man under the arm.

Lucy ran to her son, verging on hysteria, her bathrobe falling open. Charlie glimpsed her breasts before Lucy took him in her arms, kissing his cheeks and neck and head.

"Charlie! Charlie! Charlie! Charlie!"

He had rarely seen his mother without her artificial eye.

Hicklin had retreated to a corner, propping himself up with the help of his shotgun.

"My baby . . . my baby came home!" she panted.

Charlie embraced his mother halfheartedly, unable to think of anything appropriate to say. He dragged her to the couch in the living room. Hicklin wavered in the background, peeking through window blinds at the street outside.

Lucy glanced over her son's shoulder, turning her single eye on *him*.

Charlie's hand was quick to cover her mouth.

And stifle the scream in her throat.

They'd been in the pasture near the old pond. It was nearly dried up. Cows grazed randomly around the edges under a bright hot sun, chewing, looking at one another. Switching their tails as if it was the highlight of a long workweek. Lucy laughed and ran from her cousins, going into the barn to hide.

She wasn't paying attention as she passed the ladder to the loft with its stored bales of hay and dusty, webbed corners, the black-and-yellow daubers buzzing around. Her uncle was repairing some steps on the ladder and pieces of wood were stacked haphazardly, some with nails sticking out. When Lucy heard her cousins' voices she turned, but her foot caught on a board at the bottom of the pile.

They scattered as Lucy fell sideways. Hands instinctively extended, but they couldn't protect her face. Happened so fast. Lucy felt the nail go into her eye at an angle. She didn't scream so much as make a terrible noise. A guttural sound. At age eleven she'd had her share of scrapes and bruises but nothing as scary as that.

It felt like a wasp had stung her right on the eyeball. Lucy yanked her head away and started crying.

The sharp point of the nail tore out most of the cornea. She couldn't believe what was happening. She reached for what looked like pieces of fat on the ground. Hot tears and that terrible pain came next.

Her cousin Sara found her. Her other cousin, Dirk, ran for his father.

Lucy had lost something she could never have back. They tried to tell her she would still be pretty and eventually she would forget it had ever happened. And they were wrong. A small nail had redefined who Lucy was, and would forever be.

Sallie Crews smoked her third bummed cigarette, studying a report from the Bureau of Prisons while conferencing with her equivalent at the SBI in North Carolina. Detective Moye ran toward her with a cell phone, sprinting from twenty yards away. She hung up and watched him approach. The kid was in great shape.

"Agent Crews!"

"Tell me something worthwhile," she said.

Moye gestured with the phone. "Got a positive ID on the pickup. A rookie patrolman on call just saw who he thinks is Charlie Colquitt and the suspect at a house next door to his mother's. Ninety-seven-sixty-six Tulip Street. Ten minutes from the square. SWAT and hostage are en route."

"Ninety-seven—? That's Lucy Colquitt's address."

She took off at a run with Moye, both leaping across stones at the creek like fugitives themselves.

On the ghost road a caravan waited. They followed a local deputy to the highway and headed south, wide open with sirens and light bars.

These things used to excite her more, Crews realized. Snaking through highway traffic. A confrontation with the hunted, justifying all the hours of work, all the manpower and resources. Not eating enough. Not sleeping enough.

These things *used* to excite her.

This time she had a premonition that it was going to end badly.

"This *was a* goddamn mistake," Hicklin said, watching as Charlie eased his mother down onto the couch, trying to reassure her that everything was okay.

"*Don't you recognize him?*" Charlie said needlessly.

Hicklin just shook his head, glaring around the living room at the stupid knickknacks and collectibles, the country décor. It unsettled him in a way he couldn't have anticipated.

He hadn't trusted his better judgment. The *other* voice was nagging him.

Off them both and get the fuck out of here!

Charlie remained on the couch, soothing his mother with gentle pats and strokes. Lucy clutched him, moaning, rocking. Hicklin peered between curtains, looking up and down the street. He hustled to the kitchen. Drew the blinds. In the living room again he removed the bulletproof tactical vest from his duffel bag and struggled into it. His whole right side felt useless, but the pain was the least of his concerns at the moment. He took out four magazines procured from Lipscomb and secured them in the pockets of the vest. Charlie watched him.

"Don't you see, Momma? It's him," he said, pleading. "He needs help, Momma. He's hurt. We've got to help him."

"Just tell him to take what he wants and get out," Lucy said.

"But it's . . . Look at him!"

Lucy framed Charlie's face with her hands and kissed him gently on the forehead.

"What *happened* to you, Coma?"

"I'll tell you one day, Momma. Right now we're a family again. And we need to help him. He's got a bullet stuck in his back!"

Lucy refused to look in Hicklin's direction.

"You never had a father!" she shrieked, slapping her son with weak and flailing blows. Charlie struggled to get a grip on her wrists.

"Shut her up," Hicklin said.

He shook his head in disbelief.

"This was a huge motherfuckin' mistake."

Hicklin turned and walked into the kitchen, fingering the blinds so as to see out the window above the sink. Nice quiet street. No traffic. He began to pace.

Kill these two assholes, the voice said again.

He raised the shotgun subtly, as if to fire from the hip, aiming it at Charlie from the kitchen. *Do it. Do it and bail.*

The boy's back was to him. Lucy's one eye filling with tears behind a mess of hair.

Do them both.

Then put the goddamn 12-gauge in your mouth.

Nice little house on a quiet street. For a lot of men it was routine to be in a house like this with a wife and kid. Hicklin shuddered. He didn't need some epiphany to realize how fucked it all was for him.

He lowered the shotgun and leaned it against the kitchen table. Lit a cigarette and listened. Lucy halfway down the hole of a breakdown, Charlie trying to reason with her, talk her off the ledge. It was beyond anything Hicklin could have imagined.

What a homecoming.

He glanced at the furniture, the ceramic collectibles. Photos of Charlie everywhere. The boy was her life, pathetic as that was. Hicklin felt no real connection among the three of them. To that house. Lucy had gone on to make something of her life. Live it as best she knew how. *And what had you done?*

So was it really her? His mind was stalled. He could hardly look at her.

He could only remember Lucy like a character from a long-forgotten TV show. A mental mirror he dusted off, but the reflection remained dull. Himself at twenty, twenty-two. A mean, lost, ugly feeling came over him.

On the couch Charlie held his mother as Lucy brought her lips to his ear and whispered.

"I swear before God you never had a father!"

He pulled back, appalled, eyes plaintive and confused. He looked around for Hicklin, as if to petition him for help. But Hicklin was gone. Limping down the hallway, the keys to the pickup dangling from a finger.

Charlie heard the screen door to the carport slap shut.

Then gunfire.

The tactical responders compartmentalized the house by corners and then by window. The Peacekeeper showed up. It took twenty minutes once the call came over the radio. The eight-man tactical unit hurried down side streets. Gear next to the bed or in the trunk of a cruiser.

Honey, I've got to go and I can't say why.

The first four grouped up and made a decision to engage. They made a positive ID as Hicklin stepped out into the carport and tried to enter a pickup truck. The suspect fired twice from the carport and took cover back inside the residence. Then from compartment 1-1 three more shots were fired. Suspect was accurate. He hit one member of the tac team. The body armor saved him.

Return fire.

It terrorized the whole neighborhood. More units arrived. People were urged to go back inside their homes. The neighbors retreated reluctantly, disappointed, as if they wanted to watch a ball game from the pitcher's mound.

More units arrived. Inner and outer perimeters were established. The command bus was en route.

The APV sat idling. Another twenty minutes passed. A quiet street turned into a live-fire training ground. It turned into a circus.

Explosive entry experts consulted with their squad leader. Armor-plated vehicles were parked strategically along the perimeter.

State and Federal were fifteen minutes out.

The street was overtaken by law enforcement. Some asshole had already called the local affiliates. Sport-utilities and cruisers arrived in a spectacle of flashing lights. A helo's blades thrummed the air above. Someone said he killed a Sheriff up in Jubilation County. Raped a kid. Burned down a church. There were two hostages inside.

The state and federal agents in charge of the investigation were five minutes out.

A tense hour passed.

By then the hostages were walking out.

Unharmed.

And the boy was yelling, imploring them not to kill the man still inside.

I *could've told Charlie a lot of things I didn't. Like who his granddaddy was. His grandmamma. Could've told him how Lucy and I met and how I was just a big bad asshole back then. But there was some normal shit going on. Downright picturesque at times. Could've taken the boy fishing. Knew so many good holes around the house up-country. Raised in a double-wide with no mailbox. Maybe take him out*

with a couple .22s and hunt squirrel. Teach him
how to fry 'em up real nice. I could have filled him
in on why I did what I did, and why it put me in
prison. And then why I did what I did there, and so
on . . .

"It's her, isn't it?"

He looked out a window. Hicklin seemed satisfied, at peace. The phone rang. He ignored it.

"It's her," he acknowledged after a moment. "But
she don't want to remember me."

Hicklin reloaded the 12-gauge. Charlie could tell
he was in a lot of pain.

Hicklin looked up at him and smiled.

"Now it's time to say good-bye, Charlie Colquitt."

His intentions registered immediately.

"You're crazy!" Charlie said. "Why not make a
deal with them? Don't you want to live? Just give
up."

"I am giving up. My own way."

There was no more arguing. Hicklin raised the
shotgun and pointed it at Charlie.

"Gather up your mother, Son. Let's go."

Another firefight ensued, Hicklin burning up the
shotgun, the SWAT returning fire. He was lucky to
survive the barrage. A salvo of rounds shredded the
windows and blinds, the frame house getting thor-
oughly ventilated. He momentarily thought about

packing it in, thinking about what he was up against.

They stared down iron sights of G36 assault rifles, firing controlled bursts.

Beautiful weapons.

Glass popped above and around him. He glimpsed little black helmets shaped around the ears, body armor, big yellow letters identifying them as not to be fucked with.

He ducked into the bedroom. The bathroom. Put a large bath towel in the sink and soaked it. He saw Lucy's artificial eye bobbing in a bowl on the counter. The water in the bowl shimmered to the vibrations from the helicopter blades overhead. The whole house shook.

Thankfully Charlie was outside and safe. To Hicklin that was what mattered most. Saving himself seemed a dim possibility. Hardly necessary.

He crawled below the window frames, staying out of sight. Cuts from the broken glass were unavoidable, his body already bruised and wracked with fever. To the front door and down the hall to the living room. He flipped the coffee table over and summoned enough strength to drag the couch around the corner to the carport entrance, forming a makeshift barricade. He worked the pump of the shotgun. Could feel warm blood and sweat soaking through his shirt, through the vest. He took a look inside the kitchen. Fired through the bay windows.

Let's just shake things up outside, shall we? Keep them piggies off-balance.

Hicklin quickly ducked and withdrew into the living room. Here it comes, he thought. And it did come. A barrage of .223 loads, some frangible rounds mixed in, breaking apart as they struck the fridge and cupboard. Followed by a salvo of jacketed rounds that tore ass through everything. He hit the floor and covered his head, sensing the house coming apart all around him.

It finally went quiet.

He glimpsed a command bus rolling beyond the first perimeter of vehicles, hoping that Charlie was okay in all that mess.

Hicklin squatted where the couch used to be and lit a cigarette. Blood dripped from an elbow, but he didn't feel a thing. Adrenaline had him jacked up. He could have sawn off his own leg and probably not felt it. Figured he could just go on and try and kill as many law officers as possible. They had the best hand, although he'd absorbed enough tear gas in prison to be able to handle it now. Had plenty of tolerance for the stuff, built up like antibiotics in his system.

No choice but to wait for them. Their firepower was superior. He couldn't compete with assault rifles and flash bangs.

He smoked, watching the now-silent television. Chanced upon the remote on the floor and changed the channel a couple times. Stopping for a Western. Gary Cooper was talking to a beautiful blonde. The actor looked mean and hard and angry.

A bullhorn voice from outside.

Hicklin got up gingerly and walked to the nearest

window, admiring the pandemonium he was responsible for.

The phone rang.

Charlie yelled at Hicklin, demanding to remain with him inside the house. Lucy pulled at her son's arm like she would at a child having a temper tantrum. Hicklin pushed them out, jabbing with the muzzle of the shotgun.

Once they were in the front yard Hicklin retreated, standing on the threshold, shotgun still trained on Charlie and Lucy. He wrestled free of his mother as armed responders approached. He faced Hicklin, who shook his head, then cracked a weak smile and kicked the front door shut.

Officers grabbed Charlie and ran with him across the street. He was hustled between vehicles, followed by paramedics and police. Everyone had a gun drawn.

Charlie puked. Someone put a blanket around him. A woman spoke gently to him. He couldn't understand her above the noise and shouting. He didn't know where they had taken his mother. He wiped his mouth on the blanket and looked back at the house, eyes stinging from tears.

Sallie Crews and her convoy arrived, adding to the jam on Tulip Street, the growing chaos. She opened the door of the Bureau sport-utility and sprinted to the command bus. The Lieutenant briefed her.

Hostages were safe. A lone gunman remained. Three tactical teams in place, the APV on standby. A negotiator in the bus was trying to make contact.

Crews looked at Hicklin's file on a computer screen. H. Hicklin, the H for Hobe.

She looked at the Lieutenant, who nodded.

This one wasn't coming out alive.

Hicklin answered the phone.

Who's this?

My name is Larry Schoenbaum. I'm with the Crisis Negotiation Unit. How are you, Hobe?

How the hell ye think I am?

I see your point, Hobe. Hobe? That's an interesting name.

Not if your family's from Jubilation County. Reckon you're the Crisis Negotiator?

Yes.

Because this here probably qualifies as a crisis.

It's what you're willing to make of it, Hobe. Just call it a situation that can be resolved with no harm done. Can we talk?

Sure.

I like that. You can't imagine how badly these deals usually start. I feel like we're having a drink together.

I could go for a beer myself.

It's against protocol, Hobe, but if I could I'd grab a six-pack and come in. We could talk, Hobe. Minus that 12-gauge, of course.

Every time you call me by my name, I just get all weepy and want to be loved.

What are you thinking about right now?

Well, Larry. I'm thinking 'bout killin' as many of y'all as I can before I get killed. Pure and simple, wouldn't you say?

Not what I wanted to hear, Hobe.

I'll bet. But you still got my attention.

Good. Any way I can change your mind about how you're feeling right now?

Something you said about a six-pack?

You want a beer?

Goddamn right. Bottle of Wild Turkey got blasted to hell. All the woman has here in the house is schnapps. Jesus Christ. You ever taste that shit? I ain't that desperate.

If I bring you some beer what will you give me?

I guess I might not aim so straight in your direction.

That's not what I wanted to hear, Hobe.

You might want to go back to negotiator school, get yourself another playbook.

What we need to consider here are the options available to you, Hobe.

I'm listening, Larry.

By the way, you a smoker?

Lifelong.

I just started again.

Well, I'm awfully sorry about that, Larry. I somehow feel responsible.

Hold on while I light this cigarette.

What're you smoking?

A Marlboro Medium.

Yeah, them don't kill you as quick as the Reds. The Ultra Lights make me cough real bad.

Those Ultra Lights are for sorority girls and chesters, Hobe.

Chesters? Haven't heard that one in a while.

Oh yeah?

Why? You know some?

I've put away quite a few, Hobe.

You worked pedophiles? CAP? A detective?

Yeah.

How's the boy?

Who?

That young man I sent out. Charlie Colquitt.

He's fine, Hobe. Shaken up but being taken care of. He asked about you.

He did?

Yeah.

What'd he say?

He wanted to know if we were going to kill you.

What did you tell him?

I said of course not.

You lied.

Lie? That's not what I do. He's pretty upset. Seems he took a real liking to you.

Well, I did to him. Take good care of him.

We will. Maybe when we work this thing out, you could see him again.

I ain't wanting to see him again.

But you obviously care about him.

Exactly. If I didn't care I'd want to see him again, and that just ain't the answer.

Answer to what?

It's between me and him.

I understand.

Do you?

Yes, I think so.

Damn if I ain't thinking you're a good man, Larry. Mexicans I dealt with inside called folks like you buena gente. "Good people."

Well, thank you, Hobe. I like you, too. I'd hate to see this go down how it's leaning right now. Why don't we take a break and then talk some more? Think about options. I know we can work it out without any shooting. What's the worst that can happen? You go back to prison for life? Seems like you did all right there. You can hack it. And you'll be able to see Charlie.

I can't go back inside. No fuckin' way.

Well, maybe something else can be worked out. There's plenty of people here interested in what you might have to tell. FBI, GBI, DEA, Bureau of Prisons. All of them would like to know more about your associations inside. We understand you're not some small-time peckerwood. In fact, the word "deal" might come up.

Shittin' me?

No way, Hobe.

A deal.

For information you've been privileged to. They'd take care of you.

I seen how snitches get took care of. I got more friends inside I got blood.

Like what? The Brotherhood? Then why'd you

jump the score at the bank? It set this whole thing off. They found your partners. Those dead guys on the mountain. Why did you do them, Hobe?

Silence.

I'm trying to understand you, Hobe.

Are you?

Just talk to me.

So I reckon y'all got what, three, four tactical units out there? Next pump some gas in here. Some of that pepper spray. Whatever toys y'all have. Then come right through the front door?

Let's not get off-course here, Hobe. Nobody's coming in. Not while I'm talking to you. Like I say, why don't we take a break and then I'll call you back in about fifteen minutes. I might put you on the phone with some other people who are in a position to really help you out.

Meantime no beer, huh?

Better raid the fridge, bud.

That you, Hobe?

Who else?

Just checking.

Go on.

Hobe, I've got some people here. A special agent from the state. Others. They want to talk.

Tell 'em I ain't of a mind to.

Just hear me out, Hobe. Depending on what you tell them, it could go a long way for you. You could really benefit.

Larry?

Yeah, Hobe.

I can tell a good man by his handshake, the look in his eyes, and by the tone of his voice. I ain't shook your hand nor looked you in the eye. But I know you for a good man.

Thanks, Hobe.

And I still don't care to talk to anybody else.

Silence.

That the way it is, Hobe?

For sure.

Well, what do you want to talk to me about?

Just make sure that boy is taken good care of.

You have my word.

Now come in and get me.

Charlie's head filled with the past. Down the street there was a dead end he had played in as a child. He launched gyro bombs there. Ignited Wolf Packs and Saturn Missiles.

Tatatattattattaattatata!

Momma used to drive him every July to Alabama to buy fireworks. Take I-20 West. Other times they'd head up I-75 and go to Tennessee. She'd give him ten bucks, tell him to make it last. There'd be a whole gang of kids in the cul-de-sac. Charlie would fill an old Radio Flyer with dirt, plant a row of Roman candles and light them all at the same time. The parents would unfold lawn chairs and sip lemonades. Sometimes those lemonades had whiskey or vodka in them. They'd take pictures. Hoot and holler and videotape it all.

Sometimes they'd start yelling at one another. Charlie figured it was the stuff they were cutting the lemonade with.

Sallie Crews introduced herself to Charlie. He didn't know why, but he asked to see her credentials. How could he not trust these people? After all that had happened?

She was dressed casually except for the gun on her belt. Not just another cop, though, but somebody important. All the other cops kept approaching her, asking her questions.

Charlie was old enough to buy beer, old enough to vote, but felt as if he were back in sixth grade. They had kid gloves on around him. That look he got, as if no one quite knew what to make of him. He sat inside an ambulance eating a granola bar, sweating and shaky. He tried to see over the roofs of squad cars and SUVs. Knowing Hicklin was still in there.

Well-armed SWAT personnel wearing body armor and flak jackets were waiting for the signal to move in. The sight of them gave Charlie a cold cramp in his stomach and he threw the rest of the granola bar away.

Sallie Crews had been friendly enough toward him but still intimidating. She hoped to talk to him at greater length, the sooner the better. But now wasn't such a good time, she said with a touch of regret.

Still he and Crews talked. Charlie listened to

himself sounding eloquent and in control. Some hard, unavoidable truths came out of his mouth. The cottage, Hummingbird, Flock and Lipscomb. It was awkward explaining with all those people standing around. Charlie could tell Crews was listening carefully.

A memory of being nine years old struck him. His mother bought condoms, white bread and sandwich meat and a bottle of wine at a convenience store. Real cheap wine that clung to her breath for days on end. Lotion for her skin. Men would come over to the house. In his room he'd hear them. Lucy always reminded him to lock his door. He'd play with his Erector or chemistry set. Look through his book with all the pictures of rockets and spacecraft.

Sallie offered a cup of coffee. Charlie snapped out of his daydream and reached for the Styrofoam cup with an unsteady hand.

He asked Crews not to hurt him, a refrain she found curious.

Why'd he bring you here? she said.

He didn't want to give a straight answer.

For leverage, he told Crews. Hicklin knew he needed a refuge, needed some hostages.

Charlie could tell she didn't buy his version. She smiled at him anyway. A smile you'd have for a sick person, after telling them they had cancer. A brutal fatigue was catching up with him. His neck hurt, his shoulders stiff from tension. He hated the questions about himself and asked Crews about the man at the church.

How did you know the Sheriff was shot? Crews said.

Hicklin told me.

Did he tell you he was the shooter?

I saw them shooting at each other. Daddy had no choice. But I don't want anything bad to happen to that Sheriff, either.

Lang's in the hospital. I hope he'll live. Did you say your daddy? Crews said.

Yes. Hicklin. He's my dad.

Charlie jumped. The tac teams were breaking the ground-floor windows with crowbars. They fired tear gas into the house.

He screamed. Crews grabbed his arm but needed help to keep Charlie from leaping out of the ambulance. The SWAT moved toward Lucy Colquitt's home. Automatic weapons fire was answered by big nasty wallops from the shotgun. The guys in black took cover.

Hicklin was fighting back.

And Charlie smiled despite his sadness.

The canisters were thick and black. They hissed as the aerosol was dispersed, gas filling the kitchen and hallway first. Hicklin hunkered in the bedroom. He'd cut the bath towel and secured it around his mouth with a rubber band.

He shattered one of the windows with the muzzle of the .45 and fired three rounds, ducking as return fire sprayed the walls. He rolled, put the handgun in the only space available and popped off another three rounds. A tight grouping that hit the driver's side door of a squad car.

They couldn't know what he had.

Tear gas spread through the house. Could have been any prison yard he was in for the last decade.

He took shallow breaths.

Ran a tongue along the inside of the towel.

More return fire. Hicklin heard rounds chunking away at the house's exterior.

He had two angles on the SWAT's possible entry. He dropped free the expended magazine and reloaded the HK. They strafed the front of the house again, a high-velocity peppering, hot and nasty hole punchers.

For a moment he wondered if the cops would say to hell with this and just set the house on fire.

He leaned over to the window adjacent to the front door and raised a defiant middle finger, waving it at the inner perimeter of law enforcement. A tendon-twisting pain surged through his shoulder. He didn't care. The agony kept him conscious.

He crawled back to the bedroom and deftly fired four rounds through the window. Double taps that resonated like flams on a drumhead.

Keeping them honest.

Because it wouldn't be long now.

Back in prison it was isolation that challenged him the most. Solitary confinement. Time became slippery and slimy for Hicklin. That's about the only *way he could describe it. Those monthlong stretches nearly killed him. But the only person who knew that was him.*

They had to let him out of the hole eventually.

All for not talking. But they tried to get him to snitch. A dank cell with no window, a steel toilet, a concrete slab for a bed. Hicklin learned to sleep longer and longer. When his brain got active and unruly, when the fear came on, he'd focus all that activity into one place and keep it there. He'd see light from under the door. But for the most part it was dark. A darkness he found largely indescribable.

He saw things that weren't there. Time oozed by. It dripped like a leaky faucet. Eventually, time hit the edge of a cliff and changed direction.

Down. Down. Down.

He wasn't entirely immune to the chemical irritants. His nose drained mucus like a spigot. He tightened the towel over his face.

The boys in black were getting more pissed by the minute. There was an unexpected lull.

The phone rang. Hicklin crawled to it.

Not now. I'm busy.

Breathing became difficult. He blew his nose. His eyes burned. The stuff was all over him.

And it hurt like hell.

Hicklin managed to reload five rounds into the shotgun with one eye swelling shut. He racked the pump. Needed some Maalox or milk to bathe his eyes. *Should have thought of this back when he was entertaining himself on the phone.*

A little tear gas was all. Just an inconvenience.

SWAT positioned themselves along the north wall, another team outside the carport and one near the front door. Explosive entry experts stationed on either side of the house espied possible blind spots through the windows.

Green light.

They pulled the detonation cords. The charges rocked Lucy Colquitt's home, as intended. The living room was the primary focus of flash bangs and concussion grenades. The primary team waited a beat, then destroyed the front door with a ram. As did the three-man unit at the carport entrance.

Nine men entered the house with practiced, dizzying efficiency.

A brilliant, flash caught Hicklin by surprise. The blast deafened him instantly. Ghosts appeared in his field of vision, in his mind, as if a nuclear weapon had gone off, his shadow imprinted on the carpet. Again he thought of Charlie. Something the boy had said back in the motel room while they played Lowball. Just bullshitting.

You are the universe.

The impact of the concussion grenades was like an earthquake turning his bones to putty, weakening him further. Hicklin tried to stand, partially-blind, but he had no balance. The fluid in the semicircular canals of his ears had been disturbed by the explosives. He could sense the floor coming at him again, his body following the baited directions of his inner ear. With no sense of balance he crumpled.

Men in black replaced the ghost swarm. From his knees he inexplicably grinned at them and raised the HK in their direction. Next he felt the impact of the tac team's .223-caliber rounds. His own body armor failed. Another team entered the living room, firing.

Hicklin never knew they were there, as the front of his head erupted.

This is what the end looks like.
Darkness covers the cities and towns.
A broken man with a gun in his hand
Looking for the last light to shoot out.

FOURTEEN

Charlie *spent much* of the days that followed being debriefed by law enforcement. He met with Sallie Crews in an office down by the square, not far from his mother's house. There were cameras and a tape recorder. Crews bought coffee. When Charlie requested a certain brand of cigarettes, she didn't think twice about buying them for him, too. If it wasn't okay to smoke in the room she didn't say so.

He told Crews everything that happened, never intending to exaggerate or mollify some of the lurid details of his experience. He had seen a doctor, been thoroughly examined and thankfully had nothing more than scrapes, bruises and a mild concussion. Crews struggled to hide her shock when he told her about Hummingbird and Hicklin. Like those from a fever dream, some details were difficult to recall. As if they'd happened to someone else, a Charlie he found it not so easy to think about anymore

Crews responded by telling him how brave and strong he'd been. His cooperation was immensely important to their investigation. She was worried about Charlie, even recommended he see a state-assigned mental health worker.

At his request, she took Charlie up to the Tri-County Medical Center to visit Tommy Lang.

Charlie sat with him in the IC room. Lang had been through three surgeries to clean out dead tissue surrounding the snakebites, with a fasciotomy scheduled for the following day and skin grafts in the coming weeks. He was semiconscious and silent, his body bloated. Charlie studied the monitors, every tube and blinking, beating machine keeping Lang alive.

Lucy Colquitt also had been hospitalized.

Charlie spent afternoons visiting his mother. She refused to speak of anything that had happened, having convinced herself that some minor medical emergency had put her in the hospital. Most visits she just stared out the window. Crossed her legs and shook her foot uncontrollably until the slipper came off. Her baby, Coma, had been gone to camp all that time, she sometimes insisted. Charlie tried to comfort her, but he knew—and had been told by doctors—how her mental state had deteriorated badly.

He even wondered if she recognized him anymore.

Charlie focused on the three-week ordeal while putting his life together. A new life no less, a project worth pursuing. He had to reenroll at the university. Bank management had agreed to pay him another month's salary, along with a generous bonus; Charlie agreed in return not to sue or publicly criticize the North Georgia Savings & Loan for its less-than-stellar Saturday security practices.

His mother's house had to be repaired and professionally cleaned, although much of the furniture, drapes and carpeting was hopeless and trucked to the dump. He thought a time or two about moving back into the old house, in spite of what had gone on there.

Celebrity was another challenge he couldn't avoid. It seemed everyone in the major media wanted to talk to Charlie Colquitt, a hostage of any kind offering an easy bump in the ratings. He didn't even think about changing his phone number until the calls began.

When the movie and TV and book agents inquired about rights to his life story, Charlie realized he needed to hire someone to field all the requests. There was real money to be made from Charlie's ordeal. Money he could use to finish paying for school, take care of his mother. Maybe he could find them a new house in a neighborhood where nobody knew them. Set up a gym with weights and other exercise equipment. Build a model rocket workshop from scratch. Hit Hobby Town with a wad of cash and buy new supplies, payloads, body tubes, motors and transitions.

What he wanted ultimately was space and privacy, to launch his rockets uninterrupted as often as he pleased.

———

Bᴜᴛ *in the* days following the siege on Tulip Street something else weighed heavily on Charlie's mind. The first night back in his old apartment he went to the local convenience store to buy the beer Hicklin drank and the cigarettes Hicklin smoked. Charlie rearranged the small living room of his apartment to resemble the cottage up in the mountains. He turned his cell phone off and disabled the smoke alarm.

Then Charlie spent the evening smoking and drinking, flicking ashes into an empty can. His only company the quiet hum of a radio.

For moments at a time it felt real again.

He slept in binges, no matter what time of day or night it was. There were instances when he woke himself with screams.

His first and second tattoos itched as they healed. He started jogging and eventually added a routine of push-ups, pull-ups, dips and sit-ups. He bought a bench press. At first it was hard work. But Charlie learned to enjoy the pain. Weight dropped off him almost effortlessly.

Weeks passed before Charlie worked up the nerve to call Sallie Crews. Explain to her what he wanted. She said that it could be done, but he'd need a lawyer. His request would have to go through the courts.

Sʜᴇ *was ten* minutes late. Charlie was sitting in the corner of the campus coffee shop. His appearance startled Crews at first. His head was shaved and there was a rather intricate gray-green tattoo on his right forearm. He was reading a book called *The Psychopathic God,* a cup of tea before him. He looked up at Crews and smiled.

"Sorry I'm late," she said. "I told you it would take some time. And lawyers, too. But I got it."

"Thank you, Sallie."

She slid a manila envelope across the table to him.

"You look good, Charlie. Been working out?"

"Two hours every day. Without fail."

"Good for you. I saw you on television the other day."

Charlie nodded bashfully. She could tell he still wasn't quite comfortable with all the attention. Students in the coffee shop were looking in their direction. She changed the subject.

"How's your mother?"

He shook his head forlornly.

"How's Sheriff Lang?" he said after a moment.

Now it was Crews' turn to blush.

"He's as tough as they come. Up and walking around now. Ready to get out of that hospital," she said, then gesturing to the envelope, "Do you want me to explain the test results?"

"I think I can figure it out. Thank you, though. Thanks for everything you've done."

"I didn't look by the way."

"I'll tell you soon," Charlie reassured her. "There's just something I've got to do first."

They shook hands. Charlie got up to leave. Crews watched him go, biting her lip nervously. As if from sadness.

And concern.

───────

T*he cemetery was* on a hill behind a small stone Baptist church in the heart of Jubilation County. His mother had taken him there when he was a child. Memories of Easter egg hunts, the stiff starchy Sunday clothes his momma made him wear. She always took pictures.

Purple and white lilacs grew unchecked along the path up to the gates. Weeds and wild grass overran the older part of the cemetery. A stiff wind revealed a community of chest and table tombs, long neglected.

When he reached the newer headstones everything was more orderly. Fresh memorials adorned the stones with chiseled biblical verses and crosses and cherubs. Nearby there was a big possumwood tree filled with noisy birds. The sky was clear, the kind of deep blue that comes after three days of rain. Yellow jackets darted through the air. When Charlie came to the grave marker with Hobe Hicklin's name, he stopped as if surprised, appreciating for the first time the simple bronze plate he'd chosen.

He carried a duffel bag with a model rocket kit inside. He put the bag down on the ground. Produced a cigarette and lit it. Smoking was as easy now as if he'd been doing it all his life. He liked the rush the nicotine gave him, the jump start for his brain.

He stared at the ground, half-expecting the grave at his feet to give way. For Hicklin to rise up with a wink and a grin and motion for Charlie to come down and visit awhile. He smiled faintly, smoking, a breeze cool against his buzz cut.

Should have brought beer, he thought.

He opened the duffel bag and removed the manila envelope. Inside was a single sheet of paper with the results of the DNA test. Lab letterhead. He read them silently once again, as if he might have missed something. Reading aloud the results of the test for himself—for Hicklin. Charlie's voice, grown huskier over the weeks, was a man's voice.

After reading he folded the paper several times and put it in his wallet.

The Bullpup was thirty inches long, with a large hollow nose cone and big quarter-inch fins, all laser-cut. Charlie had left all the decals off the rocket. Instead he took a permanent marker and crudely wrote the word Lowball along the body tube. He took out the launchpad from the bag, a quality mid-power deal that could handle a large model like the Bullpup. It had a four-foot launch rod, a blast deflector disk that was almost eleven inches in diameter. Extrawide legs, a low center of gravity.

Charlie connected the ignition wire and spooled it away from the rocket. Then he inserted the safety key into the control box. A buzzer went off to indicate a complete circuit through the igniter. He punched the large red button on the control box and looked up to see the Lowball move slowly and steadily off the launchpad, lifting up the rod and rocketing skyward.

Charlie tracked the rocket's soaring trajectory, a hand shielding his eyes from the sun, figuring it had hit eight hundred feet above the cemetery. He thought about all the sanding and sealing he'd done, the custom modifications.

The *Lowball* was way up now, teetering a bit before the nylon parachute recovery was released. He watched the parachute catch the air and float effortlessly against a blue vault of sky.

He spoke again and wondered if somewhere Hicklin was privileged to be aware of him. Wondered if Hicklin would believe him.

Charlie ran a hand over his buzzed scalp. He pulled another cigarette from the yellow hard pack and rolled the length of it between his thumb and forefinger before lighting the end.

A ritual that had always fascinated him, which now he'd made his own.

Tommy Lang's world looked to him as though it'd been wrapped in gauze. He was in a hospital room. Great pain on the right side of his body. He tried to focus, but nothing came clear. He knew someone was in the room with him. Lang imagined that his own son had come. If it was his Danny, then maybe the rest of Tommy's family would also be there. His girls, his ex-wife.

The visitor moved forward as if to offer something. Lang kept thinking it his son. A tall young man, still with plenty of time to figure life out. But Lang's vision worsened. He was aware, if only for a moment, that he was slipping back into darkness. He carried with him the hope of getting things right, if he was going to have another chance.

Forge

Award-winning authors
Compelling stories

. . . .

Please join us at the website
below for more information
about this author and other great
Forge selections, and to sign up for
our monthly newsletter!